Scruplez

GRITTY, POWERFUL AND MYSTERIOUSLY PROFOUND

JOHN MOORE & MAYNE DAVIS

SCRUPLEZ
GRITTY, POWERFUL AND MYSTERIOUSLY PROFOUND

iUniverse books may be ordered through booksellers or by contacting:

iUniverse
1663 Liberty Drive
Bloomington, IN 47403
www.iuniverse.com
844-349-9409

ISBN: 978-1-6632-2116-2 (sc)
ISBN: 978-1-6632-2117-9 (e)

Library of Congress Control Number: 2023903301

Print information available on the last page.

iUniverse rev. date: 01/25/2024

Dedications

John Moore, thank you for your time, your friendship, wisdom, integrity, patience, and philosophy on life, it has been a remarkable journey. You will always be a great man in our hearts. Stay strong soldier.

"**_Our Metamorphosis_**," (By, Mayne Davis, Co-Author, and Executive Producer of "**_The Davis Project_**," _LLC_,) curiosity surrounds many of our thoughts, passion explains some people's attitude, but fearsome wonder is most of our reality. Chronological or alphabetical order is how you must carefully prioritize whom, and what is the most important thing, or things in one's life. During so, instantaneously one must come to grasp that loyalty provides its own guidelines without specific definition; therefore, one must be able to seek out the good, great, and the unique characteristics in any individual. Levelheaded thinking, positive attitude, and the will to want to succeed are necessary when using methods in doing so.

We as human beings make some serious mistakes, bad decisions, and difficult choices when chosen whom to love. We must now comprehend as adults that if we fail or fall down, we are able to continue in riding that horse, bike, or life unforeseen obstacles. The breath of existence is something we are all provided with. Oxygen enters through our nose, mouth, and windpipe to travel throughout the rest of our body the same way regardless if we were ill or healthy, black or white, fat or skinny, Christian,

Catholic, or Muslim, or whether or not if we were financially secure, or had no security at all. *The way of life and time, or the development of nature, slows down for nothing, nor no one.*

Emotions, unfortunately, is upgraded on a different level. A broken heart can sometimes destroy a person's spirit or mind simply because one is unable to handle the lost. To lose the one person you truly, love is a very painful thing, whereas, it is up to the individual and how they are willing to deal with such a lost. The lost will openly challenge your strength, willpower and your mental balanced structure; nevertheless, regardless of how it comes, one should always remain strong in dealing with their emotions.

The Almighty knows that most of us are still being mentally, physically, and emotionally challenged throughout ways of the, **Devil.** Fortunately, for us, we can utilize the Devil's crafty work to find out who we really are. Personally, I have utilized his creative skill to acknowledge his wisdom. I believe that I am better equipped for more promising options, and opportunities. As of today, life from me will bring to the table a good man, a soft spoken man with education from both sides of the world, (*first bad, now good*). I now have a very adventurous style, big heart and charm, enjoyment and a spontaneous personality. I know that I am a unique individual because I am true to who I am as a man. I am willing to speak openly to whomever is willing to listen. I am willing to go as far as it takes in becoming legendary in my time.

Like many great people, I have failed many times, but each, and every time I failed, I have learned a new lesson. I come to realize that I can move on from the lost of a good friend. I can get rid of old photos. I can even decrease the amount of excess body weight I provide; but fortunately, I can never get rid of my knowledge. Knowledge is here to stay; moreover, it is only good when given to another. This is a dedication to you, *the reader*, the reason or reasons why we are here today; simply, to inform people of your magnitude, that, **"we are all the same in many ways."** Please enjoy, **"Scruplez."**

Contents

One

Introduction

Kay was smiling, appreciating her cousin's compliment. Stew had always been there for her, even when they were younger. Today, she played a bigger part of Kay's life by moving into the house with her and helping out with the bills. Hard times fell hard on Kay all at once; the police had killed her daughter's father Jason/Jay, and her mother suddenly died from cancer. At the tender age of twenty, Kay definitely had her hands full. The rest of her family was not as supportive as Stew. In fact, they had distanced themselves to the point of literally becoming strangers. The one thing that they managed to do was consistently harass Kay, trying to get her to rent the house out and use the money to secure a living somewhere cheaper. The idea was not a bad one, but Kay knew that they would knock on her door every month borrowing, begging, and asking for money that they had no intentions on paying back. Furthermore, the house meant too much to her. All of her fonder memories were in the house, and she only had another year to pay-off the mortgage. She did not want to risk letting someone else stay there and depend on their income to secure the mortgage payments.

"Are you sure, Stew?" Kay continued, while turning in the

mirror to see the reflection of her ass, then turning back around to suck in her stomach.

"Look bitch, I said you look good," Stew said in a jokingly manner.

"Alright, alright I'll stop. Thanks for watching the kids tonight. I know you usually like to swing," avowed Kay.

"Look Kay, for a whole year you've been watching my two little brats while I went out to shake my ass. Not to mention the times I did not come home, straight caught up on a good piece of action. Shit girl, I owe you this much. You have not given yourself anything, besides being in this big ass house doing nothing. That is so corny! You were really tripping. You have not been in the arms of a man in a while, and don't think I don't know about Dilly either," Stew acknowledged.

Kay looked surprised and half puzzled. "What, girl! You are tripping. Who in the hell is Dilly?"

"No sweetheart, it's not who, it's what," Stew said. She jumped up, rummaged through Kay's dresser drawer, and pulled out a dildo, waving it side to side as she chuckled.

"Ooh, girl, give me that. Stop, playing, Stew. How you know?" Kay said, with a smirk, feeling slightly embarrassed.

"I heard your little nasty ass in the bathroom the other day. I started to scare the shit out of you, but I know how it feels when your groove gets busted." Stew said.

"Yeah, I'm glad you didn't, because I would have fucked you up. Girl, I was putting my weight on it!" Kay informed, smiling and demonstrating her act.

"Aw, go head, girl. Don't be using my little sayings." Stew was flattered that Kay would even notice anything she said.

"Girl, fuck you. I was putting my weight on it!" Kay gave her cousin a high five while they laughed.

A car horn beeped three times before someone yelled Kay's name.

"There they go, girl. Have a good time," Stew, said while

giving her cousin a big hug. She was very happy to see Kay taking a step towards regaining control of her life. If anyone ever knew life was short, it was Stew.

"Be careful. Oh yeah, seriously Kay, when the people see you, they are going to flock like flies on shit. You look really nice cousin." Stew assured her.

"Thank you!" Kay replied.

Kay wore a tight-fitted, black Prada cat suit with a tan and black Prada scarf wrapped around her waist, tying the knot to the side of her hip. Her shoes were tan Manolo Timberlands, and she was ready for her first night out in over a year. It was already in her mind to let go, and not worry about any problems.

After a day of hard raining, the weather became pleasant. Stepping outside the door, she quickly glanced down at her feet for a double check.

"Aw shit! Go ahead, girl. Look at you," her friend Vita said, smiling as Kay opened her arms, then placed her hands on her hips in a model-like pose. Many people had told Kay that her body was similar, if not better, than *Jennifer Lopez's* was, but for some reason, this was the only night she felt that they were not lying. This was the only night that she felt the weight gained from her second child was not a bad thing. She continued to model her outfit.

"Yeah, that's right, girl. Take a picture. This shit here is all women!" said Kay excitedly, twirling around in circles.

"Yes you are, girl. Now get your ass in this car before you change your mind," Vita said.

Vita was proud to see her longtime girlfriend in good spirits. She tried time, and time again to get Kay to go out with her, but Kay would never feel up to it. When she finally said yes to a proposal of a night out, Vita felt relieved. "Come on, girl, let's roll," she said, as she watched Kay walk to the car tiptoeing.

"Girl, I don't know about these damn boots." Kay confirmed, looking down at her feet.

"Girl, stop playing, you're cool."

"Naw, they're cute and all, but they're hurting my damn feet." Kay informed, moving around her toes to get a comfortable feel.

They would always dare each other to do things whenever they were together. The dare would be a substitute for a suggestion, request, or demand. It started from listening to the song by *Black Rob* ~ who was on the '*Bad Boys*' record label ~ called "*I Dare You*." Since then, they have incorporated the term "I dare you" in a completely different manner. They each laughed periodically; taking looks at each other as they sang along to Amyl's verse on the song '*Can I Get A*' by *Jay-Z*.

Kay was just as proud of Vita as, Vita was of her. She too lost her mother to some sort of sickness. Kay had always admired the strength in Vita to move forward, no matter how afraid or uncertain she was of the future result behind her decision-making. The two were together since childhood, not only behind the deaths of their mothers, but through the trials and tribulations that comes with family values and responsibilities.

Vita's situation was slightly different however; fortunately, she had inherited insurance money behind her mother's death. Therefore, her ambitious business minded personality illuminated. She opened up a mini soul food takeout restaurant in North Philadelphia called '*Vita's Vicious Platters*.' With her outstanding cooking styles also inherited from her mother, she had the grand opening of her place and unsurprisingly was doing very well within the first few months of its operation.

Finally, they pulled into a parking space in their old neighborhood.

"Hell no, no you didn't Vita!" Kay shouted, looking around nervously.

"No I didn't what?" Vita surprisingly, asked.

"You know '*Woody's*' place is not happening tonight." Kay quickly, assured.

"Girl, I told you, you have been in that house for too long. You did not even realize it is not, '*Woody's*' anymore. Read, Girl,"

'The Tail Feather' she pointed to the sign that hung high above the entrance. "Plus, little Tony/Tab, is having a birthday party in there," Vita updated, grabbing her belongings.

"Little Tab, Who's that?" Kay wondered.

"Girl, you know the song they be playing on the radio. It is like: Break crews, break, break… something," she explained, trying to give Kay a singing example of how the song goes.

Kay laughed. "Girl, you're fucking that song all up. I know whom you are talking about though. Isn't he from Diamond Street?" Kay wonderd.

"Yeah, him and his fine-ass friend and partner Knocks." Vita began biting down on her bottom lip, imagining herself having her way with Tab's friend.

They exited the automobile in glamorous precision, directing them-selves toward the entrance. Although this timeless ordeal took place during the evening of summer, the chilly breeze within the nighttime atmosphere marched its way throughout Kay's body. This was due to the aftermath of rain. The summertime temperament captivates the attention of inner city communities, especially when it thunderstorm and suddenly stop. Individuals from every age bracket would come parading, smiling, and entertaining themselves with joy. Apparently, this night was not any different.

The street lights spotlighted majority of the area. The music from within the environment could be heard from outside. It gave Kay an instant jolt of excitement. Had it not been for Vita maintaining a slow pace while walking toward the entrance, Kay's legs would have practically raced her into the bar to become a part of the action. She took in a deep breath of the crispy, night air to allow her heart to stop its fluttering. People were everywhere as if there was a block party. Some were in groups and some were standing individually, smoking marijuana and cigarettes. Customized cars and jeeps paraded up and down the blocks as if a car show was taking place.

A group of five people lingered in front of the entrance. Vita led, Kay through their mini huddle.

"Goddamn! Beautiful, you're a brick house for real!" someone hollered from a crowd. Kay walked past with her arms to the side and stiff from the goose bumps.

"I'll keep you warm Ma-Ma!" another yelled, from the group. She pretended to ignore the comments but gave a grin, heavily fighting a full smile. She desperately wanted to stop to suddenly give some attention to the hounding or simply to observe everyone of them, seeing if one could fit her criteria of a good man, sadly, the chances were very high of them being dogs. Fortunately for her, she knew better than to go for the problematic characters that always stood outside of the bars and clubs hoping to see who and what entered and exited. It was more than likely that they were not looking for a love affair, but a quick opportunity at a chance for a one-night stand.

The inside of this establishment was just as fashionable as the outside. A disco-ball hung high from the ceiling. Red, green, and yellow lights flashed, on and off every so often while the ball maintained rotation, allowing its reflection to glare upon the walls. This place was packed. The small dance floor was overwhelmed with hot bodies mixing and dancing as close as they could, allowing the maximum movement of your basic two-step dance to be the move of the night. The people were dressed accordingly; some with your decorative attire, some with your expensive, latest fashion, but the classy people stood out separately. The grown and sexy conducted themselves with your traditional well-mannered grace of presence; they observed the ones whom dressed provocatively with close to nothing on.

The men dressed simpler than women did. They wore jeans, sneakers, and boots of some sort, depending on their style of linen.

Kay and Vita walked over to sit down next to the DJ's booth where the rest of Vita's girlfriends were. Kay knew only two of them because they lived on the same block where her daughter's father lived. She would speak to them periodically when picking up or dropping off her daughter Asr. They knew Jay for some time, therefore, they would watch Asr sometimes during the weekends when Jay's sister couldn't or suddenly had to run an errand.

"Kay, you already know Cee, and Trace/Tray. This is Shelly and Liz," Vita said, pointing to each one, as their names were, addressed. Vita introduced Kay to the other girls, threw her hand in the air, and yelled at the barmaid to get her two shots of Hennessey on ice. Kay shook their hands and gave a comforting smile. Being in the company of North Philly girls was different; at least it felt that way with her. Especially when comparing them to the girls in her Ogontz, West Oak Lane neighborhood. Her cousin Stew was from North Philly; furthermore, Kay knew from experience that most of the girls in that area knew how to have a good time, on the "whatever" side of things, and this is what she needed, a moment to let go. Of course, you have these types of females all over the city; unfortunately, Kay just did not know any of them from her own community.

Vita returned with the two shots of Hennessey and immediately gave one to Kay.

"Damn. Are you treating?" Liz blurted in a joking manner.

"No! I see you every day," Vita replied, laughing as she handed Liz a fifty for coverage of Shelly, Cee, and Tracey's drinks. "You got the next round bitch!" she yelled as Liz quickly came into shouting distance.

Many people could not understand how or why they would continuously address themselves as *bitches* all the time, but it was a term they would used to show a close bond. You could determine its level of offensiveness; by the way, it is expressed or responded.

Liz returned, damn near fumbling as she tried not to spill drinks. "Come on y'all," she said, as she handed the drinks to everyone. They each held their drinks in front of them as if making a toast. On Liz's three-count, they drank the Hennessy straight, each making whatever face needed to swallow it. When they finished, they each held the shot glasses back in front of them and began dancing in a circle amongst each other to *Missy Elliot's* song *'Work It.'*

After two more rounds, Kay was good and loose, enjoying her night. Everyone who was somebody was there mingling, modeling their outfits, spending top dollar on Moet, and flashing their jewelry via any means imaginable. It was not long before Kay fixed her eyes on a few of Jay's friends standing counter clockwise across the bar. One person in particular, Bernard/Brim, was supposed to be the godfather of Asr. She continued to look in his direction until he noticed her. He quickly made his way through the crowd over to where she stood.

The last time the two encountered, she was pregnant and waiting for the bus. He just happened to be passing her by. At first he was reluctant to stop because of his illegal activities, besides, he was in his Bonneville, a matter that could have instantaneously enhanced a dangerous situations probability. Picking her up could have easily subjected her to all kinds of unnecessary drama, therefore, he decided to go against his better judgment and pick her up anyway. Being that nice person, he in fact finished last. She had many places to go. He thought that maybe she was heading to Jays' sisters, house or uptown; consequently, it was none of the above. She had to first, pick up pictures from K-Mart, and then ride downtown to get her hair and nails done, pick up clothing, and so forth. He definitely wanted to help her out; he held no intention on being her personal chauffeur. He stood with integrity however, and knowing she was his dead friends, daughter's mother, he felt the obligation of lying to her rather than telling her he couldn't take her, especially when she was already in the car.

He conjured up a story about having a slow leak, so he needed to go to the tire shop to get a new tire. She immediately recognized that getting a ride from him would save her a lot of time, so she offered to give him seventy dollars for the flat. However, she made it clear that he had to meet her at Jay sisters' house the next day to give the money back. It was a desperate attempt. She needed a ride to K-Mart. Catching the bus back downtown was not a problem. She just needed to get the photos she had taken or they would have charge her extra for holding them any longer. It is an offer he could not refuse. He drove her to K-Mart, dropped her off, and went on his way. He knew that he should not have taken the money in the first place, and somehow he knew his honest mistake would turn and bite him in the ass, and tonight was that night. Brim slid in front of the girls, invading their circumference. He already knew Vita and the others from the neighborhood and became use to seeing them every day, so he did not bother to acknowledge them too much. His focus was on Kay.

"Damn, what's up, Kay?" he asked, expressing his cheerful smile.

Kay looked him up and down with her lips twisted. "Umm-humm, yeah, what's up, Brim?" she blurted before rolling her eyes, and turning her back to him.

He looked at the immaculate figure of her body and could not help but to bite down on his lip. The last time he had seen her, she definitely was not as thick as she was standing before him. He placed his hand on her right shoulder.

"What's all that about, Kay? What you tripping for?" Brim asked, questionably.

"You know why I'm tripping. Don't play stupid." Kay informed. She rolled her shoulder backward in a circular motion to break loose of his touch, then motioned her way through the crowd and sat down on the stool. He followed her with his eyes stuck on her ass.

"I came to pay homage and..."

"Don't talk that monkey shit to me!" she said, stopping him. "Homage, where was the homage when you took the seventy dollars! Where was the respect in that? And you say, Jay was your friend." She angrily informed pointing her finger at him.

"Damn! You acting out over seventy dollars? I thought we were much bigger than that. I honestly forgot all about it, seriously." Brim declared, looking into her eyes.

"The seventy ones weren't shit! Do not try to make the situation look petty. I needed that money to get Asr's shoes off layaway. You knew Easter was that weekend, besides, I shouldn't have had to give you anything for a ride! But since you wanted to lie about a flat, I gave you the cash," she addressed.

"I did have a flat," he replied, hopping to cut her off.

Kay began twisting her lips in disbelief. "Okay, whatever!"

"I know you don't believe me, it's cool though, seriously," Brim added.

"Seriously, when are you going to get serious about Asr? She supposed to be your goddaughter and you do not do anything for her. Nevertheless, when Jay was alive, you acted as if she was your own daughter. I guess you were faking it, to make it. Tell me, how real is that?" Kay asked, demanding an answer.

She succeeded in her mission to make him feel bad. He knew how she was, and he expected to be blasted verbally, but not that harshly. He realized that she was like any other girl who knew that they were right about something, pounding each opinion and perception about the situation into his head. A simple, *I agree* or *an apology* would never suffice.

He reached into his pocket and pulled out a knot of money. "Alright, take this Kay, and I'll stop past your house sometime next week. I'll have something for you."

"You mean that you'll have something for Asr, right?" Key corrected.

"Whatever Kay, you win." Brim said shaking his head in disbelief.

Kay smirked. "Why are you getting upset? Can it be because you know I am right?" she asked.

"I'm getting upset because you snapped out for nothing. I said it was my fault the first time," he told her in a frustrated tone of voice.

The barmaid suddenly walked over, interrupting their conversation. She made it her duty to look at Brim seductively before asking if they wanted to order any drinks. She was not trying to flirt; she picked exactly the right time to ask about buying drinks. Just as she anticipated, Brim reached back into his pocket and pulled out his knot of money.

"Yes, can I have a shot of Alize and Vodka, and give her what she's drinking," he said, pointing to Kay.

Kay smiled, "just give me a Vodka Tonic." She turned to see where Vita was at, but in the process, she made it her duty to check Brim out. She particularly like how he was dressed in the Gucci dark-denim blue jeans with red and green half-inch stripes alone the side, a white Gucci t-shirt, and pair of S-Dot Carters. The chrome Gucci belt made out of G's had taken the cake. To her, he definitely was wearing it.

When Brim turned his attention back to Kay, he noticed the barmaid approaching from the corner of his eye. While placing the drinks on the counter, she put on her sexy look and attempted to give him his change.

"No, keep the change," he said, returning the same sexy look as she turned and walked away. Kay nudged him in the shoulder with her index finger.

"Y'all some dirty dick dudes," Kay stated, turning up her nose in dislike.

"Why we got to be all that?" Brim wondered, grabbing his drink.

"Some men will stick their penis in anything. Y'all going to mess around and catch something. STD's is out here like crazy. Just remember, you cannot come back from having full blown AIDS," she affirmed, grabbing her drink.

"Girl, don't anybody be just sticking anything. I'm not pressed," he assured.

"Whatever, that's why you are sitting there grinning." Her statement was from missing Jay so much. Brim reminded her of him in many ways. The way he dressed, his attitude, and that distinctive swagger he had with him that always demanded a woman's attention. Brim returned to the company of his boys. The Vodka Tonic had pushed Kay past her personal level of intoxication, but she seemed to handle it well. After a few minutes of sitting alone, Vita and the others joined her at the counter to get more drinks.

"Girl, why must you be over here all by yourself?" Vita pondered.

"I'm cool, Vita. Matter fact, I'm fucked up for real," Kay announced.

"Oh, I forgot you not a real drinker. Do not be spitting up in here. If you feel you have to, alert one of us, and we'll go to the bathroom with you." Vita said.

"Looking how you look, you should be over there hoping to put one of them men in pocket," Cee, ordered.

Trace, pulled a bottle of Corona down from her lips, swallowed, and sucked her teeth. "Cee, shut up, everybody not like you. That's the reason why you have four kids right now."

Cee, stared aggressively, "I got four children because this pussy good. Don't get that fucked up, men will and have killed over this pussy." Cee, informed.

"Hush up, Cee! I would not be telling people that. What if they came and locked you up about something, then what? Plus, that's not anything to be proud of," Liz added, while hi-fiving Shelly.

"Who asked you to add your two cents? You know what, it do not even matter. My, name is Cee. I will put this pussy right on Tab little ass. Turn him straight out. Put this weight on him. Eaarrrrly." Cee announced moving her body seductively. The other girls had no choice but to laugh with her. She was always outspoken and up-front with hers.

"That's right, Cee. And I dare y'all to leave her alone," said Kay, extending a clenched fist to give Cee, a pound.

"Oh, that's how you playing? Well, I dare you to make that ass clap, right here on this counter," said Vita while bobbing her head to the song '*Pump it Up*' *by Joe Budden.*

"On the counter? Girl, you got to be drunk." Kay said, looking at Vita.

"Come on, Kay, have some fun. You act like you don't get down." Vita stated, pulling Kay's arm.

"I'm not sayin' I don't get down, But...," Kay was, interrupted.

"But what?" Vita asked, smiling. "If you don't, you're going to owe me two dares for not taking this one, come on, Kay-Kay, before the song goes off." Vita urged Kay, knowing that eventually Kay would give in. She knew that once Kay got on the bar, all the people in there were going to gravitate to where they were.

The girls moved everything on the bar out of Kay's way and helped her climb onto the bar using the stool. "Go Kay-Kay! Go Kay-Kay!" they chanted as she stood motionless and towering over everyone. The whole bar began to chant "Go Kay-Kay!" along with the girls. Vita took the initiative to pull out a twenty and put it into an empty beer pitcher. Kay couldn't understand how she even let herself get dared this far, but she was determined to make the best of it and let Vita know that she was still the best at taking and giving dares.

Kay took a deep breath and zoned everything out until it was just her and the music. She practiced this all the time, naked in the mirror at home. Placing her hands on her knees in a squat-like position, she turned toward the crowd that quickly formed and began dropping it, like it was hot. Her ass snapped up and down to the music. The fact that she had on no panties made her cat suit give her ass its rightful form.Vita began holding the pitcher out for people to put money in it; it became full in no time. So much so, that Cee, and Liz had grabbed pitchers as well. The mini-crowd became larger and Kay continued to switch dances. She even juggled her buttocks, making each cheek go up and down at separate times. The crowd began to chant, "Take it off! Take it off!" she enjoyed the attention and began to accommodate them by taking her cat suit off.

While on the counter, Kay felt as if she was one with the crowd. As the "Take it off!" chants continued, her attempt to strip came to an instant halt when Brim yanked her down from the counter.

"What the fuck do you think you're doing?" he asked aggressively. He continued. "Oh, so you coyote ugly now, huh?" he wondered, while holding her arm in a tight clutch.

Kay angrily snatched her arm away. "Brim, get the fuck off of my arm like that! What do you mean, what am I doing? What do it look like I'm doing?" she said, face frowned up, as sweat began to form on her forehead.

"I'm just saying, you shouldn't be up there like that, that's not even you." Brim assured her, checking her character. In so many ways, he was right, but he could never understand the connection she felt with the crowd. Standing on the counter gave her a sense of power over men. It pushed her self-esteem to another level, after having lost it for some time.

After Brim finished telling her about her sudden abnormal behavior, he looked her up and down, and then shook his head in disgust while walking away.

"Girl, you were doing it," Cee quickly said. "Look how much money these trick-ass dudes gave up." Cee counted the last bill collected, and gave it to Kay.

"Yeah, you was hurtin' 'em," Vita added, while also counting money. She handed the money to Kay, "Here, girl. You know I already dared myself to take a breakdown, since I started the collection."

"How much did you take?" Kay asked with a smile on her face.

"Shut up. You know I did not hurt you, that is all yours. You definitely earned it, because I would not have been able to do that shit." Vita stated, shaking her head.

Kay put the money in her handbag and they all stepped outside for a piece of air. While standing in a huddle and smoking cigarettes, Cee, took the liberty to bring to Kay's attention that Brim, was across the street.

"Oh my God, why is he staring at you that way? He acts like you two are fucking or something." Cee, announced with curiosity.

"Girl, come on with all that. You know that was Jay's friend," replied Kay.

"Whatever! If he isn't tapping that, he sure wants to," alerted Cee.

"Cee, shut your nasty ass up." Liz interrupted while rolling her eyes.

She and Cee always went at each other's throat, but the love they had for each other was strong.

"Fuck you Liz; you know I am not lying. You know them looks men be giving. Hell. Let him look at me like that ~ I'm talking about eaarrrrly!" Cee, quickly thrust her hips in a circular motion to demonstrate her bedroom tactics.

My cousin is not even trying to fuck with you again," Tray suddenly blurted.

"Get off his dick! You are always talking that cousin shit. Nobody wants to hear that. All of a sudden, Brim is your cousin because he has money. If he was not doing good; matter fact, his uncle was just putting pipe in your mom for a few years. Honestly speaking, no one agrees with that common-law wife stuff. A dude has to give a bitch a ring these days; make shit official. You probably mad because he turned you down. Your fat ass could not even be his kissing cousin. Talking that cousin shit, please!" Cee informed. Everyone just remained quiet. Then Vita tried to jump in to ease the tension. She could see that Cee was getting angry.

"Alright, Cee! Damn! You didn't have to say all that." Vita interrupted.

"No Vita, you know this bitch always acting like she the shit," Cee, said.

"Vita, it's cool. That's why I didn't want to come, because she never knows how to act," Tray replied, walking away.

"Look, I act how I act," Cee, said, then put her middle finger up and twisted her lips.

Tray was right behind the comments Cee, had made. She wanted desperately to kick Cee ass. However, Cee, was her girl, not to mention she knew that she'd probable get her ass whipped instead. Cee, was a girl who could back her mouth up with a lot of physical ability.

Kay remained quiet throughout the dispute. She knew what Brim's looks were about, and deep inside she felt slightly ashamed; never imagining that she was being observed, at all. At that moment, she realized the look he displayed was more of a shocked and disappointed look. She did not owe anyone anything, however, his expression made her sort of regret completely the ass-shaking ordeal. Nevertheless, instead of giving in to the semi-regrets, she stared across the street at him and rolled her eyes. What did he know; he was just Jay's friend. Whether he expected better behavior or not, it was her night out and she promised herself to let go, so she did.

Two

The Unthinkable

tew decided to check on the kids before settling down and watching a good movie on DVD. She put all of them in the same room to save herself from an extra tour of the house. Walking through the house while no one else was there was not appealing. It was a three-story house, equipped with seven rooms, and at night, if it were quiet enough, the voices of the neighbors would sometimes echo.

It had been a long time since she had actually baby-sat. She almost forgot how time consuming it was just trying to get kids to fall asleep. Her sons were under control. She had gotten them all cleaned up and settled into bed, but Kay's children gave her a hard time. Asr, the oldest, was pretty much in pocket after a little yelling and screaming; however, Charity, the youngest, insisted on seeing her mommy, but eventually cried herself to sleep.

When Stew finally was able to get into total relaxation, she heard someone calling her name from outside of the house. She instantly sucked her teeth recognizing the voice as her kids' father Crab. She sat motionless, wondering if she should open the door. She loved him very much, but she was not in the mood to put up with any of his dumb crap. Often she asked herself why she believed in him after he proved a countless number of times to be unworthy of any belief at all. Still, for her children's sake, she maintained hope that he would get himself together and get away from snorting heroin.

"Stew, open the fucking door!" he yelled while repeatedly beating on the door. After becoming sick and tired of the beating, she decided to walk to the front door to open it.

"Can you stop beating on the fucking door like that? It's kids in here sleeping!" Stew yelled, in agitation.

Having his life together was a thought that she easily erased. She could tell by his voice that he was high. Much had changed in her life in the last four months that he had been missing in action. The fact that he was high did not really matter at that point. She had something to tell him that probably would snap his mental into sobriety, news that would affect the remaining years of his life. For her, it was now or never. His disappearing acts left her no choice but to tell him of her discovery of contracting full-blown AIDS two months ago.

Standing in the vestibule, Stew let out a sigh before opening the door with her game-face on. "What is wrong with you?" she yelled.

Before she could say another word, Crab pushed past her and into the house with three people following and pointing guns at him. His appearance had fallen from her last sighting of him. Dirt and deep-darkened oil soaked his clothes, his hair was dusty looking, he smelled of a stench that came from a potty, and his face brandished a new scar with crusty, dry blood around it.

"Uh-uh, what y'all doing?" asked Stew as she watched the men hold their guns, thinking it had to be a joke Crab had fixed. One of the assailants had quickly placed his whole hand over her face and shoved her.

"Shut up bitch," the man said as he forcefully entered her home with a gun.

Stew was beginning to get scared. She realized that it was

not a game, and sadly, she desperately harbored hopes, and traits of denial.

"Crab, what is this? Get these criminals, up out of my house!" Stew shouted.

"We need to talk to you, and I'm not in the mood for your games," one of the three men stated.

"Tell them to put their guns away," she said, while walking across the living room, intending to grab Crab's hand. She was hoping for a one-on-one chat.

The perpetrators were from her neighborhood. One in particular used to be Crab's best friend. His name is Bobby. The other two were young Corey and Little Ron.

"Oh, you think this shit is a joke, huh?" said Bobby, before he cracked Crab over the head with his pistol. The sight and the sound of the pistol hitting Crab's head immediately made Stew jump.

"What did he do, Bobby?" Stew questioned with complete nervousness. Her voice trembled with fear. The angry game-face that once was on display had quickly turned into a sad face fighting heavy tears. Crab's voice also quivered with fear when he spoke. His eyes were watery and his face resembled the look of a guilty man caught in the act.

"Listen, baby…," Crab tried to say.

"Baby!" she interrupted. "I'm not your fucking baby Crab. What the hell did you do now?" she wondered, upset, and deeply discussed

"I didn't do anything. If you would just listen…," he tried again.

"Listen, what am I listening to Crab? You have people storming in here pointing guns, smacking you in the head, and now you have the audacity to sit there and tell me you didn't do shit!" Stew screamed. Her face was red and displayed veins on her forehead from all the excitement.

"Baby, I need that money I told you to hold." Crab stated, hoping for confirmation.

Crab looked her in the face and gave his right eye a small twitch, hoping that she would acknowledge that he had a plan and play along. Nevertheless, the stakes were too high. She did not feel like playing money games with people who were waving guns. She made it perfectly clear that he did not give her any money.

"I don't know what he told y'all, but I don't have anything," Stew informed. She hoped they would listen to her cries; unfortunately, the three of them had money on the brain and did not care where, or how they got it.

Bobby looked at her angrily. "Look, Stew," he started, "that's between y'all. All I know is that he owes us a nice piece of change and he said he gave it to you. Now, one of you is going to get that money. He should be happy he is still alive." Bobby said, pointing his finger in her face, as if to hit her.

"Bobby, I swear on my boys, he never gave me anything, and I would never swear on my children if I didn't mean it," she continues, "Crab, why would you tell them this bullshit; most importantly, why would you jeopardize our life?" she questioned her children's father.

Suddenly, Young Corey became impatient. He rushed across the room, pointing his gun, and slammed the barrel into Crab's forehead with every intention of ending his life.

"Please! No! Bobby, please don't do this!" cries Stew.

Lil' Ron hurried and pushed Corey's trigger hand to the floor, away from Crab's head. Both of them had money tied into the loss that Crab was costing, and they desperately wanted to regain their interest. However, they were also new to the hustling game and anxious to make an example of the first individual who played with their money. At fifteen years old, shooting someone about money would send a loud message, especially a person like Crab. Despite his terrible addiction, he had a reputation that well preceded him as a wild cowboy.

Young Corey and Lil' Ron were far from being in conflict with making Crab an example, but he knew if Corey would have killed Crab, then Stew would have had to catch it also. He was not ready to kill a twenty-one-year-old mother of two.

Bobby stood staring into Young Corey's face. He realized going into a partnership with younger men was a bad idea. Seeing Corey with the itchy finger, just dying to kill, was all he needed to see. He quickly thought of an idea before things got out of hand and Corey gave in to the ills of his criminal desire. It was a good thing that he knew about the Social Security check Stew received each month behind the death of her father. Bobby suggested that the money is paid through a payment plan. Corey was not exactly, too enthused about the suggestion.

"A payment plan; what if she doesn't pay, and we can't find this dude?" Corey asked, in disagreement.

"Then, I will deal with him myself," Bobby added.

Again, Corey raised his gun to Crab's forehead, "I'm going to say this once, if we leave here without any collateral, we'll never see neither one of them again," he continues, "so let me ask this question. If they decide to skip town, which one of you will pay what he owes?" Corey wondered, from his criminal codefendants. Bobby and Corey stared relentlessly across the room into each other's eyes without blinking.

"Whatever! Like I said, you're not going to kill anybody!" Bobby told him. Bobby then walked across the room to look Corey in the eye at close range.

Ron stood still for sixty seconds before speaking. "Come on, y'all, let's roll out of here." He slowly walked between the both of them and pushed Bobby away, separating the intense moment.

"Alright, we can play that way; matter fact, tell her to bend over," said Corey, moving in Stew's direction. With the gun in his right hand pointing down by his side, he began loosening his jeans. He was determined to leave with something, even if it was just a piece of flesh.

Stew looked at Bobby in despair. "What's up with him!" she asked, eyes widely open. "Oh my God, please no, I said I would pay the money," yelled Stew, frightened, confused, and in disbelief. She continued, "You know this shit not right, Bobby! Please, don't let him do this!" Stew continued to yell to the top of her lungs hoping for some relief, however, none was there for answering.

Ron began to say anything he could to try to get Corey to change his mind, but Corey was serious. He pointed the gun to the ceiling and shot once, *"Bang!"* followed with more words. "Look, I don't want to hear anything from anybody," he expressed, loudly. "Her man owes money and she's going to deliver. If not, I am going to kill both of them," he stated in aggravation. He raced across the room to where Stew stood and yanked her to the floor. She squirmed, kicked, bit at his hands, and punched until he struck her in the face with his pistol. Her ears began ringing and her head had a gash over the left eye. Crab tried to lunge, and was met with a few more blows to the head from Ron's gun.

"I got AIDS!" Stew yelled, warning the assaulter of her sickness.

Corey ignored the warning. "Oh, you got AIDS now, huh bitch!" he mocked, with his teeth clenched shut. He yanked her panties down and fumbled with his penis as he entered her womb from behind. Stew had not had sex since she learned of her disease, and the pain was almost unbearable. He pounded back and forth, in and out of her tight hole, seeking to maximize his pleasure. She clenched her teeth together and cried while looking into Crab's eyes. His eyes were half-shut and swollen. With each whimper she made, tears ran down Crab's face. His struggle to get up from the floor was a hard one. Ron was practically standing on his neck. All he wished for was Crab not to force his hand. He did not plan to shoot anyone, but he knew if Crab were not subdued, Corey would have a lot to deal with.

Crab was feeling less than a man for putting his family in such a situation. The disappointing look Stew expressed on her face with tears, were, felt with every fiber of his being. She always told him that snorting heroin was going to be his downfall, but he never in a million years thought he would hit rock bottom in this manner. *Damn, Stew. I am sorry ~ what was I thinking,* he silently thought as he squeezed his eyes shut to keep from watching his sweetheart being raped.

Stew's emotions were, horribly mixed up. Crab was an addict and a major fuck-up, but he was still her children's father, and she knew that he truly loved her. Having to watch the violent episode has hurt him more than she could ever imagine.

You really fucked-up this time, she said to herself, implying that Corey's actions were consequential. Stew closed her eyes and began moving in participation of the sex act. Becoming completely overwhelmed with emotion drove her to this point, but she also wanted to make Corey regret ever screwing with her, or her family. She reached back and began pulling him toward her. She moved as if she was enjoying it, throwing her ass into it, forcing him to pound harder and climax while thrusting from behind. For Corey, it was one hell of an episode, but for Stew, it was a sentence to death by giving him every speck of the AIDS virus within her body. Young Corey quickly pulled his pants up after exiting her womb, and then led his partners out of the house. Bobby felt disgusted with himself while leaving. He wondered how he could have let it get that far.

Stew lay in a fetal position, emotionally distraught. Her womb ached and throbbed with the equivalency of a headache. She had done plenty of crazy and outrageous things in her life, but the thought of actually passing off AIDS to someone, made her vomit.

When Crab, finally came around to slowly getting up, he felt the aches the assailants had dished out. Although he hurt, nothing was a match to the heartfelt pain he had caused his family. As he stood and began trying to help Stew to her feet, tears rolled from his eyes.

"Get the fuck off of me! You make me sick!" she screamed while digging deep for the strength to stand independently. She shouted, "Oh My God!" Suddenly, she made a dash for the steps to check on the kids. She stormed into the room to find Kay's girls sound asleep, but her three-year-old son was sitting up in the bed, quietly staring at his five-year-old brother lying on his back in a puddle of blood.

The single shot that Corey had aimed up into the ceiling turned into the fatal shot that took a little boy's life. The sight of seeing her son shot in the back instantly traumatized Stew. All she could do was scream Crab's name.

Three

A Moment to Rejoice

B ack inside of the bar, Kay ordered two spring waters to lessen her level of intoxication. She was enjoying her night, and being drunk for the first time in almost a year was fun, but she hated going to sleep that way because it was hell waking up with a hangover. The girls sat in the corner at a table, laughing and listening to the music until 2:30 a.m. when the party began to wind down. Almost everyone who had attended was heading to the Marriott for the hotel after-party, and Kay wanted to be wherever the fun was. Unfortunately, everyone except for Cee, was party pooped and wanted to call it a night. Kay had no choice but to respect their decision, so she and Cee, hopped into Cee's car and headed to the hotel.

The environment in the hotel was nothing like at the bar, certainly not what Kay had imagined it to be. She thought that they would ride the elevator to a specific floor and walk into a ballroom full of people dancing. Of course, she and Cee, rode the elevator to a specific floor, but instead of one ballroom, every room on the floor, occupied with a host of people enjoying themselves.

The first room they entered is for gambling. They bobbed and weaved through a crowd of people in tuxedos and evening gowns that were standing around a poker, blackjack, and a dice table. Weed, cigarette and cigar smoke lingered in the midst of the oxygen. Champagne was being sipped on and big bets were being placed. Thousands amongst thousands, of dollars in cold, hard cash lay on each table. It was almost like Vegas but without the chips to cash in; besides, no one in the room looked to be a day over thirty-five years old.

Cee, and Kay's abrupt entrance had briefly interrupted the atmosphere of the room. Every male in the entire room had; if only for a minute, stopped what they were doing to fix their eyes on the sensational body figures that stood motionless in the crowd. A well-dressed, dark-skinned door attendant immediately approached them. "Excuse me," he said in a deep voice, "how are you ladies doing tonight? Will you be joining us?"

Kay looked down at the cat suit she had on, then to the tight apple-bottom jeans that fitted around Cee's ass, and she sadly shook her head.

"No, we are going to have to pass," Kay, informed.

"Unless you are going to give us some money to play with," Cee, joked, looking at the door attendant seductively.

"No, I don't think so. It's *B.Y.O.M*, bring your own money," he informed.

"Alright then, I guess we're gone," Cee agreed, while opening the door, and allowing the light from the hallway to extinguish the red-light darkness of the room. They had run smack into a strip-tease/swingers type of environment, and the sudden lighting enabled them to see people letting go of their discretion.

Again, they stood at the door. A sense of shock had taken over their consciousness. In front of them, no more than two feet away, they watched as a man's penis went in and out of a woman who was in a doggy-style position. The force of his strokes against her backside made a clapping sound. They could hear heavy panting, growls from men, and moans from women nearby. Suddenly, he climaxed. He pulled out of the woman, took his condom off, and stood with his manhood hanging with cum dangling from its head. He walked toward Kay and Cee, strong and upright. The way he expressed his confidence definitely intimidated them, but they were unable to move. Trying desperately not to look at his Johnson, they stood stiff, fighting off the child-like snickers and laughs.

Kay grabbed Cee's arm and pulled her. "He is coming! Girl, hurry up," Kay ordered. They ran out of the room, laughing and carrying on as if they were in high school again.

After following the sound of yet another thumping beat, Kay and Cee, finally found a room that was civil ~ a place with mild conversation and people wearing the same kind of clothes categorized to fit their attire. They entered the room, bobbing their heads to the music that played.

The mood of this room eases their tension, now in complete relaxation, Cee, noticed Brim and a few other men from the neighborhood scattered throughout the room. She nudged Kay with the elbow. "There go Brim over there. You should go holler at him." Cee suggested, now smiling in Kay's face.

Kay thought for a while and decided not to go over and talk to him. It was not a bad suggestion, but she would not have known what say, so she stared across the room, wanting badly for him to break the ice. For the life of her, she could not understand why she was feeling such an emotional response behind his behavior toward her. It was not as if they were seeing each other in an intimate way. Furthermore, he was the only person she felt close to since Jay had gotten himself shot up. Deep within, she knew that if she were going to give anyone the pussy, it probably would be him. Even so, she still felt slightly uneasy behind one fact: knowing such an act would totally disrespect loyalty. It did not matter if Jay was dead or not, half of her heart remained six feet with him. The rules were not to fuck any of his friends, and she intended to make good with the rule, but she was starting to weaken.

Brim stood with his back against the wall, showing a game-face expression. Sweat began to appear slightly across his forehead while he continued to make a good observation of who was inside of the room. He was not a stranger to the world of toting guns and robbing people, he just wanted everything to go well. It was his first time trying to pull something of such magnitude. He wondered if things would go smooth without any casualties or injuries. He had his room secured and he trusted that his crew would not shoot anyone, but he did not feel the same about the people in the other rooms.

He peeked at his watch, looked around at his crew, and nodded slightly. Within seconds, they pulled from their persons automatic weapons.

"Don't anybody move! Get down! Get down! Get down!" they yelled, waving their guns and threatening people's lives. The room had turned into mass hysteria. Women were yelling and screaming hiding behind their boyfriends or any other male that they thought could protect them. Members of the crew were hitting men over the head with their guns. Some were bleeding profusely and some fell to the floor with mild concussions.

Seven gunmen secured the room while three men hurried to relieve the people of their belongings. They took everything from jewelry and money, to cell phones and then left in less than five minutes flat. The seven men ran into the hallway, and met with the other bandits who were also exiting the hotel rooms with bags of merchandise. A group of thirty men raced down the stairwell of the Marriott, exited the building, and escaped in three black vans.

Kay and Cee, stood up and swept themselves of the dirt from the floor in which they lay. They could not believe what had just take place. Everything happened so fast. The whole ordeal explained why Brim, acted as if he did not know them, and why his facial expression was so serious.

The moment everyone realized it was safe to get up from the floor, the room burst into complete chaos, the halls as well.

People were trying to leave as quickly as possible. Some were even talking to the police, giving descriptions of the perpetrators. Many waited just to let the officers know exactly what was, taken from them. They were law-abiding citizens that happened to be in the wrong place at the wrong time. The not-so-law-abiding citizens did not bother. They knew to chalk it up and charge it to the game.

"Oooh, girl, come on," said Cee, quickly grabbing Kay's hand and pulling her in the direction to exit the room.

Kay was trying to keep up with her while in her heels. "Girl, hold up, damn! Where are you taking me?" she asked. She followed Cee, out of the building, through the commotion, and into Cee's car where she peeled out of the parking spot. They both remained quiet while cruising on the expressway until Cee, abruptly burst into laughter.

"How about Blacky?" she recalled.

Kay's face looked puzzled. "Who the hell is Blacky?" she asked.

"You know," Cee, continued, shrugging her shoulders up in an attempt to mimic a male's posture and speaking with a deep voice, "how y'all ladies doing tonight?"

"Oh, you're talking about that husky guy. Yeah, he was, built like one of them Amistad dudes. That guy in the other room was built nice, too." Kay stated.

"Built nice?" Cee, twisted her lips. "Come on with that built nice shit. That dude was fine as hell, and he had a big ass dick!"

"I know. Did you see it?" Key asked, closing her eyes.

"Did I see it? Did you see the look on that girl's face? He was tearing her little coochie up." Cee, implied laughing loudly.

"He was putting his weight on it." Kay added.

"Yes he was," said Cee, while focusing on the road.

Twenty-five, bumper-to-bumper minutes later, they were parking in front of a beautiful home with a front lawn. Cee, was smiling while anxiously getting out of the car.

"Come on," Cee told Kay.

"Uh-uh, girl, where are we? I don't be going places that I don't know where I'm at!" Kay slowly got out of the car, animating her reluctance to follow Cee.

"Come on, girl. Hurry up before we wake these neighbors," Cee, urged.

They were in an upscale neighborhood. A place where the paperboy still came by throwing his latest edition of news on the steps, and the milkman still was got chased by the dogs. The neighbors who lived there were the kind that would knock on your door and greet you with a freshly baked apple cobbler for purposes of welcoming you to their community. They would ask such questions like, '*Where are you from?*' and, '*What line of work are you in?*' Not because they are truly interested in a person's life, but to monitor them, and to know whom they are letting into their community.

"Who house is this?" Kay whispered, admiring the architectural work of the house. She particularly admired the big-circled window on the first floor, with the second-floor windows being the normal rectangular kind. She thought the house looked like a face with the mouth open. "Girl, whose fucking house, is this?" Kay continued to ask.

Cee, ignored Kay and rang the doorbell. "He is going to trip, watch," she said while waiting for someone to answer the door.

Kay quickly got back into the car however; she still left the passenger door open. From afar, she watched as Brim answered the door, holding a gun in his hand and mouthing off to Cee, about coming to his house. She wondered if she should get out of the car or just wait until he ceased with the madness.

Cee, turned her back to him and signaled for Kay. "Kay, come on. This dude making all this damn noise, knowing he got neighbors and shit!" Cee faced Brim and pushed past his body entering his home. "Move," she said.

Kay admired her bravery, but she still was not about to go into his home uninvited.

"Are you coming or what?" Brim questioned, while holding the door open and looking both ways, making sure no one was out there to ambush him. Kay got out of the car, shut the door, and slowly walked toward the house while thoroughly checking out his body. All of a sudden, the gun was not a problem. In fact, she thought he looked damn good standing in the door with no shirt on and holding a gun. To her, he looked Rambo-ish.

Since Jay had been dead, she had fantasized about Brim being on top of her quite a few times; even so, she never in her wildest dreams would have imagined him to be so, nicely built. She looked him up and down and let her eyes roam to his crotch area as she walked past, entering his home.

The inside was a little more than Kay had expected. She had long ago labeled him as a player, so she expected to see an empty house with a bed in the middle of the living room floor. Instead, she walked into a nice set-up. She noticed the oak wood floors first. They were burgundy, varnished, waxed and reflecting a glare from the kitchen's lighting. The stairs were white around the base and oak-wood burgundy on the top. To her right, a fifty-two-inch flat-screen sat alone on the wall. Its chrome trimming matched the oval, glass coffee table with chrome legs and the five black, leather high chairs with chrome legs that were sitting in front of his mini-bar. A black leather sofa, a leather adjustable chair, and a leather beanbag were, positioned around the coffee table. There were no pictures on the walls, except for a refrigerator and a microwave. The house was definitely a bachelor crib; however, it was better than a bed in the middle of the floor.

Kay sat on the soft leather sofa and immediately thought of rest. She had planned this night out, but still, she felt guilty about being awake in the wee hours of the morning, losing beauty sleep. Her body truly felt tired, but she knew she could not fall asleep if she tried. There was too much excitement generating adrenaline through her veins.

She continued to secretly lust off Brim's body, wondering if she could ever allow herself to let go of her honor and loyalty to her dead boyfriend to pursue a life of happiness. She already understood the power of her pussy, and she knew how to mesmerize. If a cat thought that all she had was a pretty face and outstanding body, he was in trouble once she got him behind closed doors. She had a distinct power over men, and Brim was, considered lucky for not being at her mercy already.

"Cee, get out of my refrigerator!" he yelled, toward the back of the kitchen.

"This is bad," said Cee, holding a Chinese container of five-day-old beef Yok. "I'm throwing it away. You need a woman's touch up in this piece. If you pay me, I'll come clean this joint," Cee offered, whipping her finger amongst the kitchen cabinets.

"All I need is for you to get out of my Frig. Why is she so crazy?" Brim asked Kay, shaking his head at Cee's demeanor.

"Uh-huh," Kay replied, admiring the home, and agreeing with him.

"What's wrong with you? What, the cat got your tongue? Why do you have that crazy look?" He asked, redirecting his attention towards Kay.

Kay then realized that her lust for him that she thought was a secret had become noticeable in a small way.

"There's nothing wrong with me. I do have a question though," Kay replied, intuitively.

"And, what's that?" Brim asked suductively, wondering what could possibly be her question.

"Can we have our things back you took from us?" Kay wondered, smiling and hoping he would confirm her request.

"Yeah, break us off!" Cee, added, determined to get a piece of his earnings. Cee knew if she pressed the issue hard enough, there would be no way he could deny her, and she had no problem holding that over his head. In so many ways, they were like Bonnie and Clyde, with an on-and-off-again love affair.

Who knows, maybe they could have tried it, but Cee, had a history that Brim could not accept. She had four kids by four different people. All of them were in the streets knee-deep just as much as he was, and too often, she failed to exhibit her place as a woman, which was one of the reasons why she was alone. Perhaps in his younger years she would have been a catch, but he had matured too much to be putting his foot in a woman's ass every time she felt the need to assume the man's role.

"Yeah, y'all can have y'all shit back. Hold up," Brim responded to Kay, looking at Cee, with a despising stare, "I knew you would hound me as soon as you walked into that hotel room." *Greedy bitch*, he thought. But he refused to argue with her, knowing it may be another time that he would need her to sleep with someone just to find out where that person hides their money.

He skipped up the steps and came back down with two small brown paper bags. He gave one to each of them. Kay's bag contained her belongings and an additional two grand. Cee, had the same in her bag: her belongings and one thousand dollars. She looked into the bag and held the money in her hand as if her hand was a scale and she could determine the weight.

"A thousand dollars! Is that all your going to give me?" Cee shouted, aggressively.

"Look, you're fucking pushing it!" Brim yelled. He continued. "You didn't lift a finger for that grand! I done told you before, I don't owe you shit!"

Cee, snickered and walked across the room, switching while waving the money in her hand. "Wooptie doo, wooptie freaking doo," she stated, stopping in front of Brim, and stared in his face with her body so close that he could feel her breath on his lips. She pointed her finger in his face and moved her head in a sassy manner in an attempt to run down her rights. "Oh, you don't owe Cee!" she argued. "That's that bullshit Brim!" she said.

"How about all the clowns I fucked for you? On the other hand, that time I told you where that guy Latney, money was at, and allowing him to beat me all, the fuck up, and you did nothing?" she asked, and continued. "Secondly, the time you asked if I could suck his dick because he was going to fuck you up, and this jackass had an STD!" Brim and Kay, sat, and listened on. Cee, pointed her finger at Brim and added. "In addition, you never came to see me in the hospital, not once. I could not even pay the bills, knowing I was going through some shit with medical coverage and them welfare people," Cee's eyes began to water with tears. "I was on all types of meds, throat looking like somebody's thigh, and you give me a get-well card, and one balloon. One fucking balloon, though! Not to mention that little girl of yours that dropped out this ass. Do I need to say more?" Cee, informed, becoming angrier, by the second.

Four

Justice

Kay lay motionless in her bed. Her alarm clock struck 5:30 a.m., further awakening her with the anthem to the morning show on Power 99 FM. Every fiber in her being, told her to just lay there and disregard every responsibility she had to take care of for that day, but she knew that too many people were counting on her. If it was not her boss at the job, it was her girls and Stew's youngest ~ not to mention Stew. It had been six months since her oldest son was murdered and she had been, raped. The pain and mental stress of the incident took an enormous toll on the disease Stew carried. For the life of her, she did not see the logic in the police arresting Crab, and charging him with Jalen's death. Despite him bringing Bobby, Young Corey, and Lil' Ron to the house, she knew he loved his son and would have never conspired to the act of her being, raped.

Within a matter of months, Crab, was push through the system and sentenced to serve four to eight years for voluntary manslaughter. The chain of events was just too much for her to shoulder. By the time, he was shipped upstate; Stew enjoyed the luxury of only one call before being, restrained to a hospital bed and restricted to a liquid diet of resource drinks. For the first three months, Kay had hired a nurse to stay over twice a week, but even that became a heavy burden on her pockets.

Fighting with all of her will, Kay let her feet practically flop off the bed as she stood to turn the music up. She knew the music was loud enough to disrupt Stew and the children's sleep, but at that moment, she could have cared less. She was half-mad at the world, mad at the rest of her family for disassociating themselves from Stew, and tired of responsibilities and the need to rebel, even if in a petty manner. Besides her kids, Cee, had become the only thing good in Kay's life. They had become best friends, and because of it, the strong bond Kay shared with Vita had deteriorated, thanks to jealousy. Kay tried hard on many occasions to assure Vita that even though she and Cee, were hanging, nothing had changed between them, but it was a losing battle. Vita had made it completely clear that she wanted Kay's undivided friendship, but Kay was refusing to kiss any ass, friend, or no friend.

With her eyes half closed, Kay lazily made her way to the bathroom. She looked into the mirror, smiled, and released a few chuckles, noticing that her facial expression was angry. Her appearance was a complete image of how she felt within. After splashing cold water on her face, she brushed her teeth, and then rolled her Yoga mat out in front of her bed to proceed with her morning ritual of keeping her body tight. It took a half hour of Yoga and a half hour of Pilates for her to feel better. She was charged and ready for the day, mentally equipped to overcome whatever bullshit she figured would creep into her life for that day.

By 7:45 a.m., Kay was dressed and serving the kids hot oatmeal for breakfast. She had to have them in school at 8:30 a.m., and be at work by nine. She was moving according to schedule. She watched the kids enjoy their food. "Y'all hurry up now, so mommy can take you guys to school," she told them, then excused her-self from the kitchen table to check on Stew. *Mommy,* she silently thought. *How could she allow Stew to talk her into letting him call her that?* Stew explained it as a way of allowing her son to grow up respecting Kay enough to listen to her. She wanted her son to feel a sense of deep attachment to Kay as a mother figure, and the title "Mom" was that way. She knew that no matter what happened Kay would always keep Stew in his head, as his biological mom, but two mothers, Stew figured was even better.

Stew lay frozen in her hospital bed with an oxygen mask on her face. She looked to the ceiling, slowly blinked, and smiled as she turned her ears into the kids' spurts of laughter. She remembered when her mother and Kay's mother used to have her and Kay sit down to eat at the same table. Now, both of their mothers were dead and she knew it was only a matter of time before she would join them.

When Kay entered the room, Stew's smile grew. Although she was dying, that in no way damaged her sense of taste when it came to fashion. She loved to see Kay dressed to impress each day, knowing that she would dazzle the heart of any man with a simple, *'hello.'*

Kay was always humble at the sight of Stew's condition. She tried to maintain a strong expression as she pulled up a chair and held Stew's hand.

"Hey, you," she said, partially smiling and barely showing her rows of perfectly white teeth. Tears began to ascend from the wells of her eyes. They were glassy, shining like the glare from a crystal ball. She held them open to keep the tears from actually falling. Stew clenched her had tighter, gave a lazy tiring smile, and shook her head as if to tell her not to cry. Kay tried but could not hold the tears back any longer. She was tired of the pain and hated seeing her cousin in such a predicament without being able to help. She literally, in her lifetime, had watched Stew transform from a child with cornrows and pigtails to a six-foot 145-pound woman ~ beautiful, voluptuous, curvy, and sexy ~ and now a 75-pound skin-and-bone frail woman whose life was slowly deteriorating.

Stew was the one Kay used to look up to, the big sister she never had; she was the one who fought Kay's battles at nine and ten years old. She introduced Kay to a sense of style at fourteen years old, bought her, her first set of thong underwear, and taught her how to walk in stilettos. In many ways, she was afraid to go on without Stew.

Kay's tears made Stew shed tears also. She pulled the oxygen mask from her face and pulled Kay's hand to her lips to kiss it. "It's okay, mommy," she whispered.

Overwhelmed by the memorable moment, Kay quickly snatched her hand back and ran into the vestibule. She leaned against the wall, slid down in squat position, and cried her heart away. Her whales were loud and uncontrollable. As she bowed her head and palmed her face with both of her hands, Cashmere had appeared. "Mommy, what's wrong?" he asked.

Kay quickly wiped her eyes and lifted her head. "Nothing," she said answered with a chuckle. She was amazed at his innocence and willingness to call her mommy because his mommy Stew had told him to do so.

Kay stood, took in a deep breath, grabbed his hand, and walked him back into the kitchen. "Are you finished your breakfast already?"

"Yup, I'm a big boy!" The child replied.

"Let me see," Kay said, looking at the empty plate. "Oh, you are a big boy!" she praised while giving him a hug. She looked at her watch and hurried to get the kids ready to leave. Everyone lined up to give Stew a kiss before heading out of the front door.

Traffic was crowed on the Schuylkill Expressway. Kay had been taking the same route for over a year and never saw as many cars backed up. As the long train of vehicles gradually moved, she later discovered that an accident had occurred. The kids were jumping around in the back seat, fascinated by the spinning lights of the ambulance and the debris caused by the wreckage. "Sit y'all asses down back there!" yelled Kay, turning at an off ramp and looking at them from the rearview mirror. She headed to a coffee shop. It was not any ol' coffee shop, but one where there was all-male customer service, the only kind in the city.

The car quickly pulled into the mini-parking lot. Kay turned the key back and took it out of the ignition. "Y'all keep still. I'll be right back," Kay told the kids while getting out of the car. As she walked towards the shop, she looked through the huge storefront window past the cursive neon coffee & pastry sign and noticed the men had smiles on their faces. The door chimes rang when she entered. She is met with a welcome of a few employees clapping. They were the steady ones, working there since the first day she entered on their grand opening three years ago. They were: *Blue, Dave, Patrick, Henry,* and *Tyrese.* The other four faces in employee uniforms were unfamiliar to her; however, they were just as handsome and well groomed as the others were.

The shop was almost, filled to the capacity. Kay navigated through the cold atmosphere, unconsciously exhibiting her signature strut, but knowing all eyes were on her. The men looked at her with lust, their natural male testosterone enabling their dicks to get brick hard. The women rolled their eyes and frowned at the nerve of her walking into the joint drawing all of the attention. Their envy deliberately stripped her of her rightful description as a black queen: strong, beautiful, and confident. In their eyes, she was deemed nothing more than, a good for nothing whore, who would probably fuck every man.

To Kay, the shop was a breath of fresh air, despite the uneasy stares and rolling of the eyes from the women. Also, was the fact that many of her potential friends had boyfriends, who at one time or another, tried to slide into her panties. When she told them of their boyfriend's disloyalty, she was always accused of wanting their man. The treatment Kay would receive from other women made her slightly turn her nose in the air with confidence and a speck of conceit. Each time she entered the shop, the floor became her fantasy-modeling debut.

The sound of her shoes hitting the floor echoed as she bypassed the long line and made her way to the counter where a man patiently waited for his order. Looking him in the eyes, she licked her permanently puckered lips and asked, "Do you mind? I'm running late," Kay, wondered.

"No, not at all, go on ahead," he answered with his eyes admiring her nice thighs.

"Thank you, I truly appreciate it," Kay politely replied giving the man a long stair.

She ordered a decaffeinated espresso and a corn muffin, then sashayed her ass out of the door, hoping each man had their eyes fixed on her ass. Her life was that lonely. She was getting sick and tired of the dildo action. She needed to feel a piece of flesh inside of her and a little companionship would have been a plus.

Kay dropped the kids off and continued her mission to make it to work on time. She listened to the tunes of *Xscape* flowing from the stereo. "What I need from you is Un-der-stan-ding," she loudly chirped, letting her voice practically drown the song while coasting down Roosevelt Boulevard. *"Damn! This was the shit,"* she commented, as if someone was in the car with her. The song reminded her of the good times, the days when Jay was alive and Asr, was a newborn,

She missed Jay dearly. At times, he would cross her mind and somehow be the voice of her conscious. Whenever she was undecided on which way to go about a situation, her decisions were loosely, based on what she thought he would tell her to do or the advice she thought he would give her. Not a day had passed without her thinking of him, and if he were alive, there would be so many things to talk about, so many things to explain ~ like Charity for instance.

Kay loved her second child, but she could not help remembering how she felt when she first became pregnant with her. All she knew was that she was torn between the thought of having a family with Charity's father ~ the one guy whom she grew to love ~ and Jay, the love of her life and the one guy she knew always had her best interest at heart. She remembered hearing Jay's voice nearly heckling at her conscious that day, *Kay do not have that baby just because you think he is going to be with you. Because that baby, is not going to change anything. He does not even deal with you too tough. Imagine how he will act when a baby gets into the picture. I am telling you Kay, he is not going to stick around.*

The words always played loudly in her mind every time she thought of that day; the day she discovered, she was to have another child. Of course, she disregarded Jay's advice and carried Charity to full term, but no soon, as she dropped her load, she was on her own.

Even before then, she had made desperate attempts to disregard Jay's voice in her mind, but every time she ignored him, he turned out to be right. Like the time she allowed herself to be talked into having a threesome. Well, she like to use *"threesome"* as the professional term for the event, but Mike and Pub had used the term *"partied"* when they told the whole senior class of William Penn High School.

....

Back then, she had just turned eighteen. Jason had been dead for almost two years and she was within a week from graduating after struggling through each report period. The grades were already submitted for the year, but the majority of the senior class stilled showed up for school to have fun, say good-bye, and sign yearbooks. Kay was not any different. That day, she stepped into William Peen High School, making not only a fashion statement, but also a statement as to remind her that her life as a teen enjoying school days was over, and a life as a woman to be, taken seriously in the world had begun.

She wore a pair of light-blue Fendi Capri Jeans, a lime-green, tight women's tank top that allowed her chest to appear perky and lime-green sandals with crisscrossing straps tying at her calves. Her hair was styled in crimps. She carried a Fendi handbag made of light-blue jean material and wore Fendi glasses with an Ice Tea tint. As usual, she mostly associated with the men, signing their books, flirting, and just having general conversation.

It was near the end of her last period. She was sitting with her legs crossed, chewing gum, and fumbling with the plastic picture case attached to her keys. She smiled at the small picture; thinking of how cute she looked the day that photo, had been taken, suddenly, Pub had pulled up a chair and started talking to her, "What up Kay?" he asked.

Kay stared for two seconds, and then popped her chewing gum before returning his greeting, "Hey, Pub, what's up?"

"Ain't shit, I'm trying to figure out why you haven't signed my book yet. You signing all these books, I just want to see where I fit in. Can I get an appointment?" Pub asked, smiling from ear to ear.

"Don't do that, Pub, you know it's not even like that. We have always been cool. Why wouldn't I sign your book?" Kay replied, embracing his smile.

"I don't know. Maybe, it is because you do not really like me anymore. We used to be alright when we was in Wanamaker, on the junior high tip," he said admiring her outfit.

"Uh-uh, don't even try it." Kay twisted her lips and let her eyes journey across his upper physique. "You the one started acting all funny when we got here, especially, when you first made the All-Public basketball team, and then when you made it again in the tenth grade; you swore you were the shit," she informed.

Pub grinned. "Come on, stop playing," he said.

"No, how about when you grew your little cuts and started looking all buff and made the team again last year? You really were thinking you the shit, Mr. Pub. I do not even know how

I started calling you that. 'Cause you still going to be Arnold Howard to me," Kay informed with a bright grin.

"That's cool wit' me, though; but, how about you getting all thick after you had your baby?" he said.

"Come on now, I am not that thick," Kay replied.

"You were way smaller than that," he said smiling.

"So were you," she fired back.

"Yeah, yeah, yeah; anyways, can I get my book signed though? I see you trying to get out of that, huh?"

"Where's it at?" Kay wondered, looking around questionably.

"I left it home, the bell is ready to ring, are you going to take a ride with me?" he wondered.

Without thinking, Kay answered, "Yes." She knew that he had his own house and figured that he was trying to get her into his bed, but she did not mind. She had wanted him throughout her entire high school years, but because he was a star point guard destined for big things, there were also too many other girls she had to compete with. As soon as the bell rang, Kay found herself taking a ten-minute ride with him to his house.

It was a one-floor, two-bedroom place. The floors were honey brown. A money-green, leather sofa and love chair sat in front of an entertainment shelf. On the shelves were a twenty-seven inch color T.V., X-box, ten-CD disc changer, and shiny basketball trophies.

Kay stood in the living room and slowly spun in a circle. To her left was a hall, which she imagined was the gateway to his love nest. To her right was a small area one might call a kitchen. She laid her handbag on a squared glass table next to the sofa.

"Come on, the book is back here," said Pub, walking down the short hall and opening the door at the end.

Kay smirked, "you think you slick," she said while following his lead. "Where is the book?"

"It's right here see," he advised.

Pub handed Kay the book. She retrieved an ink pen from her

handbag and began flipping the pages, looking for a nice space to write something. She wrote:

"...*Hey Pub, congrats on your B-ball scholarship. Stay cool, stay safe, and when reading this, always remember me, Kay-Kay, Class of '95...*"

Pub read the message and grinned. "Remember you, huh?" he asked.

"Yup," Kay answered, looking at him in the most seducing manner he had ever viewed. His heart began beating extra hard, along with the hardening of his penis. He moved in closer, taking in the aroma of her fragrance. He noticed her nipples had grown hard. She stared into his eyes, inviting him to take her. She was wet and her readiness took over. Grabbing his hand made him engage her in a passionate tongue-twirling, wet lip lock. Their bodies were warm, transferring magnetic sexual impulses. As their tongues danced in the heat of passion, their bodies grew closer. Her arms were locked around his neck, their chests were touching, and there was slow, hard grinding of their pelvic areas.

He pulled his lips away and began kissing her on the cheek, working his way to her neck while unfastening her Capri's making them drop to her ankles. His kisses were passionate, soft, and wet. Kay kept her eyes closed, listening to her heartbeat dance to the touch of his wet lips that were traveling across her right shoulder. His right hand gently rubbed her pussy while his left fingertips gracefully tickled her back. Kay quivered, "P-Pub," then let out a breathless gasp. Her arms were down to the side and her fist were balled tight. She was immobile. It was as if she could not move. "Pub," she softly whispered while opening and closing her fists, trying to control the overwhelming sensation that was running through her body.

Pub stepped back and looks her in the eyes while reaching for the bottom of his t-shirt to begin taking it off. Next were his jeans shorts, his sneakers, and then his boxer briefs. Kay looked down at his rock-hard dick, and then her eyes traveled to his stomach. She took her fingers across his six-pack, his chest, and then his traps.

His body was ripped, warm, and hard. The physique intimidated her just a little, but it did not stop her from delicately palming his sack, grabbing his dick, and proceeding to kneel.

Suddenly, Pub stood her up, grabbed her hands, and placed them back at her side. He continued his alluring stares while he took his hands around the small of her back and under her thong panties. She slowly cocked her legs open to enable him to pull them down with each hand. He kneeled and began kissing her hip ~ the same soft and wet kisses that other parts of the body had experienced. His teasing was driving her crazy. Her legs began to tremble as his kisses turned into licks. He licked and french kissed her inner thigh, and blew smoothly on the spots that he kissed. Kay was breathing loud and heavy. She could not keep still any longer. Her right hand began rubbing the muscles in his back. Finally, he pulled her legs out of the opening of her thong and Capri jeans. She instantly stepped her other leg out and used her heel to kick them behind her and out of the way. Pub had placed her right thigh over his shoulder to rest while he moved his face in and took in her aroma. Without further delay, he began passionately French kissing her pussy.

"P-P-Pub," Kay gasped, heavily fighting to pronounce his name. She had her pussy eaten before, but not like Pub was doing it. His long tongue dashed in and out. He sucked on her clitoris and finger-stroked her until she was practically begging him to stop; however, the more she begged, the more Pub intensified his treat. Like and animal, he licked and gnawed, making her love fall down in ecstasy. "Umm, Oh God! Oooh!" She yelled. She then collapsed to the floor, dizzy from the orgasm.

As Kay lay breathing heavy on the floor, her pussy muscles contracted, allowing the last of her orgasm to flow from between her legs. Pub crawled on top of her and used his knees to guide her legs spread eagle. He grabbed the bottom of her tank top and began lifting it. Kay sat up and raised her arms so that he could take it off with ease. Her breast were pointed, a firm mouthful.

He immediately began to fondle them. He kissed her, wild and sloppy, yet with an intense sexual desire that made her butterflies fly loops in the pit of her stomach. He pulled his lips away and stared into her eyes, hypnotizing her thoughts and stealing her soul. "Can you taste yourself?" he whispered.

Kay smiled. At that moment, she had never seen a man so handsome. She wanted to feel him inside her. She leaned back as he took one of her breast in his mouth and played with her clitoris with a middle finger. She trembled, wanting badly for him to stop. She just wanted him to fuck her, but he teased and played, rapidly shaking her clit and forcing her vaginal juices to gush. She tried moving her body away from him, but she could not get away. She knew that if she had another orgasm, then that would probably be it. She would be too drained to do what she wanted to do to him, but still, she could not resist getting caught up in the feeling. Her hips slowly moved in a circular rhythm. She arched her back as her body tensed. "Aaahhh!" she bellowed as she came for the second time.

Pub lifted his face from her breast, looked at her, and chuckled. Kay's eyes were lazy. She grinned and punched him in the arm.

"Boy! Why you do that?" Key, asked excitedly.

"Shut up, you know you like it," he told her.

"Yeah, but I'm saying though," Pub questioned, with concern.

"What are you saying? The day still young, you're not leaving, are you?" he asked.

"I would love to stay, but I do have a child. Let me use your phone," she asked.

Kay stood up and buckled. Her knees were weak, but she managed to strut over to the nightstand next to his bed and call Stew. She had to at least, let Stew know that she will be home in a few more hours. When she hung up the phone, she looked at Pub with a smirk on her face and rolled her eyes.

"Which one of those rooms is the bathroom, boy?" Kay wondered.

"It's the one on the right," said Pub. "What's the rolling of the eyes for though?"

Kay got up and began walking to the bathroom. "You know why, don't play stupid. I need a washcloth," Kay declares.

Pub went into his dresser drawer, gave her a washcloth, and watched her ass shake as she walked into the bathroom. While she was in there cleaning herself, Pub's best friend and roommate, Mike, had come home. Pub heard the front door opening. He hurried to put his shorts on and met Mike in the living room, just in case Mike was on his way to use the lavatory.

"Raw, what's up?" asked Pub while giving him a tight handshake.

"I haven't been doing much. I just got finished shipping the rest of my things to Georgia Tech," Mike, answered as he sat his keys on the table next to the sofa.

"Georgia? That's what's up bro, however, I still think you should have put in for Kansas with me," Pub suggested.

"Man, I'm not going way out there with them hillbillies. Besides, our scholarships are different, and I do not dribble like you. You should have come to Georgia. You get out there and start dealing with those white girls if you want, they going to…"

Mike's, sentence was interrupted, behind Pub pushing him. He angrily shook his head and placed his index finger to his lips. "Ssssshh," he whispered, than pointed into the direction of the bathroom. "Be quiet, man!" he ordered.

Mike looked down the hall and saw Kay switching her beautiful naked body out of their bathroom. Her lime-green spaghetti-strapped sandals neatly tied around her calves, complementing her mocha-colored skin tone, which magnified her natural sexiness. He grabbed himself around his crotch area. He could not believe what he was witnessing.

"Damn, who is that?" he muttered, in an overzealous manner.

"Keep it down," Pub told him.

"My apologies, but who is she, though? He whispered, making a conscious effort to be mindful that she may be listening.

"That's Kay-Kay," he answered.

"Kay-Kay! What Kay-Kay," he wondered. "Not Kay from school?" Raw asked. Pub, in a sinister fashion, smiled.

"What's that pussy like," Mike asked, and continued. "Is it as good as it is?" he wondered, "I mean, she be walking around like that shit is the best in the world."

"I didn't fuck her yet," he responded, with a devilish look.

"Please explain to me why not?" Raw asked.

"I was trying some things different," Pub replied, looking down the hallway.

Mike "Raw" chuckled. "You must've been reading one of them nasty as books again?"

"Don't worry 'bout all that. You stay all in my business," Pub replied.

"What's up with her though?" Mike inquired, in an overwhelmed way.

"Why, what's up with you? Do you want to party her?" Pub, offered.

Mike's face showed surprised. "Yeah right, my dude. You must be playing, I know you don't have it like that."

"Uh-humm, watch this," he suggested. Pub slowly walked into his room and found Kay sitting on the edge of his bed, fumbling through pages of his book titled *Giving Her Multiple Waves of Sensation*.

Kay stood and walked over to put the book back on top of the dresser. She turned and gave him a disapproving twist of the lips. He was embarrassed that she had to learn he was stealing his moves from an author, but still, he grabbed her and held her close to him with confidence. For sixty seconds they stood in the middle of the floor kissing, allowing their bodies to regenerate a warm heat of passion. To Kay, his kisses were the best. The soft touch of his lips made her pussy moist again. This time around, she was determined to feel him inside of her. Determined not to let a *how to,* book cheat her out of her turn at bat.

Horny and anxious, she grabbed his hand leading him, as the two of them lay down on the bed simultaneously. She dropped her heels on the floor and cocked open her legs widely. "I want you really bad," she loudly whispered, leaning back on an elbow while touching her clitoris. She was trying her best to turn him wild.

Pub watched with excitement racing through his body. She looks good and tasty he thought. Her head tilted to the side with a few strips of crimpled hair partially covering one eye. She stared seductively, moaning and biting her bottom lip while seemingly playing peek-a-boo by hiding behind her hair. He wanted her badly to himself, but Mike was in the other room waiting patiently.

He continued to stare, appreciating that simple moment in time as it was both peaceful and pleasant with lustful intentions, watching her perform on herself before introducing such an inadequate question.

"Hey, Kay, listen," Pub, said with seriousness. She remained focused even observing his hard penis. He continued while his mind was fighting between enjoying her entertainment versus the right words to say to have her accept Mike as a participant in their episode. "My man Mike out there, and to be honest with you, we both want to spend that special time with you, simply to enjoy this special moment." He paused shortly, and continued. Key looked him calmly in the face. "We are on our way to college and we thought that maybe you could bless us tonight. Kind of like a big going away present." She opened her concerns to see where he was going. "If you do me this favor, I'll never forget you Kay-Kay," he said with a boyish look.

Kay immediately stopped, sat up, and closed her legs to try an understand the question, although, her womanhood were aggressively tingling.

"What!" she said surprised. Her face wrinkled, showing the

deepest expression of disappointment. "You are playing right, Pub?" she shouted.

Pub shook his head. "No, Kay, I'm not playin'. We are really hoping to make this night right. Can you do this for us, for me?" Pub wondered.

Kay looked into his eyes. They were sad and sincere, reminding her of a whining puppy, cute and innocent. For the life of her, she could not understand why she suddenly felt the need to grant his wish. She felt sorry for him. She stared and wondered how many girls he tagged with the same guilt and responsibility, that if she did not agree, it would destroy him. Instead of college, he would end up dead or in jail like other's she knew whose hoop dreams had deflated.

Pub walked in close so that the crotch of his jean shorts was staring in Kay's face. "So what's up? Can we do something? I know this supposed to be about us, but circumstances change all the time," Pub informed.

"Look," Kay interrupted, "there's no need to say all that. Where's he at?" Kay ordered, giving him the comprehension of a woman who did not need explaining.

"Hold on," Pub said, walking out the room. Pub went to get Mike. While he was gone, Kay began to hear Jay's voice. *Do not be so damn stupid!* It said. *You know if you do this, they going to run their faces. You cannot trust 'em. Moreover, you do not even know Mike like that.*

Kay shook her head of Jason's voice. When Pub and Mike entered the bedroom, Pub, as usual, looked serious; which assured Kay that he was in control of the situation. Mike was all smiles as he admired Kay's nude body. Initiating the episode, Pub loosened his shorts, let them drop to his ankles, and stepped out of the legs. Kay looked at his Johnson and leaned back, inviting him to take her with her legs cocked open. He climbed on top of her and began with his wet kisses, and then he took hold of his manhood and teased her, rubbing the head softly up and down the wetness of her ready pussy lips before inserting.

Kay gasped at the feel of him inside of her. Finally, it slid as deep as it could, easing through like a hot butter knife melting into a stick of margarine. Her eyes rolled in sensation as he slowly pushed and pulled his length. She slowly humped, joining his gentle strokes. Each motion made her secret lubrication all over his love muscle. Her pussy was warm, yet tight, clutching his thickness.

Mike had taken off his clothes and stood watching and waiting for them to include him. It was like as if he was on the set of a porno shoot. Kay wrapped her legs around Pub's body and bit onto his shoulder as he stroked hard and fast. He breathed heavy and growled as he pumped faster and faster until he exploded inside of her.

He lay still on top of her for thirty seconds. He pulled his softening rod out of her and stood with it hanging limp. His breaths were still heavy.

"Go ahead, Raw, he said, attempting to step back and let his friend get a turn.

Mike stepped up with his penis ready to taste paradise. Suddenly Kay sat up. Her mentality had transformed into a true lioness. She identified Pub as a wounded opponent and went in for the kill.

"Uh-uh, hold up," she said, grabbing hold of Pub by the hips and taking his softness into her warm mouth. She toyed with the head of his dick with her tongue, alerting his sexual senses and making blood race into his manhood, to once again, stand like a soldier. Pub trembled from the sensational feeling. Her mouth felt just as warm and wet as her vagina. He was practically busting out of his skin from his hardness. She sucked on him like a maniac, driving him crazy. He tried to push her head away, but she had a hold of his ass cheeks, forcing him to withstand the sensation. Suddenly, unidentified emotion overwhelmed his body.

"Sssshhit, girl! Damn!" he blurted, angry and confused behind the tears that began to drop from his eyes. He was in heaven. She let loose of his buttocks and gently fondled his sacks with her left hand.

Mike watched attentively. Finally, Kay reached her right hand out, used her index finger to signal him to move closer. Following her gesture, he placed his penis in her hand allowing her to stroke him. Her soft, manicured hand jerked him pleasingly as she continued to gobble Pub. Both he and Mike were in bliss. The feeling of control made Kay extra magnificent, she was into it. She took her mouth away from Pub's soldier and sucked his sacks. With a penis in both hands and nuts in her mouth, she orchestrated their climax.

Pub came first. Mike was well on his way to follow when Kay stood to sit Pub on the bed so that she could mount him. She wanted to concentrate on making sure that he'd never forget her. Slowly, she lowered herself, burying him deep inside of her while taking Mike into her mouth, as it sat comfortably within her oral cave.

"Shit!" he blurted, looking down to watch her pretty lips ravish his baby-maker. She slowly moved to, and fro, making Pub gasp and pant. Suddenly, Mike let out a growl as he squirted semen into her mouth. She continued to deep throat him, draining every speck of his energy until he quickly pulled away from her. "Damn!" Mike, chuckled.

Kay looked at him and captured his soul. It was as if he could not look anywhere else. He suddenly felt intimidated, conquered, and inferior. She continued to stare deeply as her hips gyrated to, and fro in a circular motion. Her hands were propped upon Pub's lap. She rode him as if she was sitting on a mechanical bull, working her body until her g-spot was touched.

"Oh…ummm…ummm," she moaned in total enjoyment, moving slow, fast, and hard so that her spot was touched each time she buried him. Finally, she had the ultimate orgasm. Her white, creamy love fell upon Pub's rod like snow on a winter day, sending goose bumps along his forearm. "Uuuhh!" he growled as he released inside of her for the second time.

That day, Kay would have never thought that Jay's voice was the voice of reason to listen to, until she was, forced to stop going to school because of everyone knowing about her sexual indiscretion. Weeks later, Kay was dressed in a white cap and gown, sitting amongst the rest of the class of '95 and waiting for her name to be called. Stew sat in the audience with a camcorder, proud of her cousin's struggling achievement. As the announcer called Kay's, name to accept her diploma, every male in the senior class cheered, hooted, whistled, and hollered uncontrollably. Kay was surprised. She stood and began strutting like a model, walking towards the announcer. The cheers grew louder. She smiled as she took her diploma, waved it in the air, and continued to strut. Suddenly, she stopped in front of the seated graduates, squatted, placed both hands on her knees, and did the booty-pop for three seconds. The boys were going crazy as she stood and continued her imitation of a runway model. She figured that what has, been done was done.

....

The closer Kay began to get to her job, her mental state of life and experiences in ignoring Jay's voices had transcended to a more-focused thought on present reality. She had been late more than enough times to be fired. She looked at her watch and noticed that she would be late once again. She worried that if she were fired then it would be extra hard to find a job. Not only were there close to millions of females qualified to do clerical work, but she did not exactly build up good references throughout her places of employment.

At last, she arrived at work, cruising in her Ford Taurus two miles per hour in the parking lot while trying to find a place to park. Her only option was near the entrance of the building that she worked in, which was one of six others. The Neshaminy Complex was a six-building community, that Kay dreaded visiting most of the time.

Kay sat in the car and looked through the mirror installed in the car's sun visor, making sure that her appearance was up to par.

"What's up Kay," a male co-worker said as he walked past the car. Kay peeked away from the mirror.

"Oh, hey, Pete," she returned before flipping the visor up, letting out a big sigh, and exiting the car.

Dressed in a pair of Donna Karen navy-blue linen pants, a rust-colored Donna Karen blouse, and her rust-colored Nine West Ostrich shoes, she artistically walked through the maze of secretarial cubicles. She was half annoyed by the phone ringing and the click-clack of hands consistently pressing on keys of their computers.

As usual, almost all of the females that worked there disliked Kay, but the men always acknowledged her in a way that showed their appreciation for her gracing the office with her presence. "Looking good, Kay," voices echoed from a group of men standing at a water fountain."

"Oh, hey y'all," Kay responded, acting surprised as if she did not see them. Before sitting in her personal cubicle, she looked at the girl whose cubicle was across from hers and rolled her eyes with contempt. Deep down, she really had nothing against the girl, but the girl looked at Kay with hate in her eyes. Kay was not a fighter, but she had quite a few dances under her belt. The gesture of rolling her eyes was to let the girl know that she was not a coward, and she had the distinct will to kick ass at the drop of a dime.

Before she knew it, Kay had sat down and dove into a pool of papers stacked on top of her desk. She read the written instructions that her supervisor left on little yellow post-it and followed them to the letter. Seven and a half hours flew, and the day had gone smooth without her being, confronted about lateness. Again, she made a mental note to be on point, just as she had the other times she turned up late. She quickly began cleaning her cubicle to get ready for punch-out time.

Finally, the clock struck five. Kay rushed to punch out with her kids on her mind. She smiled in amazement at how she always felt tired of them when she was around them, but missed them when she was away from them more than four hours. While leaving the office building, she bumped into the same co-worker that she had seen in the parking lot that morning. If she did not know any better, she would have thought that he was stalking her, but it turned out to be a case of major car trouble. In addition, Pete was not the stalker type. He was the romantic kind who wined and dined before a night of lovemaking. She was almost certain of his character, making the assessment from the few times he had practically broken his neck to open a door for her, not to mention the singing telegram she received when he asked her to go out with him.

Being wined and dined was something Kay would like, especially considering the fact that she had not had any sex in over a year. So, when she was getting her freak on, her mates had proven to be too shallow by giving her a Cinderella fairy-tale. Pete was different, though. He was cute, handsome, and sexy all in one breath. With the way that she felt, she was sure to throw the pussy on him extra crazy, but he was too much of a nice person and she was not looking to settle. What she needed was stamina and enough strength for a man not to, be attached.

Just as Kay started her car and put the seat belt on, Pete tapped on the driver's side window. "Hold up, Kay! Kay, hold up!" he yelled in an attempt to make sure that she heard him through the possibly soundproof closed windows.

Kay turned and could not help not to look at the print of his penis as he stood back waiting for her to let the window down. "What's up, Pete?" she asked.

"Damn! Are you just going to leave? You see I am having trouble over there with my car! Is it like that? I mean damn, I know you don't want to go out with me, and that's cool, but can I at least get a ride home?" He stated, with a smile.

"Come on now! Don't get all crazy with me like I am the one who broke your shit!" Kay shouted back, smirked while sassing her head back and forth. "Besides, you have not said anything, I'm not a mind reader you know." Kay was happy to be in a direct conversation with him. She smiled endlessly. "That's right, I was going to leave you," she told him.

Pete laughed, "Damn, you're a tough something, huh?" He began walking around the front of the car and getting into the passenger seat. Kay looked at him and smiled while rolling her eyes. "I didn't say you could get in my car either," she informed him, with a delightful look on her face, welcoming him in with open arms. The fragrance of his cologne shot through her nostrils, awakening her hormonal desires. "What kind of cologne is that?" she asked

"Why, does it stink?" Pete asked, looking deeply into her eyes.

"No, it smells good," Kay answered.

Pete's face suddenly displayed a cocky grin. "Oh, you like that, huh?" he asked, expressing his boyish whites.

"Yeah, it's nice," Kay, continued, briefly taking her eyes off the road to get a good look at him. *You just know you fine as hell, don't you?* She silently thought.

Pete was half-Indian and Black; light-brown skinned, six feet and one inch tall and well built. He wore his hair low with waves spiraling in a 360-degree pattern, and the only facial hair he had was a mustache that he kept sharply trimmed. "What's wrong with you?" he asked, noticing that she had a grin on her face.

"There's nothing wrong with me, what's wrong with you?" she sarcastically mocked, trying to escape what seemed to be his natural charisma. Her heart pumped faster than ever. The butterflies she felt in her stomach would no longer allow her confidence to live in denial. She was feeling him but was afraid to show it.

Pete and Kay were from different cultural backgrounds. In her mind, she concluded that, that were not a good match, so she always projected the "I'm not interested" attitude. Pete had grown up in Alaska. He was 28 years old, a college graduate who majored in liberal arts, and seemingly, family oriented with stern values and principles.

Kay, on the other hand, was the first high school graduate in her dysfunctional family. Growing up, she had to bear the burden of being mentally strong to deal with a mother who expected too much of her as a child. She had many dreams and aspirations, but no plans on how to get there. Growing up in a rough neighborhood somewhat forced her to live day by day, and those dreams were easily diminished to thoughts. She surely did not want to complicate his life by bringing him into her world. *No way,* there was no chance he would ever understand her life, but she still wanted him and knew that if he ever decided to ask her to go out with him again she would accept.

"You do know that I see through your Linda Carter act, right?" said Pete while fumbling with his cell phone against his lap. He was admiring the length of her hair that was stretching an inch past her shoulders.

Kay eased the car up to the red light and looked at him with a smile on her face. "What are you talking 'bout now?"

"Girl, you know what I'm talking about," said, Pete.

"No, I really don't. Why don't you enlighten me?" she answered staring into his face.

"I'm talking about you playing hard to get. I see you checking me out," Pete stated, rubbing the top of his head, maintaining the flow of waves that sat there.

"There's nobody checking you out! And if I was, what does Linda Carter have to do with it?" Kay became curious.

"Because you are not the Wonder Woman, that you portray to be," he explained, looking away from her and waiting to hear a response.

"Oohh, you got jokes. Wonder Woman, huh?" she said. "Well, I guess I am Wonder Woman, today; because, I saved your ass from walking, didn't I?" she politely sassed, as she pulled off as the light turned green.

"Ok yeah, that reminds me." He quickly began dialing the number to Triple 'A' Towing Service, so his car could be towed to the garage to be fixed.

"See, tell me I'm not Wonder Woman, when I just helped you to remember," Key affirmed, laughing loudly.

During the rest of the drive, they quietly entertained thoughts of each other. With the help of Pete pointing directions, they arrived at his house. Kay instantly visualized the woman's touch she would put on the front of his home while she pulled behind the back of a candy-apple-red Lexus GS sitting in the driveway.

She figured she would first turn the soil of the front lawn so that the sunflowers she would plant had a good chance of surviving. Then she would acid wash the dull, grey paint away to give the house its natural, tarnish brick color. She was quite impressed with Pete being so down to earth. She was no longer intimidated by him.

"So, can I call you or what? He asked after getting out of the car and sticking his head through the window of the passenger side.

Kay looked into his eyes, noticing for the first time that they were hazel brown, fairly complementing his skin. She wanted to scream behind him being so cute. Instead, she twisted her lips as if she did not believe that he really wanted to call her.

"Yeah, Pete, you can call me," Key allowed.

"The number still the same?" he asked.

"The number is still the same, Pete," she answered before

looking at him with twisted lips and backing out of the driveway to start home.

The peaceful night of good rest had only lasted four hours before Kay, became awakened by the loud cries of Cashmere. She lay still in her bed and looked to the ceiling with an angry expression on her face. Every piece of her body was telling her not to bother. Looking at her clock radio on the nightstand made her sigh. It was 2:00 a.m., and she was scheduled to get up in another four hours, somehow she knew that it would be hard for her to dive back into slumber once she was fully awake.

Suddenly, Kay began going through the motions as if she was a person chronically battling insomnia. She tossed, turned, and threw the pillow over her head in attempts to muzzle Cashmere's cries. After two minutes, she sucked her teeth, deeply sighed, and kicked the covers off in a tantrum. ***This damn boy,*** she thought as she stomped into his room. "What's wrong with you, boy?" she asked.

Cashmere sat with his head tilted back while looking up at her. Tears fluently ran from his eyes and his arms were stretched out indicating that he wanted to be picked up.

"Mmom," he cried. "M-mom, mommeee."

Kay could not help but to cater to the emotions that Cashmere had exhibited. For the life of her, she could not guess what was wrong, but she knew that she had to hurry and pacify him if she was to get any more rest for the night. She tugged the legs of her pajamas up, squatted, and picked him up.

"Ooh, boy, you are heavy. You are getting too big for me to be picking you up." She sat on his bed and rocked and rocked, humming the words to Regina Belle's hit single "IF I could" until she became sleepy and snuggled in the bed with him.

The distant, low sounds of the clock radio alerted Kay's senses, and just that fast she had to get up and get the kids together for school. Half asleep, she walked down the stairs and sat a box of Fruity Pebbles cereal and a gallon of milk on the kitchen table for the kid's breakfast. She decided to skip her usual workout session for the day. She was tired, and the only thing she had on her mind was a cup of coffee ~ not to mention the marvelous time she had with Pete just hours ago.

It was yet another night he wined and dined her in a fabulous five-star restaurant and took her dancing. Then he dropped her off at her house, where he walked her to the door and dashed his tongue in and out of her mouth as he kissed her. They had been seeing each other for four months, and though she hated to express it, she knew that he was her boyfriend. This is what troubled her often. There it was; a man, who had her dangling off his every word. He was far from being intimidated. The only person, who treated her with class, never even taking a chance at her panties; of course, he had eaten her pussy twice, but he showed little interest in her cookie and much interest in her mind, and that turned her on.

Kay went into the refrigerator and grabbed two cold Resource drinks for Stew's breakfast. While shaking them up, she smiled as she thought of picking out an outfit for Pete to see her in for the first time. She was especially excited to flaunt her way through the office cubicles, knowing that she was hated on, furthermore, within the four months that she and Pete had been dating, Pete had been promoted to Assistant Building Executive and Floor General. With that came a nice office room for Kay, and a position as his personal secretary. Indeed, every woman that worked in the office reasonably concluded that she had sucked and fucked herself into her occupation. Kay was aware of their suspicions, but it didn't bother her, besides, she knew that if she had done such an act to be promoted, then she would be the Assistant Building Executive and Floor General Manager, leaving Pete to be *her* personal secretary.

As Kay began pouring cereal in the kids' bowls, she hollered up the steps, "Asr, Cashmere, and Charity! Y'all come on and eat breakfast. It's you guys favorite, Fruity Pebbles!"

The smile on her face grew as she listened to the bumping and rumbling of the kids' footsteps shuffling to be the first at the table. When they became seated Kay poured their milk, and then headed into the dining room to attend to Stew. When she entered, a slight chill overcame her body. She shook and rubbed her arms to rid the goose bumps and quickly checked the thermostat. "Shit, it's cold in here," she blurted while placing her hand in front of the heat vent on the floor to make sure it was working. Again, she shook the Resource drinks. "Okay, cousin, time to wake up for your breakfast. This time it's blueberry," she encouraged.

Stew did not move. It was as if the rest she was getting couldn't and wouldn't be disrupted, not even by the sense of humor Kay was trying to display. She motioned over to Stew's bedside and gently touched her shoulder, trying to wake her.

"Come on, girl, get up, you," she teased. Still, Stew gave no response. Her eyes lay peacefully shut as if her ears were listening to the relaxing tunes of jazz. Her oxygen mask dangled halfway off her face, partially covering her lips. Kay felt her hand and noticed that it was unusually cold. Just then, she recognized the discolored complexion of Stew's face. Kay reluctantly felt the pulse of Stew's wrist and buckled. Her cousin, her big sister, the seemingly only family she had, was dead.

With her heart weighing as heavy as a boulder, she unconsciously wept in silence while hugging Stew's lifeless, frail body. Her tears trickled between the touching of their cheeks. She had tried to prepare herself for that moment, but her preparation was no match for the emotions that death had brought. Kay cried from sorrow, from happiness of knowing that Stew was no longer suffering, and from fear of the responsibility of raising Cashmere. Satisfaction grew tighter with each thought that raced in her head. Her life was suddenly different. Whom could she count on now? Stew hadn't been mobile for some time, but just her being alive worked wonders for Kay's esteem to achieve certain things in life.

Finally, she released herself from the light embrace, thinking she had better start making calls to inform the rest of so-called family and make funeral arrangements. She turned and there Cashmere was, standing in the doorway just as innocent as can be. His eyes shifted from Kay to his mother's hospital bed and back to Kay before he motioned his way towards her. His face was expressionless, yet serious. He stretched his arms out and embraced her. Kay held tight while still weeping. For an odd reason, it seemed as if she didn't have to tell him that his mother was dead. She felt weird. Here was a young boy who had just lost his mother to AIDS, and he turned out to be the comforter instead of her comforting him.

When they finally finished hugging, Kay, announced that they were going to have a free day off from school, which naturally excited Cashmere. At the blink of an eye, he dashed back into the kitchen and relayed the news to Asr and Charity. "No school today!" he yelled. "No school, no school, no school." Kay watched him and snickered at his exhibition of his "no school" dance, and then she began making her calls.

The first call was to Pete. She wanted to alert him that, unfortunately, she would not be gracing the office with her presence for the day. The next call was to the city coroner's department to pick-up Stew's body, get it preserved and prepared for the funeral arrangements, therefore, she called Cee. It would do Kay some good to hear a friendly voice. Cee, answered the phone. "Hello?"

"Hey, girl," Kay sadly answered.

"Hey girl, what's up with you?" Cee asked, continuing with, "either you sound like you're sick, or I need to call up a few of my friends to have somebody fucked up. 'Cause only a man can make a girl sound like that, and you know the best way to heal a broken heart is to replace it with a bigger and better one," Kay remained silent, "What did he do, child?" Cee, questioned, over-talking with assumptions

Kay laughed a little, trying to hide the pain she felt. "It's nothing like that girl, but Stew died," she informed. A ten-second moment of silence came about before Cee, spoke again, "Damn," she sorrowfully whispered, "my bad, here I am talking 'bout a man and you done lost your cousin'. I am so sorry, girl. You know I just don't know what to say out my mouth sometimes. Are you okay?"

"I guess I'm alright. It's not as if I didn't know it was coming, but it still feels funny. I am going to need your help doing the funeral preparation. Can you help me?" Kay muttered, knowing Cee would do anything for her.

"Come on now girl, you know I got you covered. Just let a bitch wash her ass first, oh yeah, you know Brim back in town! Yes, he showed up last night with a rock-hard dick, girl. I put my weight on him...eearrrily! Seriously Kay, who am I kidding, I do not care how many dudes I've laid down with, that's still the best piece of dick I ever had." Cee, continues to talk and Kay just holds the phone, not really listening, but respecting what her girlfriend needed to express. "However, he'll never know it. I don't care if he doesn't realize that this is the finest piece of feline he'll ever get." Cee, suddenly realizes her blabbering off a little too much. "Oops, here I go again. Let me get off this phone, girl, I'll be there as soon as I get dressed," Cee stated, shaking her own head for running her mouth so much.

When they hung up the phone, Kay began thinking about Vita. She and Vita may have had their differences, but she knew that Vita and Stew are good acquaintances. She felt that it was her duty to make sure, that many of Stew's friends had the opportunity to pay their last respects. She sighed and reluctantly allowed her fingers to dial Vita's phone number. When she heard Vita's voice, her vocals suddenly failed to utter a word. Her mind formulated a hello, her tongue, and lips moved, but Vita heard nothing. "Hello! Who is there?" Vita inquired in an agitated tone. She waited patiently for someone to say something, but the prolonged silence forced her to hang up the phone.

Less than sixty seconds later, Kay found herself dialing Vita's number again. The very instant she heard hello she blurted the news, "Stew died!" Again, a prolonged silence took over the airwaves. Vita was speechless. While Kay listened, Vita rewound the statement back in her mind before responding, "Oh my God! Are you okay? When did she die?"

"I don't know. Last night I guess. I found her dead this morning." Kay shared, trying her hardest to fight back tears, but it was too hard.

Vita quietly listened to Kay weep and sniffle until she herself began crying along with her. "It's going to be alright Kay, I'm here. I'm on my way right now." She hung up the phone, grabbed her car keys, and raced out of her front door. Her actions were done purely off instinct. She and Kay had been friends since they were kids, since they were little girls wearing Jelly Bean Sandals with corn rows, running to the mom-and-pop corner store to go half on a fifty-cent pickle. A history such as that was not easy to let go of, and death had reminded her of that unforgettable history.

When Kay went through her series of calls to her family, the reactions she received were shocking. She long ago understood that the family bond diminished, but she never imagined that even death wouldn't mend the distant relations. Out of a host of aunts and uncles, no one cared enough to offer to assist in the funeral arrangement. There was her uncle Harry, who battled in and out of addiction and always angled in ways to get a dollar. Of course, when he found out that Stew had life insurance, he had the nerve to ask Kay how much. Then there was Aunt Sissy, who at the age of 62, was still caught up in her own world ~ so much so ~ that she was bold enough to announce that she had to check her calendar book to see if she was free to make the funeral. Lastly, there were her Cousin ~ Adam, Lil' Harry, Coupe, Aisha, and Fatima ~ who were all coldhearted and unemotional to the news. The distance in their family had grown that deep, to the point that they were only family according to their bloodline, and the love that they had for friends was stronger than the love they had for each other.

Disgusted and hurt, Kay hung up the phone, walked, and stood in the dining room entrance while staring at Stew. All at once, the doorbell rang and she snapped herself out of the trance and rushed to answer it. She opened the door to see Cee, standing there. Behind her were three men who had arrived to take the body away. She and Cee, exchanged a strong embrace. "Hey, girl, how are you holding up?" asked Cee.

"I'm okay," said Kay, pulling her to one side of the vestibule so that the men could do their job. "Y'all can come on in. She's in the dining room," she told the men. While the men entered her home, she yelled up the steps for the kids not to come down. She didn't want to risk them seeing Stew's body, being carried away.

"Ooh, damn," said Cee, in a low-pitched voice, "I forgot all about Cashmere. Is he okay?

"Yeah, he's alright. You know he's young, so he doesn't really understand what's happening," Kay told her.

"Uh-hmm, child, you know I know," Cee answers.

"I just pray that I do right by him," Kay wonder, looking to the floor.

"What you mean? You have been doing right by him all this time, what's the difference?" asked Cee.

Kay thought for a minute, and before she had a chance to answer, one of the workers handed her a clipboard to sign. As she let her eyes roam the paper, she noticed that it said that Stew had been dead for seven hours. If that was so, then that meant she died around 2 a.m., Kay slowly gazed at the ceiling, thinking about Cashmere. "Girl, stop trippin'. Sign the board," said Cee, as she watched and wondered what had suddenly demanded Kay's undivided thoughts. Kay said nothing. She looked at Cee with her mouth slightly open.

"Excuse me, ma'am," alerted the worker in an attempt to bring her back from wherever she went.

"Here, I'll sign for it," said Cee, smiling as she took the clipboard out of Kay's hands and put her John Hancock on the paper.

"Thank you ma'am," the worker obliged.

"You're welcome, but I am not anyone's ma'am though. Don't be giving me that old title. I'm young, but I do be having them call me mommy sometimes." Cee, looked him up and down and winked, being loud and inappropriate.

The worker grabbed the clipboard out of her hand and gave her a flirty grin. He had walked away just before his manhood rose. He could not believe how forward she was being. He quickly turned to get another peek at her physique. She was fine as hell, dressed athletically and sexy in her pink Baby Phat, low-riding sweat suit. Although ethically immoral, if he had the chance, he would have fucked her right in the middle of doing his job.

Cee, saw the workers to the door. While carrying Stew's body out of the house, Vita was on her way in. "What's up Cee?" she greeted.

"Nothing much," Cee, responded.

"How is she? Vita whispered.

"I don't know. She was cool when I got here, but when the dude gave her the death papers, or whatever to sign, she went into a trance. I had to take the board out of her hand and sign the thing," said, Cee.

"Where is she?" asked Vita.

"In there." Cee, replied pointing in a particular direction.

Vita walked past Cee, and rushed into the dining room where Kay sat with her head bowed into the palms of her hands. She walked closer, stood over the top of her, and gently rubbed her back. "Hey, you," she said. "I dare you to stand up and give me a hug."

Kay lifted her head and gave a bright smile before standing and tightly embracing Vita in her arms. They each burst into tears while admitting to each other that it has been such a long time since they seen or even spoke to each other.

Cee, stood at the dining entrance watching them. She felt jealousy rising from within. For the past nine months, she and Kay had become very close friends. She even considered Kay to be her best friend. Before Kay came along, Cee's friends consist mostly of men who were willing to pay a heavy price for her panties, and as for the women, they really didn't like her either, but dealt with her anyway. Now, there she was feeling shut out, as if all of the confiding in Kay she had done was in light of a possible illusion, one mistaken to be a friendship.

A crash sounded above their heads, followed by a thump, and then the loud cries of one of the children who were upstairs playing. Kay sucked her teeth, looked to the ceiling, and rolled her eyes. "Y'all sit your asses down somewhere!" she yelled. "Don't make me come up there!"

When Kay stood and motioned her way toward the door, Cee, held her hand out and halted her. She leaned her head to the side to look past her and focused on Vita to roll her eyes.

"Kay, you stay here. I'll check on them," Cee said, walking toward to stairs.

When Cee, went up the steps, Vita decided to comment about her. "I don't know what's up with your buddy," she said sarcastically, "but she better check her attitude. 'Cause she ain't all they say she is, and I can fight just enough."

Kay says nothing. She wasn't in the mood for a tug-of-war match between the two of them. When Cee returned, she was just in time to hear Kay explain her mysterious experience concerning the death. "I'm telling y'all," she summoned, "when, I woke up, he was just crying. He kept hollering, 'Mommy, Mommy.' I thought he was talking about me, but what if he knew Stew had died somehow. 'Cause the paper said that she was dead for seven hours. That means two o'clock, right? Well, what if Stew's spirit had touched him, to say good-bye?"

Cee, looked at her, as if she was crazy. "Uh-uh, girl, now you know you're crazy with this spooky shit." Cee, said.

"No, I'm serious. It sounds crazy, but that is how it happened. I mean, he was just standing there when I found out she was dead. He held his arms out for a hug like he already knew his mother was dead," Kay, said hoping to make some sense of the situation.

"Yeah, but I need you to stop talking 'bout spirits and stuff. I damn near caught a heart attack seeing them men carrying Stew's body," said Vita.

"I know. One of them was cute as hell, too," Cee, added.

After shaking their heads at Cee's statement, the girls sat, drank Vodka, and chatted for the rest of the day.

Moving Forward

T he funeral was finally over. It was the longest seventy
minutes Kay had ever lived through. A bunch of people
she knew that did not like her cousin surrounded her. She
hated watching them wail, fall to the floor kicking and screaming,
and carrying on as if they loved Stew. It made her sort of regret
even having a funeral. The overemotional theatrics made her
realize that the tears they cried were from shame, shame of not
showing Stew any support. They were the same so-called friends
and family who never went to see Stew in her hospital bed or
never inquired about her well-being when they saw Kay in traffic.
They never even had the decency to send a Hallmark card telling
her to get well. Yet, they were there, fashionably sitting in the
pews with feathers sticking out of their tightly fitted hats with
wide, flexible brims.

Kay thought about how she wanted to scream. She wanted
to stand in the middle of the church and tell all of them to get to
steppin'. She realized that the only ones who should have been
there were her and the kids, and at the most, Vita and Cee, for
moral support. The others had no right being there. She felt that
Stew would be cursing her out for inviting them.

While riding and thinking in the back of the limo with her

head on Pete's shoulder, Kay sadly stared at the children. The funeral had apparently taken a toll on their bodies. Peacefully, they slept stretched out along the seats, their bodies as still as a parked car, and their breaths deep and silent. She watched, as their frames grew larger with each inhale and smaller when exhaling. Suddenly, she lifted her head from Pete's shoulder, looked at the side of his face, and kissed his cheek as he stared into a daydream. He smiled and returned the kiss, but on top of her head along the thick strands of honey-colored hair, styled to the back.

"Will you," he whispered into her ear softly and sexily.

Kay sucked her teeth and slapped his knee after giving an embarrassing chuckle. "I know...I know, Pete. Please just give me a little time to think," she whispered.

"I just want to make the right decision, Pete."

"The right decision? So what, you're not sure of the love we share?" he asked, looking deeply into her eyes.

"I know I love you, but I just don't want you to be marrying me out of pity. I mean, you did ask me after I told you about Stew's death," Kay said, countering his look.

"That's bullshit, Kay!" he yelled, moving his body closer to where she sat.

"Hush, be quiet, please. The kids are right there," Kay informed, now getting agitated.

Pete remained silent for a moment and then began again. "You know that's bullshit!" he whispered, in a direct manner, "If you're scared, then say you're scared. Please, do not sit here and make all these excuses and to question the love I have for you is crazy," he announce. "Okay, so what if I asked you to marry me after the news of Stew's death. All that means is that I love you. When you are hurting, I am hurting. What is so wrong with a man wanting to take care of you?" Kay looks on with eyes of a confused woman. "I don't see any of these dudes out here doing what I'm trying to do," he states.

"I know, but Pete just..."

"No, Kay, "he interrupted, "what are you waiting for?"

As the limo pulled in front of her home, Kay stared into Pete's face with fluttered emotions and a blank mind. He was right. What was she waiting for? She thought hard of what to say to him. Everything good she ever learned in a relationship, Pete gave her. The life she always dreamed of would finally be in her possession, and all she had to do was say yes; still, she couldn't say it. Suddenly her cell phone rang. *Damn,* she thought, *saved by the bell.* She kissed Pete on the cheek, gave a partial smile, and answered, "Hello?"

"Yeah, girl, it's Cee. Vita and I is about to come get you."

"Wait, what? You two are now hanging together. I know I must be dreaming now," Kay replied.

"Girl, shut up. She got a lot of shit wit' her, but she still alright when she want to be," Cee, answers laughing at Kay's statement.

"Umm-hum, I know that's right. Where are we going?" Kay asked intensely.

"I don't know yet," responded Cee.

"Okay, I need to ask Pete to watch the children." Kay looked at Pete's frowning expression while holding the phone to her ear with her shoulder. Her hands placed together in a prayer formation. By saddening her face and silently saying *please,* she begged him to watch the kids. Pete's frown remained. The nerve of her asking him to sit at home and watch the kids as a husband would do. The more he watched her plead, the angrier he became. It seemed to him that she wanted all of the benefits of a husband without even being married: weekend gifts, flowers just because, and the hundreds of notes and messages left around her house all in the name of love. He loved her a lot, but he was not about to sit around and wait for her to make up her mind.

Finally, he suppressed his anger, looked at the kids, and reluctantly threw his hands in the air as if to say, *Whatever, I'll watch them.* Kay smiled and lightly clapped her hands in excitement. She immediately spoke into the phone, interrupting Cee, who has not stopped talking since Kay had answered.

"Cee...Cee! Damn, girl, slow the hell down. Pete is going to watch the kids, but I still got to get some comfortable clothes on," Kay shouted in happiness.

"Alright, well hurry up 'cause we like ten minutes away, if that."

When Kay hung up the phone, she shook the kids from their slumber and exited the car. Peter followed, carrying Charity in his arms. Once the front door had opened, the kids raced inside and up the steps to play video games. "Y'all better not be playing that game, and you guys better have changed out them clothes!" Kay yelled, while in her room preparing for a well-needed day of fun with the girls. She threw on a pair of dark-blue denim jeans, a tan woman's blazer, and a Kangol, cool cap. By the time she began walking down the steps of her home, Cee, and Vita had rung the doorbell.

Before Kay answered the door, she walked into the living room where Pete sat on the corner of the leather couch with his arm resting on the armrest. Kay strutted over to him and stood. She noticed that he still had an attitude and wanted to ease the tension before she headed out. "Baby, you mad?" she asked as she grabbed his hand and stood him up. She let her hands gently rub his chest and make their way down his dress pants to fondle his manhood. "Don't be mad at me, baby," she pled.

Pete snatched her hand out his pants. "Kay!" he irritably yelled. "This shit is ridiculous!"

"Sshh! Pete, you know them kids is in here!" she alerted.

Pete quickly calmed himself and angrily whispered back to her, "This is ridiculous, Kay! You act as if I haven't said shit to you. I asked you to marry me, do you remember that?"

Suddenly the bell rang and again Kay was saved. Pete looked at her with the most disappointing face she had ever seen. He was disgusted at the way she was avoiding the subject. Kay knew it but did not help but to selfishly pursue her day of relief. She wanted to forget about the seriousness of life, and if it meant avoiding the subject of marriage, then so be it.

Pete's anger easily turned into ready-to-drop tears. He was a man though, and even though she hadn't had sex with him yet, no thug she had ever been with could compare to him. No thug would be willing to stay home and watch three kids that are not his while his woman went out with her girls either, but he was no thug.

As Kay grabbed a hold of his necktie and began tightening the knot, she tried to reassure him that she weren't disregarding his concerns. "Please don't be upset," she said, "we can talk about it when I get back."

Pete looked on and said nothing. As Kay tried to pull him closer by using the tail of his tie, he placed his hand on her shoulders and kept her at bay. "Look, Kay," he started, "just go, and do whatever it is you're trying to do, we will definitely talk when you get back, 'cause this here is bullshit. I'm not going to play this game with you," he informed, hoping to walk away from her.

"What game?" she asked, looking at him concerned.

"You know what game!"

"Come on now, nobody's playing games," she assured him truthfully.

"Look, are you going out or what? Because I can be elsewhere doing more things that are more important. Now go 'head, 'fo I change my mind," Pete, ordered.

Kay kissed the corner of his lips and rushed to the front door. "Love you, Pete!" she yelled while exiting the house. The moment she stepped into the bright sunshine, she took in a deep breath and exhaled. The autumn breeze gently wrestled with the fallen leaves, making them dance along the sidewalk. At times, its force would increase, sending the leaves into loops in the air.

It was a perfect day to spend with the genuine love that Cee, and Vita were giving.

"Damn, girl," said Cee, "you all jazzed up. We only going for a drink and maybe hit Franklin Mills to see if they got anything on sale for winter."

Kay smiled and looked down at herself. "Child, please, I just threw something on real quick. I don't have any money to be playing up in the mall all crazy, though."

"What? Yeah right. I know that man in there didn't allow you to leave without greasing your palms, especially with all that money he got," Cee announced in a jokingly manner.

"What money?" Kay, asked curious about the statement.

Vita looked at Kay with her lips twisted. "Oh, come on now," she added. "He's driving that Lexus GS, plus I seen him in a Mercedes-Benz last week. Don't let him tell you he broke," she informed, smiling as if she knows Pete business.

"I know," chimed Cee. "You need to go put your weight on him real quick, we'll wait... earrrrly!"

"Uh-uh, girl, you don't think about nothing else, do you?" Kay asked, deep down inside wishing Pete would allow her to put her thing on him.

"Yeah, I think about how I'm going to get enough money so I'll never have to work again. And have a fine-ass, husky male maid wit' cuts and rips all over, running around the house catering to Cee." Cee took her palms across her ass, around to the hips, up her stomach, and rested them on her breast. "Beause y'all know I'm worth it."

"Please!" said, Vita. "All those damn kids you got. Girl, don't nobody want to be picking up after their bad asses."

"Shit, I can have your man doing it if I put this pussy on him...I said, 'cause I'm worth it. Now, bitch! Please that!" Cee, replied nonchalantly.

Kay began walking to Vita's car. "Come on, y'all; let's get away from this house before Pete changes his mind. Do not look now, but he up in the window watching, so let's just hurry up, because he already has an attitude," Kay told them.

The three of them hopped into the car and began their day of quality time. "Where are we going first?" asked Vita, bobbing her head to the radio while focusing on the road.

"I don't know," Cee said, it's all about Kay right now.

"Where am I going girl?" Vita, asked Kay.

Kay thought for a minute and threw up her hands. "I don't know either, anywhere."

"I know where," Vita said. She then navigated her way to a sports bar & grill, that was located on South Street. They found a parking space a block away and began walking.

Within four minutes, they were sitting in spinning high chairs and ordering double shots of 151 on the rocks and making personal assessments of the people who sat at the tables. The environment reminded Kay, of a spot, that one of her previous male friends would have labeled a secret place to cheat, and not worry too much about anyone seeing you.

A low-pitched R&B tune played from the jukebox, drawing Kay deeper into the scheme of the place, a romantic hideout. With her shot glass in hand, she slowly turned in the chair, grading the interior designing. It was something she had obsessed with since a child. She tried to find something wrong, but the place was perfect: charcoal-colored granite-marbled floor, spacey, and old styled tables and benches attached to the wall along the perimeter, which reminded her of an old 70's sitcoms like Happy Days and What's Happening.

Kay sucked the last bit of her drink through the thin straw and finally broke the silence between them. "Why is everyone so quiet?"

Cee, sucked her teeth and turned from the direction that her attention was focused and answered. "Girl, I'm sitting here checking out that corny-ass Hal over there in the corner."

"What Hal?" asked Vita.

"Hal, he's from our neighbor," Cee answered

"Where is he at?" asked Kay.

"Over there," pointed Cee.

"Damn, I know it's time for me to pick a different chill spot now," Vita stated, shaking her head.

"What for?" asked Kay.

"Yeah, what for?" followed Cee.

"Because, when people like Hal, start hanging in places like this, it won't be long before a whole gang of them start hanging in these places; damaging the place credibility, just tearing the establishment down," Vita warned.

Cee, looked at Vita with a confused expression. "Here you go with that uppity shit."

"Cee, don't even start. You know I did not mean it like that. I come here all the time to get a peace of mind, and sometimes I even do a little paperwork concerning my restaurant. If I wanted to be around corner guys, I would have gone to a corner bar…you know what I'm saying?" Vita implied, sipping her drink.

"Yeah, I feel you Vita," Kay affirmed.

"Yeah, me too," Cee, admitted. "He probably wants her to fuck him."

Kay and Vita looked at each other, and then Cee as if she had cursed one too many times. Cee, stared back. "What?" She began. "What everybody looking at me like that for?" she wondered.

"Stop playing, Cee. Do not say that about him," Vita told her.

Cee looked on with intensity, put a hand on her hip and the other in the air to signify an oath. "I swear girls, you know I am not lying."

Vita had to take a swig of her drink behind the shocking news. "Hold up, bitch…so you trying to tell me…"

"That's just what I'm tellin' you," Cee interrupted. "That man probably take more dick than you can even stand."

"So he likes men?" Kay asked, in a shocking manner.

"Well, he might as well, 'cause when I went to his crib, he

pulls out a strap-on... about a nine-inch joint. I buried that shit all the way in him," Cee demonstrated.

Kay looked over at him and fell in disbelief. "Are you serious, Cee?"

"Earrrly! He was really into it. He gave out a grand, and had the nerve to ask if I could see him again," Cee declared, picking up her drink.

"Hell, if that's what he likes, no judgment!" responded Vita. They shared their first laugh for the day, ordered another shot of liquor, and chatted away. Before long, Kay decided to confide in them about her decision to get married or not. She made it clear that she loved Pete and would not mind being his wife. However, the sacrifice that might come attached to the title of being a wife was frightening.

Pete was the kind of person who would eventually want her to become a stay-at-home wife, one who has the house clean, and dinner waiting on the table when he arrives at home from work. That's an idea Kay, could possibly be willing to mode herself to. What about her own dreams, because she wanted to pursue a career in interior decorating, earning her own keep, and not have to depend on a man for anything, but love.

Intoxicated and bewildered, Kay lazily stared into space while circling her index finger around the brim of the shot glass.

"Look, girl," Vita shared, "You have to do what your heart feels. We cannot make that decision for you. We can sit here and tell you something, but you're going to have to do what you think is best for you and your kids."

Kay looked at her and burst into tears. "I just don't want to lose him. He's been the best thing that happened to me for the longest, and I've been stringing him along and he doesn't even deserve it."

"Look, girl," Cee interrupted, "fuck what Vita is saying," we can make the decision. He got money, and he's fine as hell. I don't know what his stick game is like, 'Cause if he slammin' that ass right, I say go for it girl."

Kay immediately chuckled and wiped her eyes. She could always count on Cee, to humor a serious situation. "Cee, you so stupid, but thanks," Kay said.

"No, but seriously, he really love you. On some real shit, bitches wait their whole lives to find a man like that, therefore, I say go for it, you only live once," Cee, confirmed. "Besides, you don't want to live your life wondering what it would have been like, and trust me, I know you got expirations."

"Its aspirations," chimed Vita, correcting Cee's pronunciation.

Cee looked at her and rolled her eyes. "Whatever, bitch."

"Before we were rudely interrupted, as-per-rations... you can work all that stuff out. The bottom line is, love," Cee acknowledged.

Kay heeded to the words of wisdom from her girls; by that time, it was time to go to the mall, and she was mentally, drained. She insisted on being, taken home. Out of all the things Cee had ever said to her, Kay never thought that Cee's reasoning would be the one to weigh the heaviest on her decision. After Cee's words, Kay excitingly made the choice to tell Pete that she would be happy to take his hand in marriage.

Happiness

The bells of the Community Baptist Church, located in the East Falls section of Philadelphia, rang loud. The pigeons flapped their wings and danced loops in the air around the cross that sat on top of the church's steeple. Although the weather was only 70 degrees, an increase in temperature is approaching considering the sun had established its luster. At 9:30 a.m., the rays intensely fell upon the city, making a simple pair of shades a necessity for the day. In front of the church ~ amongst a stretch limousine decorated with wedding accessories ~ were many automobile's of all sorts of sizes, and colors parked as far as a two-block radius. A group of hired photographers patiently waited for the married couple to exit the church. They strategically positioned themselves and marked their territory with tripods.

At last, the church doors opened at 10:30 a.m., and the attendants of the ceremony spilled out of the entrance like bees exiting their hive. As they formed parallel lines to await the newlyweds exit, they cheered congratulations with hands full of ready-to-be thrown rice. Many of the women cried at the sight of Kay and Pete standing at the top of the church steps holding hands with smiles. Kay is, draped in her trendy halter-topped wedding gown, and Pete looked handsomely polished in a traditional black tuxedo. They laughed and giggled while gracefully marching down the steps of the church, squinting and seemingly trying to duck the hails of rice. The photographers hastily focused their lenses and snapped away second after second. They walked the aisle made up of family, friends, and coworkers until reaching a chauffeur, who politely smiled, tipped his hat, and opened the limo door for them.

Once they were inside, Kay sat across from Pete, quickly kicked her shoes off, and let out a holler of excitement. Pete gave a masculine chuckle while pouring two glasses of champagne. After giving Kay a glass, he held his hand out and proposed a toast. "To, my baby *Kay* or *Kaleen* and now, *Mrs. Peter Frazier,* I love you with all my heart. May you be happy, and full of spirit; may God bless you to live long with many great moments to share. You are truly the best friend in the whole world."

Kay was flushed with tears. She immediately knocked back the drink and held her glass out for another.

"Now my turn," she said, as her face sparkled from the lip-gloss, and make-up she had on "To, my husband, *Mr. Pete Frazier.* I never felt this kind of love before. Thank you, for the love that you have been providing me since the beginning. I am young, madly in love, and afraid; however, I know that with you by my side, somehow things will always be okay. I ask that you never stop loving me, and as time go on, I will probably make many mistakes, I only ask in advance, that you forgive me for my shortcomings and/or defective ways. I am so looking forward towards this journey with you. You as my husband is the best gift a woman could ever ask for."

Again, they tapped their glasses of champagne, and then Pete turned the volume knob on the door of the limo so that they could hear relaxing melodies of wedding songs compiled on a CD. He stared into Kay's eyes with lust while taking his tuxedo blazer off. She attentively allowed her body to get ready for whatever Pete had in mind. Whatever he wanted and however he wanted to do it. Therefore, she aimed to be submissive. Anticipation of having sex with him had long invaded her cerebral each time he would get close to her; each time he touched her, each time she allowed him to dash his tongue in and out of her mouth when French kissing.

Without delay or any form of foreplay, Pete slid from his seat onto his knees while maintaining eye contact. He crawled the short distance with his heart pounding at the sight of his love, his mouth dry, and thirsty to drink the gushes from the well of her pussy. The touch of his palms upon Kay's knees made her quiver, sending a sensational chill through her body that drew her legs open.

Slowly, his hands journeyed to the bottom of her wedding gown to hike it up. He gave one last look at her, winked his eye, and dove under the gown as if he was putting on a t-shirt. He hadn't so much as touched her before she began panting and squirming. Her scent had released the animalistic hunger in him, and before long, he was sucking on her clitoris as a baby would a pacifier while ramming his middle finger in and out.

Kay's eyes opened, and closed and rolled to the back of her head. She scratched at the leather limo seat trying to resist the work of his tongue, but it had become a lost cause. Pete had graduated from just a finger to two fingers, and three.

"Ooh, Pete," she heavenly whispered. "I'm cu...I'm cu..." before she could get the words out, her juices fell down, making her body jolt like she was having a mild seizure. Pete pulled his head from under her gown with a smirk on his face and sweat on his forehead. He wiped his mouth, gave a peck on the corner of her lips, and flopped beside her. Kay looked at him with a deeper level of love. He was her husband. She adored every inch of his handsome face, from his bone structure to the way that his always sharp-shaped-up haircuts played a part in his appearance. *Damn,* she thought, *I am married...I'm really fuckin' married.*

The chauffeur pulled the limo onto a landing area a quarter

mile from the Philadelphia Airport where a rented helicopter awaited. After he exited the car and loaded the helicopter with Pete and Kay's luggage, the pilot lifted them into the air and flew them high above the city. The speed was mild and casual, enabling them to enjoy the scenic view. It was beautiful.

Kay had never been in a motored air vehicle. She definitely never thought the city she had known to be, infested with drugs, sex, and violence was actually a beautiful place. The skyline view helped them admire the greenery that intertwined into the subtle areas and urban areas, by way of Fairmount and Hunting Park. The sight stretched far, and wide. The more she looked out of the window, she couldn't help but ask herself, *What if this damn helicopter malfunction, or a bird get caught in the engine or something?* It was then she adopted a mild fright of heights.

Kay snatched her body away from the window and threw her face into Pete's shoulder, seeking refuge from the sudden fear. Her hands clutched his shirt in her fist as she extended her voice a pitch above the noise of the propellers. "We don't even have parachutes, Pete."

Pete softly rubbed her face and began nurturing her fright. "It's cool, we're going to be alright," he said.

"How long do we have up here?" she wondered, looking out the window.

Her worriment slightly humored Pete. He gave a snicker and explained that it would be a few more minutes. He tapped the pilot and gestured his index finger to draw imaginary circles, telling the pilot to increase the speed.

Finally, Kay pried her face from his shoulder and looked him in the eye. "Where are we going?" she wondered.

Pete instantly mesmerized her with his intense stare. His eyes were in a slight squint as he rousingly bit down on the bottom of his lip before answering, "It's a surprise. Just be cool, I got you. You're my wife now." The words coming from Pete's mouth were soothing. Without another word, she laid her head upon his shoulder and began to relax.

The honeymoon for Kay was something that she had only watched on a cable show called *A Wedding Story*. After first landing the helicopter on the roof of the finest five-star hotel in, Atlantic City they were then escorted to a presidential suite where they changed their clothes, and then they were off to the casino to gamble and see the showgirls. Following the night they were, again, in the air on a private jet that was, endorsed by the company where they worked. They made a stop in Las Vegas Nevada, where Pete convinced Kay to skydive with him. Each day was a surprise: California to scuba dive, and surfing, to Colorado to mountain climb, and then horseback riding.

By the time their week of adventurous escapades has ended, Kay was tired. She missed the kids and could not wait to get home and relax in her own bed. The honeymoon had revealed much about who Pete truly was. He had shown her a different side of his life, an in-depth glimpse of his interests. Kay finally concluded that he had a lot of money, money that a Neshaminy salary couldn't match.

It was July 28, 2000, the day of Kay's 23rd birthday, when they were to head back to Philly. Although she was excited, she didn't expect anything special. The gifts she had received throughout their trip well exceeded anything she would have expected in her entire lifetime. She felt that she was winning in the game of life, and Pete had made it all possible. He also made it possible for her to wonder about why he hadn't touched her. It seemed he was plainly obsessed with going down on her ~ no blowjobs, no kind of penetration at all. For the longest, she desired to feel his love to the extent that they could be one with each other, the way most newlyweds expressed affection.

Pete's disinterest in having sex with her was an unusual experience for Kay, and it began to make her second-guess herself. She wanted to ask him why, wanted to say something to him to let him know how his actions were affecting her esteem. Since thirteen, at the first sight of puberty when her breasts had perked beyond average, and her ass, hips, and thighs had metamorphosed to take on a life of their own, she had people crawling and practically begging to get into her panties. Sadly, this was not the actions of her husband. What was wrong with him? If he hadn't been treating her so well, she would have told him that she didn't feel complete, but she didn't want to sound ungrateful. Truthfully, she felt as if none of the gifts or trips could amount to just one night in the bed with him.

As she sat on the bed in the hotel room, waiting for Pete to return from his morning jog, her thoughts of him made her hormones kick into gear. She held herself as if a cool breeze abruptly entered the room, yet her body was warm and heated from the urge to have sex. She began to feel her eager vagina moisten, and she let out a sigh behind her thoughts of intentions. She was horny and throbbing for touch. She angrily eased her hands down her sweats and under her panties to insert her middle finger inside of her womb. She thought of being caught by her husband while moaning and shifting her body in sensation. With every stroke of her finger, she prayed that Pete would just show up and give her what she needed, but she was out of luck. With imaginary visions of her husband standing there watching ~ his naked frame dripping with sweat, shining and enhancing his muscular cuts while stroking himself ~ she thrust her finger in and out of herself with desirable intentions as fast as humanly possible. Within four minutes, she climaxed and like a melting ice glacier, it fell upon her hand and even onto her wedding ring. Though no one knew of her act, however, she couldn't help herself from feeling somewhat embarrassed and ashamed when she finished. It shouldn't have to be that way. She thought.

When Pete and Kay stepped off the private jet, the same chauffeur awaited them. He greeted with the tipping of the hat and transferred their luggage from the plane to the limo.

During the entire ride to her house, Kay remained silent, staring through the light tint on the widows. She was trying to recall her honeymoon to pacify the anger she needed to subside. She was damned if she was going to start complaining that early on in her marriage. Pete deserved for her to be patient, just as he had been when waiting for her to accept his hand in life. Even so, she was certain that she also deserved to feel something inside of her. Without room for second-guessing, her sexual urges focused her mind on the dildo she had hidden in her dresser drawer. *Aint this some shit*, she thought. *Back to life, back to reality.* At that moment, she thought of how Stew had named her toy "Dilly" and couldn't help not to snicker.

Pete was smiling. "What?" he asked.

"Oh, I'm just sitting here thinking," she answered with a smile.

"I'll give you a penny for them," Pete suggested.

"A penny, for what?" she inquired inquisitively.

"For your thoughts," he replied with a smile.

Kay grinned and stared for three seconds. "It's just something Stew had said to me one time."

Pete raised his eyebrows and continued to smile while periodically bouncing his palms on his knees to be in harmony with the music that played as he looked out of the window.

Kay's heart instantly grew fonder of him. How could she stay mad with him at all? He always said the sweetest, simplest things that would take on the form of Cupid's arrow. She was wild about him and the way he unconsciously displayed his charm, moved her. The world, she was used to was definitely not full of Pete's. What she found was quiet in a world of thunder. A piece of dick was only a small percent of what a successful marriage was really about, but still, she wondered why he hadn't advanced to the deeper side of her love.

Kay's nerves were shaking with anticipation of seeing her kids. As the limo came to a halt, she anxiously got out while practically encouraging Pete with demands. "Come on, baby, let's hurry. Is the driver going to take care of the bags or what?" asked Kay, pulling her husband.

"Yes, he's going to take care of the luggage," said Pete while shutting the door and giving himself a stretch. "But listen, Kay, I need…"

His sentence was, cut short when Kay fell disinterested and redirected her attention to a Century 21 sign staked deep into the grass of her front lawn.

Her face was baffled. Her brows bent at the intersection of her nose and forehead as she slowly walked over to the sign and stared.

"Kay!" Pete called. "Hey, baby!" Kay ignored his calls and continued to stare.

Pete walked up behind her and hugged her while whispering into her ear, "I have to tell you something."

"Uh-umm, hold up!" she said, wallowing herself out of his embrace. *What the fuck they think they're doing! I've paid my last mortgage bill. They supposed to send me the owner's papers this week, and they pull this bullshit! Oh, they're really messing with the right one now,* she told herself. She violently pushed, pulled, and tried to yank the sign out of the grass. "Help me! Don't just sit there!" she yelled at Pete.

Pete rushed over and easily yanked the sign out.

"Come on," Kay demanded. "Bring that inside. I'm calling their ass right now, *today!*" She marched up the rest of her doorsteps and led Pete inside. She stomped through the short hall and turned into the living room where she was startled; a group of family and friends, yelled-out *"Surprise!"*

"Happy birthday to you, happy birthday to you!" they chanted away as Kay stood speechless. The palms of her hands covered her nose and mouth. Tears of joy raced to the bottom of her jawbone at the sight of people she hadn't seen since she was a child ~ people that, for some reason or another, couldn't make the wedding.

The view was overwhelming. Everyone wore either black or

white. A huge "*Congratulations*" banner hung above the dining room entrance. A pile of wrapped gifts of all sizes sat on the floor in the corner. Suddenly, Cee and Vita appeared, pushing a cart that had a five-layer wedding cake on it.

Kay turned and threw herself into Pete's arms and held him tight. "Thank you. Thank you," she repeated, before flopping him with kisses of appreciation. Everyone clapped, cheered, and whistled for the newlyweds.

When Kay released herself from hanging on Pete's neck, she greeted the attendants with hugs and instantly began mingling. After thirty minutes had passed and the shocking excitement had worn off, she realized that she had not even seen her children yet. Without notice, she rudely excused herself from the company of two cousins to rush and inquire about them to Pete. The party had temporarily taken her mind off them, and she at once felt irresponsible.

Pete was standing in the kitchen amongst a group of three, drinking champagne and talking sports, when Kay approached him from behind. She softly placed a hand on his shoulder and whispered into his ear, "Baby, where is my damn kids?"

Pete turned, brandishing a grin. "I was wondering when you were going to ask," he said. "They're in the yard playing with the rest of the kids."

Kay kissed the corner of his lips and aimed her mission toward the backyard. As she walked away, many guy's tried their best to only moderately stare out of respect for their friend Pete, but even that was hard, and Pete knew it. He nonchalantly turned to face the group proudly, as if to say, *Yeah, that ass be me._All of it.*

Standing in the backyard doorway watching the kids' play a friendly game of tag was a sight that made Kay slightly, feel at ease. She did not want to disrupt their fun, but her selfish desire to hug them had easily overpowered their natural right in the innocence of play. She called out their names. At the very sense of hearing her distinct voice, the three of them, though standing in different places in the yard, each began to look around, desperately trying to home in the direction of their mother's voice.

With puzzled faces, they looked to the sky with their mouths open and ears awaiting another call of their names. Their eyes carefully searched the yard for possible hiding spots, while their minds began to wonder if they had truly heard whom they thought they heard. Asr was the first to locate Kay. "Mommy!" she yelled, as she excitingly raced into Kay's arms. Cashmere and Charity followed her lead, and before she knew it, Kay was being, tackled with love.

It was 6 p.m., when Kay finished cleaning the inside of her house after the party. At the same, Pete finished breaking down the two large charcoal grills that burned in the yard, he trashed all of the foam cups, paper plates, half-eaten hot dogs and hamburgers, and other forms of debris that were left behind by the kids. They were both tired and grateful from being good host. The kids had played themselves so hard that Kay allowed them to fall asleep without a bath. Finally, the West Oak Lane block where she lived had its serenity restored. The loud music was gone and the sunset alerted the lightning bugs that it was time for them to come out. The crickets expressed themselves and the mosquitoes would soon be stalking a victim.

The newlyweds sat on the backyard steps, joined by their arms hooked like links to a chain. Kay's head rested upon Pete's shoulder while she quietly enjoyed his company. Pete had thoughts of returning to the office to catch up on his backed-up workload; Kay looked in hindsight at the conversation she had with old so-called friends and compared her life to theirs, without question, if she was a basketball player, her stats on life would have amounted to a triple double.

She suddenly realized that her furniture hadn't been returned from wherever her husband had it taken. "Baby, where's my furniture?" she asked.

Pete looked at her with tiring eyes, trying to allow her

question to register with his brain. "Oh, damn," he slurred. "I got two more surprises." He reached into his pocket and pulled out a check. "Here… I sold the house and moved all the furniture, except for the kids' stuff to a warehouse. We have to be out of here by late tomorrow."

Kay's arms were, folded. She looked at the paper in his extended hand and refused to take it. "Pete, I know you playing, right? You sold what house?"

"I sold this house," he said excitedly.

Kay's heart dropped. She recalled her encounter with the Century 21 sign and began fighting back the sad emotions that would soon shadow denial. "Pete, stop playing! This shit is not funny! I know damn well you didn't sell my house."

Pete's face was the face of a little boy who had stared into his mother's eyes after breaking her vase. He struggle with his words, "Baby, I…listen right, bab-I'm not playing though. I sold the house."

Kay stood and looked down upon him, as he remained sitting while looking up at her. She noticed that he wasn't smiling. Not even a slight grin showed on his face. Her heart rate continued to accelerate, but she tried to ease her nerves with lasting traits of denial. Deep down inside, she knew that he wouldn't lie to her about something that serious.

She snatched the check out of his hand without taking so much as a peek at it. "I know you lying, Pete," she said as she stormed into the kitchen and began searching for evidence of her husband's news being a lie. Now the smallest piece of evidence would pacify her emotions. She quickly opened the cabinets aligned above the kitchen sink, then angrily slammed them, seeing that not a plate or glass was in any of them. Not a fork, knife, ~ that she remembered seeing since she was ten ~ was gone. She bowed her head and looked at the check with an unusual and unexpected feeling of defeat. The tears that she cried were those of a mighty Queen who suddenly found out that she had been overthrown. The conspiring hand of someone whom she had loved the most had betrayed her.

A one hundred thousand-dollar check was the sum of every one of Kay's childhood memories. As she stared at the zeroes on the check, she wondered if it was all worth it. *Was her marriage worth giving up the only thing in the world she owned that was worth something? Did, Pete even have the right to wipe out a part of her life in an instant without consulting her?*

Though her sorrowful tears easily answered the questions she formulated, her mind told her that it was worth it. In the name of love, she disregarded her ill feelings, threw herself into Pete's embrace, and continued to weep.

"It's okay, baby. It's okay," said Pete as he mildly rubbed her back. "I wouldn't have done it had I known it meant this much. How can a marriage stay maintained, if we're not under the same roof? Kay, it's just not possible."

Kay's face remained relaxed upon his chest. She hadn't thought about living arrangements during the whole time that her marriage had set sail. She realized everything Pete was saying was correct. However, the more he opened his mouth to try to soothe her pain, the angrier she felt, mentally harboring explicit language with visions of her claws at his face. Again, for the sake of love, she ground her teeth and took in a short breath. "I know, baby," she feigned. "You did what you thought was best for our marriage." *It had better be best for this marriage because we could have lived here and sold your house*, she thought to herself while releasing herself from his arms to answer the ringing of the phone.

"Hello." A six-second silence had taken place before someone introduced herself. "Hello, this is Ruthie Reynolds, Assistant District Attorney. May I ask whom I'm speaking to?"

"Yes, this is Kaleen Harris...I mean Frazier," said Kay.

"Kaleen. Yes, I am calling in reference to a relative of yours, Stewart Harris," the DA addressed.

"Uh-humm, that was ~ I mean she is my cousin," Kay asnswed.

"Yes, I also have here that you were her next of kin," she wondered.

"Uh-humm, that is correct," informed Kay, as Pete looks on in wonder.

"Okay, well we are in the process of taking a Ronald Mason, a.k.a. Little Ron, and Corey Lassie, a.k.a. Young Corey, to trial. They are, charged with the rape of your cousin and the murder of her son. It would be very impressionable upon the jury if you can show up during trial proceedings. Do you think you can make it?"

"Yes, I can be there. What time should I be there and where?" Kay asked.

"It is held at the Criminal Justice Center on the 8th floor, room 822, It'd be good if you can gather all of the family and friends you can. We don't want these guys' to go free. I'll call you two days prior to trial for a follow-up," she told her.

"Okay, thank you so much. I'll be there," Kay complied.

Kay hung up the phone and slid down the wall to a sitting position. Shortly thereafter, Peter joined her. He held her hand and said nothing.

Seven

Victory

The courtrooms on television were more subtle. The defense and district attorneys would assemble at their long oak wood tables with exhibits, discovery evidence, and a defendant who was awaiting arraignment or judgment of some sort. Though her vision of court proceedings were ·an instant derivative of the thousands of episodes of "Law and Order" that she watched, everything was the same except for the commotion.

Kay sat beside Pete on the side of the courtroom reserved for the victim's family. She periodically turned looking around the room in amazement at how much publicity the case had generated. News reporters huddled to exchange opinions. Writers of newspapers and magazines anxiously sat with their pens and pads, ready to take notes. Local film directors attended with visions of the case being their bridge to Hollywood. Of course, three sketch artists were on standby, yearning to cover their art paper with the color and emotional expressions of both the jury and those who may take the stand.

With every minute that passed, the volume in the courtroom grew louder and louder. The start of trial proceedings had been long awaited by those to whom a beneficial interest of justice could determine their career ~ and by the citizens of the West Oak Lane section of Philadelphia.

The crimes of drugs and violence had plagued their neighborhood since the eighties: murder, rapes, robberies, and crack-heads walking the streets stealing any and everything not bolted to a particular surface. The nights that they fell asleep to the shots of gunfire had those awaking in the morning gripped with fear. Overall, despite the abnormal activities that from time to time crippled their peace, they still considered their neighborhood one of the best in the city. A conviction, they hoped, would surely send a psychological message to the thugs that they were tired.

When the judge finally exited his chamber and entered the courtroom, the bailiff alerted the attendants. "All rise for the Honorable Judge Corby presiding!" The courtroom immediately fell into a state of complete silence. Everyone stood and watched the judge stand imperially. His black, shoulder-padded robe draping from his body made his shoulders appear broad. His glasses hung on the edge of his nose with the arm barely hooking his ears. He robotically scanned the room before slamming the gavel and loudly voicing, "You may be seated!"

The moment the courtroom was seated, the prosecuting attorney stood and introduced herself and the case number. "Your Honor, Ruthie Reynolds, attorney for the Commonwealth, prosecuting case number 29820-98. In which defendants Ronald Mullen and Corey Laessig are both charged with one count of home invasion, rape, murder, aggravated assault, attempted murder, and recklessly endangering others' lives."

The Judge nodded his head. "Stated," he said as he again nodded toward the defense table, indicating for the attorney to introduce himself. The five-foot-nine Italian lawyer cleared his throat as he stood. "Your Honor, Arnold Angelino, attorney for both Ronald Mullen and Corey Laessig."

"Wait a minute," said the judge while removing his glasses

and pinching the bridge of his nose out of impatience. "Are you saying that you're representing both of the defendants?"

"I am, your Honor."

"Well, I only see one defendant in the courtroom. Where is the other defendant? And which defendant is present today?"

"Your Honor, here today is defendant Ronald Mullen. Defendant Corey Laessig is ill from contracting the AIDS Virus. I figure that it would be a painful process for him to come up here."

"What do you mean 'to come up here'? Are you saying that the defendant is actually in the building?"

"Well, yes, your Honor, he is. He's actually is a holding cell, but he's —"

"But he's what!" the judge interrupted. "Are you telling me that you are going to disrespect the integrity of the judicial system right here today, in my courtroom?"

"Your Honor—"

"Mr. Angelino, you are aware of your duty to effectively represent your client under the Strickland v. Washington standards, aren't you?"

"Yes, Your Honor."

"And you're also aware that any defendant who is accused of a crime has the absolute right to be present at trial proceedings, that this right is inherent within protection of the fifth, sixth, and fourteenth amendments of our very constitution, which, might I add, is the fundamental nature of why we even have court proceedings. Mr. Angelino, what are you thinking?"

"Your Honor, I—I'll just have the sheriff bring him up."

"Yes, Mr. Angelino, I suggest you do that. Meanwhile, we'll all just wait. And the next time you figure it will be best to deny a defendant his rights, make sure that it is not in my courtroom."

Kay looked on and listened closely, trying to understand the legal terminology that was being used, but it was like a very different language being spoken. It was her first time in a courtroom. She tried to suck up every small part of remembrance she could ascertain. She noticed the jobs of the little people who played a big part in the operation of the proceedings. Some seemed to get no recognition; such as, the courts stenographer, for instance, whose listening and typing skills had to be immaculate in order for the court to have proper record developed; the bailiff who administered courtroom conduct; the sheriff who escorted the defendants into the courtroom on their day of reckoning.

The experience was like being at a live taping of "Law and Order." She began to wonder how well she could do in a profession such as, law enforcement. She had been out of high school for a few years, and though she had concluded that she needed a break after graduation, she realized she should have continued her education. She was wholeheartedly full of ambition. Yet, other than the move she had made to marry, her life was stagnant. The environment full of professionals made her clearly see that she hadn't been living up to her full potential.

The side entrance to the courtroom opened. In walked the sheriff and the brittle, one hundred-pound young man. His dress shirt and pants were visibly too big, hanging from his body in the same manner they would on a hanger. His steps were painfully slow, as if a step too fast or too hard would completely shatter his frame. His neck disturbingly showed his Adams apple bulging like something the size of a plum had been stuck in his throat. Dark passion-mark blemishes decorated his baldhead and sunken face.

As the sheriff gently helped him sit at the defense table, he looked into Kay's eyes. The courtroom not only became as quiet as a theater at the very start of an opera, but the sight of the defendant hypnotically tapped into the natural, human sympathetic trait of everyone. The citizens that once hollered "death penalty, death penalty" were, now taken by the apparent suffering. Some even turned their heads away from the sight, the sight being of someone or something they had only seen on movies like "Zombie" and "Night of the Living Dead." Others, like the reporters, writers, and film producers, swallowed large gulps of saliva and allowed tears to fill their eyes. The judge and even the prosecutor's mental bearings stalled with emotions. Instead of a defendant who seemed to be a wild barbaric-behaving young man well deserving of the most harsh sentence known to mankind, before them was simply a young man who, for one reason or another, made a costly mistake that any fifteen-year-old could have made. He was a young man scared to wits, already sentenced to death by a disease that seemed to be plaguing all of America.

Kay clutched Pete's hand and squeezed tight. The sight of the young man had her reliving the distress that Stew's death had forced upon her life. As the tears trickled down her cheeks, she, too, fell in a state of sympathy. Attorney Arnold Angelino smiled on the inside. He loved the way everyone had reacted to the sight of the walking disease. What everyone actually saw was AIDS and not the defendant. He took well advantage. "Your Honor, the defendant, Corey Laessig."

"Okay, now we can begin," said the judge. "Does the defendant need any water before we start?"

"No, Your Honor," Angelino replied, swiftly.

Again, out of impatience with the lawyer, the judge pulled his glasses from his face and pinched the bridge of his nose before putting them back on. He looked at Angelino and frowned. "Well I think I'll get him some water anyway...just in case." He pointed to the bailiff and signaled for him to get some water from somewhere. "It seems as if you know exactly what's best for your client today, Mr. Angelino. Okay, Mrs. Reynolds, you may proceed with opening statements."

"Thank you, Your Honor," said Reynolds, motioning her way toward the jury. She smiled and committed to give them eye contact while parading back and forth in front of them. "Good morning, ladies, and gentlemen of the jury. Throughout these trial proceedings, the Commonwealth will prove that defendants Corey Laessig and Ronald Mullen, accompanied by a Calvin McNair, the father of Jalen Harris, invaded the home of

Stewart Harris with guns drawn, demanding money and jewelry. Perpetrator Calvin McNair will testify to this matter. He will admit that although Ms. Stewart Harris was the mother of his two sons, the motive was indeed to rob Ms. Stewart so that they could get money to buy drugs. In Addition, when Ms. Stewart refused, because she had no money, it was then defendant Corey Laessig, shot into the ceiling, and advanced to rape her. Perpetrator McNair gave way to stop the malicious rape attempt because, they were there for the money, and was attacked by the same individuals. He had been beaten and hit upside the head multiples time, which is why he sustained a mild concussion, and permanent scars on the face. The gang then made him watch as Corey Laessig was aggressively thrusting himself inside of Ms. Harris' womb."

"The Commonwealth will present the testimony of the medical examiners' professional opinion, confirming that Baby Jalen, Stewart Harris' son, died from a gunshot wound in the back. The projectile perforated the lower left lung, aorta, renal artery, and bowel. The examiner will testify that the fatal bullet crashed into Baby Jalen's organs was the bullet that came from Corey Laessig's gun. At the end of said testimonies, you will find it necessary that the defendants spend the rest of their lives in prison."

Reynolds finished and politely smiled at the jury. As she walked past the defense table to sit down, she looked Angelino in the face and rolled her eyes in disgust. Her office had already made a pact with the Defenders Association that this was a case where everyone wanted the same outcome for justice. For them, the world was better off with criminals such as Ronald Mullen and Corey Laessig contained. Not Angelino, his interest was publicity and his job was to win. He was one of few lawyers who didn't fret by the murder victim being a little boy.

He mentally prepared himself for more of the judge's personal display of disdain before standing and giving his opening argument. "Yes," he said, while fastening a button on his blazer, standing and stepping from behind his table. "This is indeed a tragic incident. I mean, no one likes to see a child die from someone's careless mistake. Today, the defense will prove to you that Corey Laessig, and Ronald Mullen did not invade the home of Stewart Harris. They were let in by Stewart herself."

"Objection!" yelled Reynolds.

Angelino turned, facing the judge. "Your Honor, I'm just giving opening remarks."

"Your Honor, Mr. Angelino mentioned to the jury that Ms. Stewart Harris let the defendants inside of her home. Who is going to testify to that?" Reynolds continued.

"The Defendants! My clients will testify to that much," Angelino stated.

Reynolds slammed her palms on the table and stood. "I guess they will! I guess they would get up there and lie! Ms. Harris herself isn't here to testify now, is she?"

After listening to the attorneys engage in their verbal sword fight, the judge commented, "Counselors, I will not allow my court to be made a mockery of. Do you not see the jury sitting there? I simply will not have it…sidebar!"

Kay watched along with the rest of her family and the public, who were excitedly making notes of every detail. Any occurrence in the case could be the turning point, fault, or evidence, which would possibly shape the end. Nothing could be measured as minute. The attorneys stood at the bench and listened to the judge. He whispered since the conversation was off the record.

"This is a high profile case," he said. "I understand the stakes in winning or losing, but as I said aloud, I will not allow the two of you to turn my courtroom into a game of Scrabble with the wordplay. Now, what is the issue behind your objection?"

"Your Honor, "Reynolds whispered, "there is nothing in discovery documents that proves Mr. McNair, who will testify that he entered the home with the defendants by force. And I do have to add, Your Honor, which this particular witness is a co-conspirator."

Angelino wasted no time chiming in. "Yes, Your Honor, he is a co-conspirator, but one who has already received a deal from the Commonwealth."

"Well, I know that much," said the judge. "But what does that have to do with this objection?"

"Well, Your Honor, my clients are willing to testify. I'm not sure, but it is a right incumbent upon the constitution for them to do so," Angelino, implied.

The judge squinted and stared through the lenses of his glasses with resentment. "I see...very well, Mr. Angelino, you do have a point. I will overrule the objection, but I am warning you, there will be no mistrials so be careful of your language."

"I will do that, Your Honor," Angelino respectfully responded.

Angelino looked at the prosecutor and winked before returning to the area before the jury. Reynolds hurried back to her seat, trying to exhibit confidence.

"The objection is overruled!" said the judge, formally updating the court of the sidebar result.

"Ladies and gentlemen of the jury," Angelino continued, "the defense will present evidence that my clients were let inside of Stewart Harris' home by Ms. Harris herself; that the act of shooting in the air was not intentional; that, in fact, the weapon discharged due to its hairline trigger or perhaps an inexperienced operator. I will prove to you that my clients could not have known anyone was upstairs in the home; therefore, the charge of recklessly endangering others' lives is just another charge that you shall not consider. The defense will prove that the defendants were forced, by threat of death, to travel to the Harris' home, threatened by a much older and street-savvy guy ~ that guy being the other unknown perpetrator, whom might I add, is the true criminal and is still out there somewhere. This older guy in question took advantage of my clients', the defendants, mental capacity and drove them into a brick wall, leaving them to suffer consequences alone. We will present the testimony of neurologist Dina Freeman, who will explain the facts of juveniles not possessing the culpability to resist influence. Yes, ladies and gentlemen, I said juveniles. Because even though they are sitting here being tried as adults in adult court, as a matter of law, they are still juveniles ~ not even eighteen yet."

"Objection!"

"Please disregard, I am finished, Your Honor!" said Angelino before the judge could have the chance to rule.

The judge bowed his head in order to stare through the top section of his lenses. "I warned you, counselor," he scowled.

"That's it, Your Honor. I am done with my opening remarks."

Angelino smirked while hurrying to take his place behind the table with the accused.

After opening remarks, the judge ordered the Commonwealth to commence with the presentation of their case. Those who took the stand were a number of officers who testified to the time in question of the 911 call, the content of its dialogue, the scene of the crime and what evidence obtained. The pathologist testified to establish cause of death, and a few neighbors took the stand to account for the disturbing noises they may have heard on the night of the crime. It was a clear-cut presentation of evidence, ending with Calvin McNair, the co-conspirator, as the chief witness.

"The Prosecution calls Calvin McNair," said Reynolds.

The sheriff opened the door to the side entrance that separated the courtroom from the holding cells. All eyes were focused on the admittance. In walked the angry-looking and serious witness. His baldhead was well polished. His eyes were half squinted, and he had a full, bushy beard that displayed heavy streaks of grey. The state-issued brown uniform hugged his body in a manner in which an athletic physique could be x-rated.

His hands were before him and cuffed to a chain that wrapped around his waist and dangled to connect with yet another chain that shackled his ankles. He walked slowly, being careful not to take large steps. The chains not only limited him to inch-like steps, but the thoughtful possibility of the cuffs cutting into his ankles also played a factor. His body swayed rhythmically with each step, as if a hardcore gangster rap played in his head.

When the sheriff freed him of his bondage, he was escorted to the stand where he was sworn in. "Will you please state your name for the court," started Reynolds.

"Calvin McNair. C-A-L-V-I-N-M-C-N-A-I-R."

"Would you please tell the court your relation to the deceased?"

"He was my son," he replied in a low and sorrowful tone.

"And for the court, what was your son's name?"

"Jalen Harris."

"And what was his mother's name?"

"Stewart Harris."

"Can you tell the court what reason you were at the home of Steward Harris in the night in question?"

Calvin cleared his throat. "Well, I had owed them some dough."

"Excuse me," the judge interrupted, "what is it that you owed them?"

"I owed them some dough."

"I take it when you say 'dough' you're implying money? Am I correct, young man?" asked the Judge.

"Uh-humm."

"Is that a yes?"

"Yes, Your Honor."

"And just for the record, so that there aren't any mix-ups later, who may I ask is them?"

"Oh...I'm talkin' 'bout Young Corey, and Little Ron."

"Would that be the defendants?" the judge wondered.

"Uh-humm."

"That would be a yes then?"

"Yes, Your Honor."

"Okay, counselor, you may continue with direct."

"Thank you, Your Honor."

Reynolds slowly migrated from before the twelve jurors to where her witness sat on the stand. She thought to comfort him with eye contact and a sense of closeness, even if only from where he stood. It wasn't easy for a young man such as Calvin to do what he was doing. After his testimony, the name Crab as he once knew it would have no street credibility. He would never be able to show his face on the stomping grounds where he made his bones ever again. Reynolds just needed him to follow through with it, and then her interest in his uneasiness would be out the window, right along with the name Crab.

"Mr. McNair, would you please answer the questions 'yes' or 'no' for clarity of the record? Now you may continue telling us what happened."

Again, Crab cleared his throat. "Well," he started, "I owed them some money, so when I was going to see my sons, they came from out of nowhere."

"So they ambushed you?"

"Objection! Leading the witness," yelled Angelino.

"Your Honor, the witness stated that the defendants came from out of nowhere, which implies an ambush."

"Sustained! You may proceed," the judge ordered.

"So they came out of nowhere with their guns drawn and told me to get in their car. They took me to Stew house, because I told them that she had money in there."

"Did Ms. Harris open the door?"

"No, we kicked the door open. The lock was weak."

"Once you were inside, what happened?" Angelino asked.

"We ransacked the house looking for the money while Stew was at gunpoint."

"Tell the court what happened when they didn't find any money."

"That's when Young Corey shot in the ceiling and killed m-m-my son."

Crab could not suppress his emotions any longer. He cried, silent and hard, with his shiny head bowed and sniffling away. The heart aching sadness throughout the room is overwhelming. Again, for the second time, the courtroom fell into a state of tranquility. It was almost as if no one was in the room at all. The tear-jerking testimony had won back the hearts of the people, and Reynolds was determined to let them see her witness weep as long as they needed to. It was her way of reminding them that a child was dead, and though one of the defendants was suffering from AIDS, justice will not serve unless the American Judicial System hands down a punishment.

Three minutes later, Reynolds was moving along with her presentation. "Would you like some water, Mr. McNair?"

"No!" he said. His face now frowned, with his hands bald tightly together. "I'm okay."

"Alright, you can continue," she implied.

"When he shot in the ceiling, they beat me in the head and made me watch them rape my son's mother."

"No further questions, your witness."

Reynolds held her head high as she walked back to her rightful place behind the attorney's table. She felt confident that the jury had eaten up Crab's testimony, and she hoped that would hold tight during cross-examination.

Angelino stood and placed his palms on the table while bowing his head, trying to hurry and finish reading a sheet of discovery evidence. He looked at the witness. "Mr. McNair, is it?"

"Yes."

"Do you ever remember talking to the police officers after the night of the murder?"

"Yes."

"And what kind of conversation did you have with the police?"

"It was a regular conversation."

"Allow me to rephrase. Did the police ask you anything?"

"Yes, they were asking me all kinds of questions."

"All kinds of questions, huh?"

"Yup."

"And you gave them all kinds of answers also, right?"

"Objection! Your Honor, is this line of questioning relevant?"

"If you give the counselor a chance, we may see the relevance of the questions. But I agree, Mr. Angelino, let's get on with it," responded the judge.

"Understood, Your Honor," Angelino responded. He toyed with an ink pen in his hand while directing his body from around the table and toward the witness stand. He stopped in front of the witness to block Crab's view of the prosecutor. "Mr. McNair, do you remember telling officers that you led my clients to your home on foot?"

"No."

"Do you remember telling the officers that your son's mother, Stewart Harris, opened the door for you all?"

"N."

"Your Honor, I'd like to present to the court the investigatory statement marked as exhibit 'A'." He rushed to the defense table and grabbed copies of the statement. He handed the D.A. (District Attorney), Crab, and the judge a copy each. "Mr. McNair, please flip through the pages. It's not many, only four. Is that your signature on the bottom?"

"Yes."

"Now, please turn to page two. Now count four lines from the top...do you see it?"

"Yeah, I see it."

"Can you read it please?"

Crab cleared his throat and began reading. "Question: then what happen. Answer: Stew opened the door."

"Okay, stop right there...so Ms. Stewart Harris did open the door?"

"No."

"Isn't that what you told the police?"

"Yes."

"So you lied then?"

"Yes."

"And aren't you lying now?"

"No."

"So everyone is lying except for you, huh?" Did the prosecutor offer you something in exchange for your testimony?"

"Yeah, they gave me a lighter sentence."

"No further questions."

The judge banged the gavel. "The court will recess until tomorrow."

Choices and Decisions

While Pete was downstairs making turkey sandwiches, Kay methodically evaluated each room on the second floor of her new home. A lot of work had to be done before she could actually feel completely comfortable calling it her home, but she was up to the task of putting her woman's touch on things. With the exception of the kids' rooms, all of them were full of boxes of things she had immediately gotten out of storage. Pete had taken her house away from her, but she was damned if she was going to allow her possessions to be taken also.

Her notepad had a number of categories in which she listed her first steps to designing the home. She had the trash category, things to save, rooms to paint, and furniture to switch, all the way to colors of shades and curtains. Everything was down to a science. She just needed to figure out which room she would start on after the master bedroom is done.

Pete had brought sandwiches up on a tray, five of them, sliced diagonally, accompanied by two glasses of homemade ice tea and a large bag of barbecue potato chips. Silently they ate, enjoying the presence of each other without as much as a word. Before they were finished, their doorbell rang. It was Cee, and Kay invited her in. Cee had hoped that Kay wasn't too busy and would take a ride with her and keep her company.

"You want one of these sandwiches?" asked Kay.

Cee stood still and let her eyes roam around in the room.

"Uh-uh, girl, how can you even eat with all these boxes all over the place?"

"Well, I don't have any choice. It's going to be this way until we sort through everything." Kay's response was Pete's cue to leave. He felt bad about selling her house without permission and knew that she would never let him forget until the house was the way she wanted it. In the ten days that they had been living together, Kay turned his home into the likes of an antique shop. Chairs and extra tables sat wherever looked like a good spot. Mounds of clothes rested on them, the banister, in the hall, and even over top of a few doors, which cut the chance of them completely shutting. Pete hated it but chalked it up as the first of many sacrifices he would make in his marriage.

Kay took a swallow of her tea to wash down the last bite of her sandwich. "Girl, if you don't stop lookin' 'round and just move some of that shit so you can sit down," she said, feeling slightly embarrassed of the disarray. "I haven't really had the chance to put my thing down in here yet, but I am going to hook this joint up."

Naw, girl. This is a beautiful spot," Cee, responded. "It's damned near out the boondocks. The neighbors probably aren't nosey ~ all up your ass about the smallest thing. Plus, it's as big as your Oak lane crib."

"Ooh, guess what, girl. You not going to believe this shit here," whispered Kay. "This dude done sold my house."

"What house! The house I am talking 'bout?"

"Yup, and I was mad as hell."

"Was? Shit, girl, I'd still be beating that ass as we speak. So don't tell me he kept the money?"

"No, I got the money."

"Oh, well just make sure you buy a new crib just in case he

acts stupid. Trust me girl, husband or no husband, men start acting stupid when you up in their spot, start acting as if they own you and things like that. Do this, do that, fix me this, cook that… like a bitch name Florence from the Jefferson's. Don't let him get sick. They act like they can't do anything by themselves; have you taking off of work just to pamper their lazy asses."

Kay listened and knew that everything Cee expressed had some truth to it. Of course, she knew that all men weren't the same, but she didn't want to rule out any possibilities just yet. Cee was right: husband or no husband. Kay respected her for having the balls to give it up raw.

Cee looked at her watch. "Damn, girl, are you riding with me or what?"

Kay immediately began shuffling to put her shoes on. "Where are we going?"

"Girl, just come on. I'll tell you on the way."

"Alright, plus, I need your advice about something."

"Well, a bitch is late, so hurry up!"

The girls rushed out of the house and drove away in Cee's car.

"Where are we going?" asked Kay.

"We're going to the county jail, girl," answered Cee as she turned onto the expressway at the Vine Street exit.

"To the County jail, for what?" Kay asked, in disbelief.

"I got to handle something for somebody. This is my last time doing this, though," Cee assured.

"Uh-uh, girl, I know you aren't ~ why you bring me if you knew you were going to be doing this bullshit?"

"Girl, I don't know. I usually have somebody with me and I was feeling like your company. You can stay in the car, though. I'll only be fifteen minutes."

"You damn right I'm staying in the car. I wish you had said all this before you let me take this ride with you! I got kids to take care of. I don't have time to be gettin' caught up 'cause you want to be a mule and trot some shit into the prison."

"I got kids too!" Cee responded loudly.

"Well, you need to act like it. What if they lock you up, Cee? What will the kids do then?"

Cee never answered the question. She didn't even bother to explain to Kay that she wasn't actually taking the drugs inside. All she had to do was drop them off to another guard, a female who wouldn't be able to recognize her if she tried.

About a mile from their destination, Cee pulled over in the lane next to the guardrail. She popped the trunk and quickly got out of the car to retrieve the drugs and her disguise. When she got back into the car, Kay, was startled by her sudden appearance in costume. She was fully, covered in women's Islamic garments. Her hands, face, feet, neck ~ not a single piece of skin showed.

Kay started in a sort of shock. "Oooh, girl, you is wrong."

"Girl, I know you're not thinking I was going to just let my face be seen."

"To tell you the truth, I didn't know what to think," Kay said.

"Uh-humm. See, I am acting like I got kids," responded, Cee.

Kay grimaced with temporary dislike. "That's bullshit! Cee, if you were acting as if you have kids, then you wouldn't even be doing this. Besides, where is my disguise? You going to pull up on state prison, thinking there isn't a million cameras watching things. All they need to do is zoom in and see my face, and I am going to jail."

"Stop trippin'. There are no cameras out there. You are going to be cool."

"You don't know what they got. Matter of fact, I'll be waiting here." Kay got out of the car and angrily sat on the guardrail with her arms crossed.

Cee leaned over and began talking to her through the passenger window. "Is you serious?"

"Bitch, you motherfucking right I'm serious." Kay stared for a second and then rolled her eyes. The sound of her tone made

Cee realize that she was deeply upset and possibly willing to go to blows, so Cee respected her decision and pulled off.

As Kay watched the car stretch into the distance, she grew angrier. For the life of her, she didn't know why she had thought that her getting out of the car would somehow change Cee's plans. She had thought their friendship was worth that kind of sacrifice and always figured that being a mother herself she wouldn't dare pull her into anything that would subject her to the horrifying possibility of being away from her kids. The ordeal had definitely placed their relationship in a different perspective, but Kay persisted not to be too judgmental. Often she wondered where would she be, or what she would be doing for money if she didn't have her clerical skills or met a guy like Pete who had been paying her way from day one. She sure hoped that Cee was being paid, because to her, there wasn't a good enough piece of dick in the world that would make her do such a thing.

Kay was worried. While impatiently pacing back and forth, a car sped past, stopped, and backed up. A voice appeared. "You need a lift, young lady?" a middle-aged man asked.

"No, thank you," Kay quickly answered, then walked toward the direction that the car was facing.

The man watched, tapping the gas enough to enable the car to move at the speed of her walk. The sight of her firm ass bouncing with her strut showed off her black thong panties that were sticking out of the white, low-riding sweats ~ along with her t-shirt pulled tightly across her stomach and knotted in the back ~ made him ask again.

"Are you sure, little lady?" I can take you anywhere you need to go, free of charge," he added, rubbing his hands together.

"Yeah, I'm sure!" Kay responded without even looking in the man's face.

"Okay, just asking." The man sped forward and resumed in the moving lanes.

Kay looked down at herself. Shit, she thought, *here I am*

standing by myself in the middle of the fucking expressway, looking like I am turning tricks or something. This bitch better hurry up."

No soon as the thoughts stopped playing in her mind, another car sped past and stopped. In it were three men who looked to be in their mid-twenties. One of them got out of the car and advanced toward Kay, who was now displaying her "don't fuck with me" poker face. He was a clean-cut, neatly dressed man. His walk was charmingly confident, his white buttoned-up short-sleeve shirt was stylishly, tucked into his khaki shorts and he wore no socks.

He slid within Kay's personal space and looked her up and down. Her arms were folded, her heart was beating with fear, and her limbs had frozen. She couldn't have moved away from him if she had tried. Instead, she returned a hard and irritated look, her eyes traveling from his head to his feet. Her thought was intense, noticing that he had on Skippy sneakers. She wondered how much of a chase he would give if she decided to run.

"What's up, sis?" he asked.

"No, I'm not lost! Thank you!" she sassed.

"Damn! Calm down. I was going to ask if you needed a ride."

"No, I don't need a ride. I'm alright. I'm waiting for somebody. Now would you please get away from me!"

The man reached into his pocket and brandished a stack of money. "It doesn't look like dude going to show up. You might as well come with us."

"What! Uh-uh, I'm cool!" Kay shouted directly.

"Well, how much for all of us then?"

Kay was disturbed at that point. She wanted to fight. Unfortunately, whom was she fooling? She was out there by herself and dressed in clothing that was alluring. How could she blame him?

Suddenly another person got out of the car and slowly began walking toward them. "How much does she want!" he yelled.

"She acting like she's not working!" the first dude yelled back.

He took his palm and rubbed it across Kay's ass. "Bitch, why you fronting?"

Kay slapped his shoulder. "Boy! Don't be doing that shit! You don't know me!"

"Shut up and tell us how much 'fore we take this shit."

"Yeah, how much?" said the second male, finally standing amongst them.

They were so close to her body that they practically were kissing her cheeks. She felt the heat from their bodies pressing against her shoulders. She was dying on the inside, scared to death, and her limbs had managed to fail her. She felt another rub across her ass, followed by a hard squeezed, and then another until the two men were groping her. Their animalistic instinct took advantage of the smell of fear. She tried to knock their hands away, but it was a lost cause. With each feel of her soft ass, their urge to plug her hole began to increase.

At the very moment that one of them expressed his aggression into rubbing her virginal area, Cee's car pulled up and halted just inches from where they stood. She noticed the harassment from a two-block distance while driving, and had it not been for Kay clearly in the way, she would have run their asses over with the car. Kay could see the front bumper of Cee's car in her peripheral view. Her inside voice screamed, "*help me*," yet her mouth ceased to move. Cee furiously watched through the windshield while rummaging through her glove compartment past a small container of antibacterial hand lotion, condoms, the title, registration, and owner's card. Under a number of unimportant pamphlets, she retrieved a black snub-nosed 357 Magnum. She grabbed the gun and exited the car, leaving her door open. The nerve of them not caring enough to stop harassing Kay, even when she was right there

"As-Salaamu-Alaikum!" (Peace Beyond to You) she yelled, holding the gun to her side and slowly raising it. "Get your hands off of her! Or I swear by Allah, (God) I'll murder you motherfuckers!"

The sight of the pistol immediately changed their minds. Cee's appearance also played a part on their psyche. She was an angry woman, fully covered in black, holding a huge black gun, and making promises of death. To them, that was synonymous to the Grim Reaper ~ Islamic garments or not. They slowly stepped back and gave a good showing of their hands.

"Alright, sis, you got it," said one of them while displaying a smirk on his face. The other remained quiet and seriously frightened.

Kay's limbs had at last enabled her to move. She ran to the passenger side of the car, goes in, and slammed the door shut. Cee was tempted to shoot one of the men, but that would have only put Kay in more danger than she had already caused her to be in, so she easily backed up, got into the car, and burned rubber.

For the first ten minutes of the drive, both Cee and Kay remained silent. Cee's thoughts were on the conversation that they had prior to her leaving Kay on the side of the road. While driving to the prison, she thought about saying to hell with the drug transaction and turning around. She really didn't want to leave Kay standing there, and now she would live to regret it for the rest of her life. She would have explained to Kay how she felt if she thought, it would have been any consolation, but the turn of events was all her fault.

As Key stared forward at a car with her eyes focused on a *"Honk if you love Jesus"* bumper sticker, her mind was reliving the sexual assault she had just experienced. She was mad at herself for not questioning further into their destination before getting into the car, mad at Cee for not respecting their relationship enough to tell her, and mad at Cee for leaving her on the side of the road. Most of all, she was mad at herself for choosing the type of clothing she had on.

For more reasons than one, she figured that maybe she had it coming to her. How many real women with three kids walked around with their thong panties showing? Doesn't it only draw unwanted attention? What kind of class and elegance was she exhibiting? Better yet, what kind of example was she setting for her girls? She suddenly burst into tears as she asked herself these questions.

"I know, girl...I know. Let it out," said Cee, holding back tears of her own and trying to be strong for her.

Instead of driving Kay home, Cee steered her way through traffic and ended up down South Street. They went to Vita's favorite sports bar-and-grill to have a drink.

"And what will you fine young ladies have?" The bartender asked while watching as the girls positioned themselves in the highchairs.

Kay remained speechless. Cee stared into the side of Kay's face, then reached into her handbag and gave the bartender a fifty. "Just give us two double shots of 151 and orange juice," she said before going to the restroom to take off her disguise.

When the drinks arrived, Cee reached over Kay, who stared in a daze, grabbed a thin straw out of a container, and began stirring Kay's drink. She picked the drink up and held the straw to Kay's lips. "Here, girl, drink."

Kay looked at her strangely, as if her face has somehow taken the form of an alien.

Cee maintained a steady hand with the shot glass, still trying to get Kay to drink. "Look, bitch," she fussed, "I'm not going to be holding this shit forever. Now, I already bought the drinks, you better not waste my damn money."

It was then that Kay had identified with whom she was with and where she was at. She looked into Cee's eyes and connected with sincerity. Without hesitation, she lazily opened her mouth and sucked through the straw while grasping a tight hold of the shot glass.

"Oooh shit! Give me another one, please!" she yelled, slamming the glass onto the marble countertop.

"Hey, hey… I got you women. Just please take it easy on the marble countertop," said the bartender.

"It's about time you came around," Cee encouraged. "I thought a bitch was traumatized."

"That was some corny-ass shit you did, Cee."

"I know, Kay. I am so sorry. That was it. I'm done with doing that shit. I heard you loud and clear. Now as you would say, I dare you to just forget about it."

Kay didn't bother to respond. She drank another double shot, and just that fast, she was able to throw the aches and pains of another experience to the back of her consciousness. Thirty minutes of laughing and joking the seriousness away, she was again confiding in Cee about her husband. The issue of him not having sex with her needed to be flushed out, and she felt that Cee would have given her an honest opinion whether she liked it or not. At that moment, honesty was what she needed.

She spun in her highchair to face Cee. "Listen, girl, you bet' not say nothing when I tell you this either."

Cee chucked. "Girl, you trippin'."

"No, I'm serious, Cee."

"Girl, who am I going to tell? I don't have any friends but you. Unless you're in need. I can reach out to one of my male friends for you."

"See…that's what I'm talking about, forget all about it."

"No…I'm just playing, damn! Come on, tell me."

Kay kept quiet for ten seconds before overcoming her embarrassment and telling her. "Look, Cee, what if I told you that I never had sex with Pete?"

"I'll say you're a fucking lie."

"Well, I am not lying. He's not pumpin' on this kitty-cat."

"Girl, you are playing, aren't you?"

"No. I'm dead serious. He ate my pussy plenty of times, but he's not penetrating me. I've been fucking Dilly all this time."

"Damn! You are cheating on him already! And, who the fuck is Dilly?"

"My dildo bitch."

Cee smiled, and shoves Kay in the shoulder. "Ooh, girl, shut up. You nasty," she teased.

"Don't even try it. I know you get down."

"Who? Shit, girl, I get plenty of sex. These guys banging down my door for this stuff." Kay was staring with twisted lips of disbelief. "Seriously, no," Cee continued, "I got four of them in my closet. A bitch needs different sizes for different occasions. 'Cause sometimes a man just isn't worthy to be bouncing up and down on this. Earrrly!"

"What's a chick to do though? I even tried to sneak some on the honeymoon and he threw me up off his ass like I had a disease or something."

"Damn, bitch! What you douching with?"

Kay chuckled. "Whatever! My, Pooh-Pooh don't stink."

"Well you need to rape his ass. Tie his ass up when he go to sleep and ride that 'thang.' That's what they do to us. I can't even count how many times I woke up and some dude done already slid his dick in."

"Girl, I am not about to catch a rap case, over no man."

"That's not rape. You are trippin'."

"Why isn't that rape? It is not consent either."

"But on something real, your husband is probably gay." Cee, suggested.

"I know, that's what I was thinking." Kay looked disappointed.

Cee grabbed a hold of her hand to comfort her. "Can his dick get hard?" she asked.

"Can it get hard? Hell yeah, that shit is up all the time."

"Then he's gay." Cee, quickly implied. "Cause I don't know

any man who wouldn't fuck his wife on their honeymoon. I mean, that's just crazy, straight unheard of."

Kay sighed, when she embraced that commit. "I never in my life thought this could happen to me. I mean, damn."

"Awww...you'll be alright? What you need, some work? 'Cause I know about four or five men I can call that's guaranteed to blow your back out of place."

Kay laughed. "No, I'm cool."

"Are you sure? Don't play, 'cause I'll hook a bitch up. Fuck that weird-ass husband of yours! Earrrly!"

Cee's words began to tear down the knight-in-shining-armor impression that Kay had always viewed Pete in. Her rock wasn't a rock anymore. He was something like Play-Doh, soft, mushy, and definitely bendable.

Nine

The Verdict

It was the second day of trial, and once again, Kay found herself sitting at what seemed to be a live recording of "Law and Order." The reporters, producers, writers, and sketch artists had poured into the courtroom earlier than usual, and everyone wanted to see how Angelino would do. His performance in cross-examination was highly criticized. Rated a poor job when compared to other cases he had handled.

With Pete seated beside her in the pews, Kay tried to clear her mind and prepare for all of the legal terms that the lawyers would soon be saying. It was hard. Pete's arm was touching hers skin to skin, and though she loved him, things had changed. She couldn't stand the smallest, simplest thought of his touch, let alone feel it. Her husband was gay and she was stuck with the fact that her life was over before it had even begun. His kisses used to make her melt, get her pussy wet, and formulate butterflies of excitement in her stomach. Now, the mere notion of a kiss made her want to puke, knowing that he probably had a man's penis in his mouth.

The judge exited his chamber. "All rise for the Honorable Judge Corby presiding," said the bailiff. Kay stood, along with the rest of the courtroom. The judge slammed his gavel and ordered everyone to be seated. When Kay sat back down, she made sure she distanced herself from Pete's closeness by placing her pocketbook between them.

For the first five minutes of the proceedings, she didn't hear anything. Her mind filled up with what to do and how to talk to Pete. When the defense recalled an officer to the stand, she was able to pay closer attention. The red-boned, full-lipped police officer took the stand and stated her name, "Officer Sullivan. Badge No. 59363."

Angelino stood before the jury while questioning. "Officer Sullivan, can you please explain to the jury for a second time what the crime scene looked like."

"Yes, after receiving communication from the dispatcher, I drove two blocks and arrived at the home. The door was slightly ajar. I radioed for backup and proceeded to enter the premises. I yelled 'Hello' and a male's voice hollered back from up the steps. I asked was anybody else in the house, then proceeded up the stairs of the home, where in the middle room stood a woman whom later identified herself as Ms. Stewart Harris. She was holding a child in her arms. I discovered that the child was unresponsive; I then administered CPR, and took precautionary measures to identify the unknown assailant, unfortunately, the child was then pronounced dead."

"Would you say that you got a fair look at the house?"

"Well, I know I should have searched the house more thoroughly, but since the male yelled, I figured--"

"What I'm asking is: did it look as if the place was robbed?"

"No."

"Was any furniture turned over?"

"No."

"Any lamps knocked down?"

"Objection! Your Honor... lamps and furniture?"

"Sustained!" ruled the judge.

Angelino immediately rephrased his questioning. "So what

you're saying is that...well, are you saying that the place was intact?"

"Yes. It seemed that there was no real disturbance, other than the yelling of the male."

"No further questions."

The judge leaned toward the officer and announced that she could leave the stand. Angelino visited the defense table. He read over a few sheets of paper and called his next witness.

"The defense calls Private Investigator Oliver Marshall to the stand."

"Objection!" yelled Reynolds, fumbling through page after page of the discovery evidence. "Your Honor, there is no Oliver Marshall here in my witness list."

Angelino walked a sheet of paper up to the judge. On it was a list of potential witnesses. "You see, Your Honor," he said. "In the middle of the list it says Detective Randy Oliver Marshall."

"Yes," answered the judge. "I see it. Objection is overruled."

Reynolds was furious with the decision. She slammed her fist in her hand and pleaded, "Your Honor! With all due respect, this is crazy! On the list I have, it says *Detective*. Today, here in the court he addressed his witness as *Private Investigator.*"

"That is correct, Mrs. Reynolds. I see that you finally discovered the name. I assume that you're making the fuss because you hadn't had the chance to investigate and interview this witness. Am I correct?"

"But, You Honor, Mr. Angelino clearly switched the titles of this witness' profession on purpose."

"Yes, I agree. However, he has in fact listed the name in a full package of potential witnesses; therefore, it was your duty to investigate. Am I correct?"

"Yes, but..."

"No 'buts', Mrs. Reynolds. Your objection is overruled."

Angelino carefully watched the jury to see their reaction behind the judge's ruling. Some had their eyebrows raised, some had them bent with a puzzled facial expression to match, while others stared clueless, trying to make sense of the whole proceeding. He focused on those ones. Chances were that the jurors with emotions written all over their faces were the very ones that already had some type of opinion as to the degree of the defendant's guilt or innocence. In contrast, the jurors that were undecided were those who looked clueless. They were to sway.

As the private investigator took the stand, Angelino marched back and forth before the jurors, periodically making intense eye contact with his marks. After stating his name for the court, the investigator committed to answering the series of questions.

"So, Mr. Marshall," Angelino began. "How long have you been in practice?"

"I've been a detective in the Philadelphia Homicide Division for 18 years and in private practice for 9…so that'll be 27 years all together."

"Could you please tell the court what drew you to investigate this case?"

"Well, my wife had first brought it to my attention when we were watching the news. She had mentioned that it didn't make any sense for the two little boys not to leave with any valuables if they had gone to the Harris home for money in the beginning."

"What did you do then?"

"Well, I sort of put it in the back of my mind until I heard it on my car radio while working. It stated that the accused were saying that they were forced to go to the home by another perpetrator. That's when I thought about what my wife said. It all made sense."

"But why this case?"

"Well, my grandson went to school with the fellas."

"Your Honor, for the record, when Mr. Marshall said fellas, he means my clients, the defendants. Okay, Mr. Marshall, you may go on." Angelino implied.

"Well, yes, they all went to school with my grandson and

they didn't seem like the kind of children that would just do such a thing. I have been on the force for some time, and I know the stakes a high-profile case brings. I thought maybe I could assure those kids just a little justice if I could do a little investigating."

"And did you investigate?" asked Angelino.

"Yes."

"And what did you find?"

"Well, I first took a peek at the initial investigatory statements and there it was, a statement signed by Ms. Steward Harris, stating that there was, in fact, three bandits."

"And did she say in the statement that she knew the assailant other than the defendants and her son's father?"

"Yes."

"And what was that name?"

"It stated that his name was Bobby."

The courtroom burst into loud murmurs and slight dispirited character. Angelino grabbed a piece of paper from his table and quickly walked it to the judge.

"Your Honor, I'd like to enter this into the court as exhibit 'B'."

Clack, clack, clack, and clack! The judge banged his gavel to restore order. After the court had calmed, he allowed the statement to be, entered as evidence.

Back in front of the jury, Angelino made eye contact with his marks before resuming with questioning. "So, Mr. Marshall, what, if anything, did you do after the discovery of this name?"

"Well, I entered it into my computer at home."

"And did you find out who this Bobby guy was?"

"Yes. His name is Bobby Wilson. He's an older guy from around in the area where the crime happened."

Again, the courtroom became discomposed with voices and murmurs louder than before. "Quiet down! Quiet down!" yelled the judge, instantly restoring the fortitude of his quarters. Angelino entered the witness findings into evidence and commenced with his unflawed performance.

"Mr. Marshall, what else did you find in your investigation?"

"Well, from years of being on the force, I know that there is always a few boxes of misplaced, or should I say miscellaneous evidence. I searched through a few of them and found two items bagged as evidence and labeled 'Oak Lane Murder/Rape' and subtitled 'Baby Jalen Harris.'"

"What was in the bag?"

"It was an ink pen and a cigarette butt found in front of the home."

"Did you test the evidence?" asked Angelino.

"Yes, I sent it to a laboratory and had it examined here in Philadelphia."

"And please tell the court what were the results."

"The fingerprints on the ink pen were that of Bobby Wilson and so was the saliva from the cigarette butt."

"No further questions."

The judge banged his gavel. "This court will be recessed and won't resume until further notice. I'll have to give the Commonwealth a chance to have the evidence tested by someone from the city lab."

As everyone stood and began to disperse, Kay threw around items inside of her pocketbook, trying to show reason why she wasn't following right behind Pete. She loitered and mixed within the crowd, keeping focus on the shirt of witness Randy Oliver Marshall. The idea had suddenly come to her that she should hire him to investigate her husband's activity. If she were to get a divorce and seek half, then she needed to pile up evidence against him that would weigh heavy in the court of law.

She finally got close enough to get his attention. She spoke softly, "Excuse me, sir... excuse me."

The light-skinned, clean-shaven man stopped and politely smiled, showing his yellow cigarette-stained teeth. "Yes, ma'am," he answered. "What can I help you with?"

"I, um...I...can you...well I'm trying to find something out about somebody, and I was wondering…" Kay paused, twisting and turning her head, bobbing her body side to side and peeking through the now-thinning crowd to make sure Pete wouldn't double back and catch her.

Marshall noticed her uneasiness and was tempted to walk away. He hated the potential clients who would insist on meeting with him under uncomfortable conditions. It always posed a high chance of him being made by his mark early on, which would eventually make him resort to irritating disguises in order to tail them. He looked at Kay with coldness in his eyes, not caring if she were to get mad or not.

"Is this somebody, actually, someone you know or what?" he started. "Because before you go any further, if you are thinking about hiring me, you must tell me the truth. Now who is this someone?"

Kay looked at him strangely, resenting him for being forward with his arrogance. She hadn't even finished saying what she needed to say before he presented his intensified personality. She would have left him standing there if she absolutely didn't need his help.

"Look, sir," she started, "I need my husband investigated."

"Okay. Who is he? Where does he work? Where does he live? How does he look? I need to know these things."

Kay grew tempered. "I am really trying to tell you. I really need you to give me a second and stop interrupting me. Maybe I'll have that chance to do so."

"Okay, lady, I apologize. Look, here is my card. Call me. Perhaps you and I can discuss matters in a more detailed fashion, under different circumstances." He placed the card in her hand and seemed to vanish into the last of the crowd. Kay slid the card into her pocketbook and rushed out of the courtroom where Pete waited in the hall for her.

When they exited the Criminal Justice Center, they were ambushed via, news reporters and writhers of all sorts of papers and magazines. Photographers snapped away with their cameras. "Ms. Harris! Ms. Harris! I'd like to interview you!" a voice yelled out of the midst of the opportunists who were shoulder to shoulder, pushing and shoving one another for position. Microphones and hand-held tape recorders were staring into Kay's face. Something as simple as managing to walk had become difficult. The eager professionals were craving for a tasty story, and Kay was it.

Pete grabbed Kay's hand and heroically pushed through the crowd. He opened the car door for her, making sure she secured, and slowly walked around to the driver's side, ignoring the reporters who followed behind him.

Kay stared at him with a fluttered heart. He was so handsome. He acted unlike any person she had ever known with the way that he spoiled her. She, have been pampered before, but it was by individuals who went bananas over her sex. Not everything given to her in her relationships, she figured, was out of love. No, the things she had received were from the desire of people hoping to keep her legs open, so that they could fuck her to death until her womb was just a hole, no flesh.

The gifts she had received from Pete weren't at all, pussy motivated. They were genuinely given, motivated by love and a natural decency to care for not just any woman, but her. Often Kay imagined the father she never knew to be of such character ~ with a constant brave and un-withering interest in her well-being. It was strange, but in many ways, she unconsciously identified Pete as the father figure in her life.

As her husband sat at the steering wheel, she continued to stare with misty eyes. *How can you be gay? Out of all the men in the world, I get a good man and he's gay! What fuckin' luck.* While she played with thoughts, Pete continuously cursed the crowd for pounding their paws on the car window as he drove away.

Ten

Suspicions

Remnants of the hot, record-breaking summer seethed the atmosphere. After all, it was the first day of fall. It was just after 1 p.m., when Marshall found a spot in the shade, under a thin tree with half-colored red and green leaves on the branches. Some hanging on the stem by a thread of an ending cycle of photosynthesis, and some had already fallen to the ground, many in which were stationed on top of the concrete bench where he optioned to sit.

He was in City Hall's Oval Park, listening to cars beep their horns while circling around the park's perimeter en route and watching a group of punk-rock skateboarders skate back and forth jumping ramps, flipping, and doing various stunts off the concrete benches. He was of course, also keeping a close eye on Pete while enjoying the guilty pleasure of a delicious chocolate bar for lunch. He was supposed to be having an egg salad sandwich and an apple juice that Sara, his wife, had prepared, but he could never tell her that he hated her salad. He finished the last of the Snickers, licked his fingers of the melted chocolate, and pulled a hand-held notepad from his shirt pocket to jot down a few notes.

His subject, Peter Frazier, sat just a few benches away, crumbling bread, and throwing it to the ground to feed the pigeons. He had been there for twenty minutes reading a newspaper and enjoying a snack of his own, a Cinnamon bun, and a fountain drink from somewhere. He stood, clapped his hands together to free them of crumbs, and started across the busy multi-lane street while talking on a cell phone.

Intrigued, Marshall trailed from half a block away. It was his first investigation of the sort. Usually he would investigate or tail typical criminal activities and maybe even retrieve specific documents, but never a husband whose wife suspected him of being a homosexual. Frankly, at this point, he was also curious of Pete's sexual proclivities. He had neglected to give Sara a feeling of Lowboy sometimes over the years in their thirty-five year marriage, but even for him, the idea of not having sex on the honeymoon was outrageous.

Marshall made certain to stay out of view by using the people who beat the downtown sidewalk as a screen while walking; from time to time, Pete liked to glance at his reflection in the storefront windows. The soft breeze, developed from cars whisking past, crept under his three-quarter fall jacket, making its back flap like a flag or even the cape of a marvel superhero.

Marshall studied his walk, trying to see if he could notice maybe an extra twitch, but there was no trace. Pete's posture was upright and soldier-like. After he watched a cable program with Sara about men on the down low, the truth was that one could never just tell by appearance. Marshall began wondering if Kay was simply fishing for reasons to divorce. However, he still found it hard to believe that Pete hadn't slid into home base with a beautiful woman like Kay. He swore to himself that if it weren't for the fact that Sara would kill him and the love he had for her, he would have taken a few Viagra pills and jumped into the race.

When the trail ended, they had already walked four blocks. Pete entered a building that looked much as if it was condemned. Its entrance was through a storefront that, according to Marshall's familiarity, had always been a place that the city was waiting to remodel. He stopped in front of the place and looked above the entrance to see if there was a name. It wasn't. The huge square foot window with deep dark, smoke was covered in tint that could not be seen through. Even after peeking with his face to the glass and using his hands as blinders, he still couldn't see inside.

When he entered, he observed the small office in one take. A familiar-looking security guard stood by an entrance leading into a hall, and a leafy tree-like plant was located in the corner of the right-hand side. On the left, a trashcan sat below a huge poster of a molecular-structured DNA diagram, along with safe sex posters across the bright white wall. Next to the trashcan was a rack full of pamphlets, and of course, a secretary sat at a metal desk, typing on the computer and popping gum. "How can I help you, sir?" she asked.

"Um, yes, I'd like to have an application," said Marshall.

The woman chuckled. "Are you married?"

"Yes."

"And I bet you have kids too, right?"

"Well, yes. As a matter of fact, I have six of them, but I don't see what that has to do with an application."

"Well, I'm sorry, but here is an address for our sister company. It's for men with children already."

He suspiciously took the card with a smile. "Okay, thank you." While leaving, he gave another glance at the security guard and walked out of the door.

Not even five steps had, been taken when the security guard found himself behind Marshall. "Hello, sir! Excuse me sir!" he yelled.

Marshall spun around and faced the guard. "Yes, son, what is it?" He was trying to remember if he knew the man.

"Mr. Marshall, right?" he asked.

"That's me."

The guard extended a hand. "About a few years ago you and

my grandfather were the two finalists in the Annual Policeman's Bowling Tournament."

Marshall looked him in the eyes and threw his hand into a firm shake with a smile. "Yes, yes...um, Rayford!" he said excitingly. "How is he?"

"Oh, he's doing fine. What about you, do you still have that excellent stroke?"

"Well, once you have it, it never really leaves you." Marshall figured, since they were talking, he should try to get a little information about the place. "So," he continued. "What's the deal with that place you work for?"

The guard hesitated. From years of experience, Marshall knew right off the bat that he wasn't going to get a straight answer.

"Sir, I really can't tell you any information, but I can tell you that it is only for those who don't have any children. Well, sir, I think I'd better be getting back. It was nice seeing you. Have a good day."

"Okay son, same to you. And tell your grandfather that I said hello." The men shared another handshake and parted ways.

Marshall of course, stood amongst a group of people half a block away. He leaned against a wall, acting as if he, too, was waiting for the bus, using their very existence as camouflage. There was a thirty-something-year-old man, tall, and lanky dressed in a full Temple University warm-up suit with headphones on his ears. An elderly woman whom was full of spunk and four Catholic-school students neatly dressed in uniform, all of whom were oblivious to the true reason that Marshall was there.

He jotted mental notes on his pad while keeping track of the time that Peter stayed in the building. He needed to find out what was going on inside, and he had blown his chances by stating that he had kids. After thinking a minute, he made a conscious decision to call on his would-be protégé Aramis. If he had any reason to call on him, now was the perfect time, but he wondered if he would prove to be reliable or prove to exhibit the know-how and skills that had been sincerely passed down to him.

Never mind the fact that he was just as close to Marshall as his own grandson. He was a young man full of himself and he couldn't manage to think outside of the pecker in his pant. Being a dark-skinned, bald-headed, physically fit underwear model placed him in a category that women, young and old, found irresistible attractive ~ which is why, because of his untamed sexual desires, he literally screwed up his last two assignments.

Marshall listened to the phone ring three times before Aramis answered. His voice was groggy and he sounded half-asleep. "Yo, what's up?"

"Is that any way to answer the phone, boy?" Marshall asked.

"Oh! Hey, Pops. What's up?"

"Well, I don't know. That depends on your mood. Do you feel like coming aboard?"

"For-real, Pops! Yeah, I want to come on board."

"Now, boy, you know what happened last time," Marshall, lectured. "You are to deal only with me. I don't want any of that hanky-panky going on. So do not, you understand; do not contact this client for nothing! Agreed?"

Aramis thought for a minute. From the sound of Marshall's tone, he knew that there was a pretty woman involved. He insistently gave himself handsome points, suspecting that Marshall knew that the girl would be dying to drop her panties at the sight of him. He sighed. "Okay, Pops, agreed."

"Are you sure?" I won't have you messing up another job for me. I try to teach you something and you want to get your little pecker wet instead of doing the job."

"Alright! Alright! I know. I'm sure. I promise that I won't seduce the client."

They shared a laugh. "Son, you are crazy," said Marshall. He gave Aramis his location and waited thirty minutes. When Aramis arrived, he pulled up along the curb in the space where the bus normally stopped. The civilians that were used as a screen were gone. Marshall was there alone, leaning against the wall in plain view. He watched as Aramis stylishly leaned with one hand on the steering wheel and the other resting on the armrest that separated the passenger from the driver.

It was a 1993 white Cadillac El Dorado, equipped with a loud stereo system and shiny chrome rims. When Marshall thought about the context of the investigation and the reason why he been hired, he looked at his protégé and laughed.

Aramis turned the loud music down. "What's wrong with you, Pops?" he asked.

Marshall eluded the question. He opened the door and sat in the passenger seat. "Go around the block. Hurry up so we don't lose him." He pulled out a picture of Pete and explained that he was the mark and that he was in the building.

"So what am I investigating him for?" asked Aramis.

"For now, just let me know why he's inside of the building," said Marshall.

They made it around the corner and halted back at the bus stop. Aramis got out of the car and fixed himself up. Marshall couldn't help not to laugh again. If only he knew that he was possibly getting ready to enter some kind of event with potentially gay men, he would have died.

"Why you keep laughing?" asked Aramis as he bent over to hear the answer from Marshall, who scooted into the driver's seat.

"Nothing, son, just go on and make me proud of you. And make sure you tell them you have no kids." Marshall pulled off in stitches. *That'll teach 'em to keep his mind out of the gutter,* he thought.

Aramis entered the establishment and at once cased the room. It was what he been taught to do. The private investigating instincts were like second nature. His assessment was that of the likes of Marshall: the dark tint on the storefront glass, the plant, and the guard, the poster, pamphlets, and of course the woman at the desk.

"Excuse me, may I help you?" the secretary asked. The sound of a woman's voice was always like music to his ears, like poison, that made him unconsciously pour it on.

"Uh, yes, you can help me. My name is Aramis," he answered softly, sexily, and flirty while motioning toward her desk. His eyes matched his voice, deep and tranquilizing, and his smile trained her thoughts.

He was fine as hell, a tall cup of hot chocolate: good, thick, and sweet. She smiled. "How are you doing, Aramis?" Sitting upright with her elbows on the desk and forearms crossed, she girlishly looked into his face with dreamy eyes. "I'm Tonya," she said, her eyes traveling to his size 14 shoe, to his crotch and back into his eyes. He had her hanging on his every word and enjoyed it.

"Tonya, huh?"

"Yup."

"Well, Tonya, I need an application."

"Do you have any kids?"

"No, I don't."

She felt a weakening in her knees. If she had been standing, she would have fallen to the floor. "And how old are you?" she continued.

"I'm old enough," he replied. "No, seriously, I'm 26. Is that a good or bad thing, Tonya?"

"It's all a good thing, sir." She played with her hair, pulling and twirling a long stand around on her finger while returning the flirtatious body language.

"Well can I have the application or are you going to make me wait for it?" he asked. His eyes searched her figure and examined her plump breasts.

"Do you mind waiting?" she sassed.

"No, not at all, especially, when I know I'm going to get the job."

"Oh, you're that confident, huh?"

"I'm well-qualified. A person would be a fool not to hire me."

Tonya chuckled. Instead of an application for a job, she handed him a plastic card used for unlocking the doors of hotel rooms. "Just walk through that door, make a right, and follow the yellow brick road."

Aramis followed directions, not knowing what to expect, but he was good at being on his toes when it came to investigatory work. As he walked, he made a mental note to be responsible and do a good job.

The hall was narrow. At the end was an opened door. Aramis could see a man walking back and forth inside the room, falling in and out of view, lecturing or giving a motivational speech of some sort. Aramis hurried with curiosity ailing his thoughts. *What is he saying? What am I walking into?* The questions were, answered when he walked, into the room and stood a foot away from the entrance. The speaker cut his speech.

"Do you have a card, sir?" he asked.

Aramis was puzzled. "Oh, yes, I do." He reached into his pocket and gave the room key to the speaker.

"Thank you. I am Doctor Lauren. Glad you can join us," he said as he punched the card into a time machine and gave it back.

Aramis returned a smile and sat in an empty chair. The room was bright and plain. There were no pictures, posters, nor plants or any other living species—except for the group, seated in circled formation. There were nine of them, five men, and four women, all of whom were dressed in a business fashion and nametags on their shirts.

He spotted his mark just two chairs away and made sure not to stare. A white woman that sat next to him suddenly began to speak. She looked to be no older than, thirty. She had a short-styled, trendy haircut, designer two-inch heels, and an olive-green woman's two-piece suit with pants that hugged and gripped her curves like the tires of a racecar gripping and hugging a track. She sniffled and patted her tearing eyes with a napkin.

"It will be my second divorce," she started. "If I don't go through with it, it will be over. I want to, but I am just so afraid."

"We are afraid, too!" the group chimed in unison.

"Yes," said the doctor. "The things you are afraid of we understand. It's not easy to have sex. We, the people in here, are special. Despite of the physiological things that made us the way that we are, being virgins isn't a bad thing."

Aramis had to do another survey of the room. He couldn't believe it. There he was sitting next to a beautiful, well shaped, twenty-something-year-old virgin, and another just four chairs away. Her red-complexioned skin, high cheekbones, and wide smile was some of what complemented the class she upheld by merely sitting in the chair looking beautiful and not saying a word.

Aramis did not need to be there any longer. He had come to find out what the function of the place was about, therefore, he accomplished his goal. He politely stood, excused himself, and exited the room. By the time he was at the end of the hall, it was too late for the doctor to encourage him to stay. Aramis sped past the security guard and Tonya and left the building.

Outside, he dialed the number to Marshall's cell phone.

"Hello," Marshall answered.

"Yeah, Pops, I'm finished," he said.

"Don't tell me you screwed things up."

"Naw, Pops, everything is alright. You wouldn't believe what kind of place that joint is."

"It's a Psychiatrist building?"

"How you know?"

"Well, I made a few calls."

"Yeah, but it's not any ol' psych joint Pops. It's a place for virgins." Aramis laughed.

"What do you mean for virgins?"

"Yes. It's a group of virgins sitting around trying to cope with the mental reasons why they haven't had sex yet," Aramis informed.

"Yeah? Well they should have a group for you about the mental reasons why you can't think but with your other brain."

A silence grew. Aramis didn't find Marshall's joke funny.

"Listen," Marshall, continued. "Thanks a lot, son. I'll send you a check in the mail."

"No, that's cool, Pops. I didn't do much. Plus, I owe you."

Marshall sassed. "Yes, you do owe me. Well, I'll be seeing you. Your car will be parked in front of your house."

"How am I supposed to get home?"

"Catch the bus. Oh, and ummm, son…"

"What's up Pops?"

"I didn't mean anything by that smart remark." Marshall stated.

"I know, Pops."

"No…I just wanted you to know that."

Marshall hung up the phone and pressed Kay's number on speed dial. Kay let the phone rang twice and picked up.

"Hello."

"Hello, Ms. Frazier? This is Detective Marshall, here."

"Hello, Mr. Marshall. How are you?" She asked. Kay's heart thumped with fear of the truth being what she had already concluded. She loved Pete so much that she wondered if she could possibly live with knowing that he was gay and still stay married to him. She just knew that she would never in her lifetime find a man like him. *Why is he calling so soon? The investigation can't be over this damn fast. What did he find?* While she asked herself questions, Marshall gave her the news of his findings.

"I am doing fine," he started. "Well I have some good news concerning your husband. He's not gay."

"Not gay?"

"Nope, not gay, he is a pure virgin. That's why you guys hadn't rolled in the sack yet."

"Are you serious?" Kay excitedly asked.

"Lady, you paid me to investigate. It's fortunate that the investigation ended so early, that is, if you still want me to investigate more, I will."

"No, that's alright. Thank you."

"Okay, if you need me for anything else, you have my contact information. I strongly suggest you find a way to make things better at home with your husband. Try to openly understand his situation and sympathize for his hardship, so you two can have a healthier marriage. Don't be so hasty to jump to conclusions when your question's isn't, answered. We are only human, and we all have issues," he said before hanging up. She stood dumbfounded; therefore, she needed to make things up for assassinating her husband's character.

Eleven

Romance

The *Passions of Pleasure shop* was located on Ludlow Street, in Center City Philadelphia. A back street usually occupied with freight trucks unloading merchandise, and large heavy trash bags. Puddles of still water sat in between the cracks, and dips, decorating the weather-eroded warped street at night. The bold alley cats and rats scurried, and competed for what little garbage left behind inside dumpsters. Despite the damp, clammy, and dreary feeling that would overcome a person when entering the block, people still found themselves ignoring the aggravating dislikes just to enter the store. On this particular night, Kay wasn't any different.

Though she had never tried most of the sexual accessories retailed in the store, Kay walked around, up and down the aisles in excitement, reading the use of items, wondering if there was any truth to what the words were saying the item could do. She looked at the boxes of different porno DVD's, and scrutinized the things that were in the showcase. From the smallest level at scented candles and edible underwear, to the largest at anal beads and strap-on dildos for women, they sold it all. Kay bought hot-and-warm strawberry motion lotion, scented massage oils along with scented candles; not one, but three hard-core porno DVD's, and even a box of pasta noodles that were shaped and designed to look like a vagina. The kids were over Vita's for the weekend, and it was going to be a night she went after her husband with both barrels blazing.

She thought of Pete's huge penis in her mouth while driving home. She couldn't wait to taste him, and the anticipation had the crotch of her pants wet, damned near seeping through the tough denim. She was glad that he wasn't gay and sort of felt like she had dishonored him by having such thoughts.

Pete was to arrive at home at 6:30 p.m., Kay got home at 4:30 p.m., to set things up. She started with the noodles. While they were on the stove simmering, she stationed candles all over the house and put on a Barry White CD. She took a steamy, hot shower at 5:45 p.m., and was anxiously waiting for Pete to enter the house at his normal time. She stood at the door wrapped in a shiny, satin, peach lingerie robe ~ its length stopping just about the bottom of her buttocks, showing not only her perfect-shaped ass shaking when she walked, but also her nicely-trimmed, fat pussy as well; a pussy that had been ready for him since their second date. Underneath, she wore black g-string panties that matched her slide-on pumps, a pair Pete had brought her on their honeymoon.

Patiently, she anticipated hearing his key entering the lock. Her hands were on her hips, her nipples clearly poked through the robe, and her womanhood was almost dripping with thoughts of her husband finally inside of her. Like clockwork, at 6:30 p.m., Pete fiddled his key into the door. He opened and there she was, looking like Miss America. The sight made him pant. His heart pace increased. The foreign scent of the candles complimented the traveling of his eyes along the curvy terrain of her body, making his penis stand erect.

Before he could say a word, Kay strutted three steps and dashed her tongue into his mouth wild and passionately while relieving him of his blazer. She looked him in the eyes and instantly intimidated him. He tried to speak, but she placed her index finger over his lips.

"Shh!" she demandingly whispered. "Don't say a word. I got this."

Her demands were out of the ordinary, but he liked it. Kay briefly dashed her tongue back into his mouth and lightly bit the bottom of his lip when finished. She continued to stare him in the eyes and yanked his necktie out of its knot. Reaching into the split between the buttons of his shirt, she tore the shirt open, making all of the buttons pop off, and then snatched the shirt off his body. She raised his arms and put her soft hands under his tank top to rub his rock-hard abs and husky chest. His body quivered with her touch and she loved it.

Each move had to be right. She wanted to keep him interestingly in the mood of traveling into uncharted waters without scaring him with too much foreplay. Finally, she went for his belt, unbuckling it, snatching it out of the loops of his pants, and snapping it to the floor like a whip before dropping it. After his pants were off and he stood decorated in boxer shorts, socks, and a tank top, she untied the knot to her robe and let the robe smoothly slide off her shoulders, down her arms and to the floor.

"Don't you dare move," she whispered as she took a walk around him twice, scrutinizing his hairy legs and tight ass. The muscles in his back were bulging and his back arms had a horseshoe print.

Kay stood back in front of him, looking down at the 10-inch, brick-hard shaft. Her nipples darted forward and her mouth watered as she slid her hand down her panties and inserted her middle finger into her gushy wetness. She pulled her hand out and put it to his nose so that he could smell her.

"Now, open up," she said, guiding the finger at his lips.

Like a good husband, he obeyed her demand, opened his mouth, and sucked the love from her finger. Suddenly, she pulled the finger from his mouth and grabbed his hand to lead him over to the table where she had his place set. She pulled his chair out.

"Have a seat. I'll be right back," she said.

She went into the kitchen and made him a plate of the pussy noodles with garlic powder, cheese, broccoli, soy sauce, and two very fine-crushed ecstasy pills. She sat the plate in front of him and motioned to sit across from him.

"Eat," she demanded.

"But aren't you…"

"Uh-umm. Uh-umm. Shh! Just eat," Kay interrupted.

Pete was getting impatient with her demands, but still bowed his head to eat the noodles. When he noticed the shaped of them, he looked up at Kay's seductive face. She shushed him while sliding her hand down her panties and inserting her finger. She played with herself while Pete ate the noodles, trying his damnedest not to pay her any mind, but it was hard. She was beautiful, sexy, and all his. He was scared but wanted everything she was willing to give him.

Before he finished his meal, Kay slid under the table and crawled over to him. She gently placed her palms on his knees while staring at his erect penis. His legs began to shiver. Quickly, he tightly grabbed her hands.

"It's okay. It's okay, baby," she said, speaking softly, assuring that he could trust her.

His mind was telling him *no,* but somehow he released his clutch, grabbed the fork on the plate, and tried to concentrate on eating the last scoops of noodles.

"I love you, Pete," said Kay, grabbing hold of his rod and licking it like an ice cream cone before making half of it disappear in her mouth.

Pete's legs stretched out before him, tight and stiff. His body continuously shivered and he grunted with the fork clenched in one hand and a glass in the other. She sucked away while juggling his sacs in her hand. She wanted to swallow all of him;

however, he was too huge and it would have only made her gag, so she worked the half, slobbering and twirling the warmth of her tongue until he exploded in her mouth.

The discharge was unlike anything Pete had ever experienced, something special like a drug tried for the first time, making him hooked and wanting more and more.

Kay wasted no time. She crawled from underneath the table and sat on his lap face-to-face. She grabbed the back of his head and placed a breast in his mouth. As he sucked and gently bit at her nipple, she groaned and gasped his name, "Pete. P-Pete." The sensation was overwhelmingly delightful.

While he fed on her breast, she reached down in front and grabbed his dick, aiming it at her juicy hole. She began to tremble as if it was her first time ever. The touch of his fat tip touching her pussy lips sent a tingling feeling through her body, and before she could get him inside her, she had came explosively. Despite her climax, she still lowered her body. His Johnson slid deep into her guts, giving her a mixture of pleasure and pain.

Kay had never felt anything inside of her that long and thick, but she was so horny that she just wanted him to pound her all night if possible.

"Oh God," she whispered in a pant as he grabbed her cheeks and bounced her up and down with speed. She hugged his neck, tilted her head back, and concentrated on more pleasure than pain. Her eyes closed, and she could feel his balls smacking against her ass each time he slammed against her body.

"Pete, Pete, Pete, Pete," she rhythmically chanted with the motion.

Suddenly, she found herself around the dining room while he was deep inside her. He laid her on the table and thrust in and out, around and around, making sure that his hammer nailed every part of her luscious, hot, creamy womb. He growled loudly. He groaned and thrust faster and harder while reaching a climax. Kay pulled his body into hers and worked her hips until she felt his dick throbbing inside as he shot sperm into her cave.

Instantly, Pete turned into a horny lion that could not get enough of his lioness. The ecstasy had dissolved into his bloodstream and he needed more sex. He yanked Kay from the table and carried her upstairs to the shower. The hot water fell upon their bodies, increasing their heated temperatures and producing steam. They could barely look in front of themselves and see their own hand. With her eyes closed, Kay concentrated on his touch, ready and willing to be his sex slave for as long as he wished to fuck.

Pete stood behind her, reached around, and rubbed her love while his other hand was full with a breast. He reached for her hair and yanked her head back with just enough force to turn her head so that he could kiss her. With each of them breathing heavily in sensation, he rubbed her shoulders, kissed her neck, and licked down her back. He guided her body to bend over as he grabbed her by the hips, kneeled, and twirled his tongue inside her womb, letting it travel to her crack where he worked his tongue as if he had never worked it. Kay reached behind and grabbed his head while moving in a frenzy and blurting loud, uncontrollable moans.

With a thumb in her hole and tongue in her ass, she came, came, and came, back to back, to back, as if she could not stop. Pete then scooped her in his arms and carried her to their bedroom, leaving the shower running, steamy, and smelling like sex. They rolled around in the bed in missionary position, and from there they went to doggy style. When it was over, Pete nodded off to sleep. Kay lay beside him, fighting her sleep, looking at him and admitting that she hadn't been, fucked liked that ever. She hadn't cum like that, nor had she ever yearned for a man so much. She finally knew how people felt after breaking a virgin in. She felt like she had conquered something, and figured for that reason she should have been, searched for a virgin. She realized that with virgins, their dick was fresher, their mouths were more respectable, they had no one to compare you to, and they were less likely to deceive you.

Twelve

The Verdict #2

I t took the Commonwealth a little over two weeks to get the evidence produced by Angelino's witness tested. They were awaiting affirmation of the results when the judge had ordered everyone into the court. The delay in trial proceedings was unprecedented, and the judge refused to keep the jury away from their normal lives ~ especially not at the expense of the court, or the taxpayer's money.

Everyone took their place in the courtroom: the judge, bailiff, defense, prosecution, the accused, the public, and, of course, the victim's family. As the judge sat quietly at the bench, he rumbled through some papers, while the two counselors strategically prepared for a closing argument. Kay and Pete hoped that justice would be served for Stew's sake; meanwhile, the accused hoped for the benefit of an acquittal, and as for the media, they didn't care since they were sure to put a spin on any outcome of said proceedings.

Before the start of proceedings, the judge opened up with remarks. "This, ladies and gentlemen," he said, "is a continuation of the proceedings that started in late August, early September. While I absolutely saw it fit to delay in order to seek the ends of justice and allow the Commonwealth to examine evidence entered in this court, I have to apologize, first to the victim's family for the delay in closure. Secondly, of course, to the jurors who have been placed in a hotel while the Commonwealth abused its delay, furthermore, I find it appalling that I have to order everyone back into this court room and still there is no result upon the Commonwealth's testing's. This kind of practice is what makes our judicial system a laughing stock. It also gives a stigma of faulty practices within a corrupt system. I, for one, Judge Corby, will not allow it! I will accept all of the evidence presented pertaining to the ink pen and the cigarette butt as true evidence. That is including the perpetrator Bobby Wilson, his existence, as well as his participation in the crime. Now on this date of September 9th 2001, I hereby order trial proceedings to begin. We are starting with closing arguments. Mr. Angelino, you may begin."

Angelino, whispered in a mini-huddle with his clients before standing. He fastened his suit jacket, took a sip of water, and began.

"Good morning ladies and gentlemen of the jury." He smiled and motioned toward them. "I know that it's been a while since you have had your mind on the facts of this case. In conjunction, with what the judge has spoken, I am also appalled, and I personally apologize as well. However, the facts are simple, the Commonwealth in her opening statement, said that she would prove that the accused, my clients, had willfully stormed into the Harris' home to rob it. Well, as the defense proved by a signed statement of the Commonwealth's chief witness, my clients did not storm into the Harris' home. In fact, Ms. Stewart Harris herself let them into the home. That there was another perpetrator involved, whom the Commonwealth did not bother to investigate. The defense discovered that this particular perpetrator's name is Bobby Wilson. This participant forced my clients to go with him into the Harris' home via, death threats. My clients did not leave their home with any money nor any valuable's of any kind; therefore, it is apparent that they weren't seeking money to get high with.

The detective that testified for the Commonwealth said, herself, that their home was intact when she arrived. That the house was not, ransacked as the Commonwealth wishes you to believe. Yes, my clients were there, but not willfully. The Commonwealth, due to the long delay, had stipulated to the findings of neurologist, Dina Freeman, who, if had testified, would have explained to you, ladies, and gentlemen of the jury, that a juvenile's brain is not fully developed to neither understand, nor appreciate the nature of their crimes. They do not possess the culpability to predict the consequences behind their actions. This is due to the scientific study of the brain and its gray matter. The judicial system is clearly aware of this fact, for a juvenile cannot enter a bar and drink, but only upon a certain age. They cannot drive, watch certain rated 'R' movies, buy cigarettes, nor vote, simply due to their particular age. This is because children can inappropriately, be influenced. My clients were influenced to go to a home and participate in a crime. The defense therefore asks that this court show mercy on my clients, and convict only of the lesser charges."

When Angelino sat down, the full jury panel was staring in amazement. It was quiet. A moment of silence given for an attorney whom many considered him as a *deal* maker. He looked at his clients and smiled while inwardly patting himself on the back for a job well done.

Reynolds flipped a few pages of a legal book then stood and gave her closing.

"Yes," she began, "it is true that I told you, ladies and gentlemen of the jury, that I would prove a number of things at the start of trial but, however, I have failed to do so. Life is all about changes. Things and people change every day. The circumstances in a case make a particular verdict just, and warranted. What if I was to be heading to work on another job way across the city, and I just so happened to get a flat tire; I call a friend, and he agrees to come and help me out. After waiting an hour, he becomes a no-show, so I call 'Triple A' to tow my car and I catch a cab to work, and, of course, I arrive late. Those are circumstances. Furthermore, the facts remained that I had to be at work and I, all though I am late, still made it. That's what this case is really, about. It's not about what I said I would do, or who presented what kind of witnesses with special degrees and numbers of years of experience. This case is about a woman, Stewart Harris who had been, raped and her son Jalen Harris, whom had been, killed by the accused. One of the defendants didn't say that they were, forced to commit that kind of act though, did they, no, one of them sat and watched while the other raped Stewart Harris. A baby is dead and a woman was, raped! Need I say more! I don't have to go on, and on about juveniles and their mental culpability to understand the nature of their crimes. Everyone in this courtroom is familiar with these phrases woman-child and man–child. The acts that these defendants committed were adult acts. They consciously raped Stewart Harris, and one of them shot into the air to let her know that he was serious. There are thousands of pedophiles on our streets of America, some in which may be mentally impaired; however, even many of the mentally impaired understand there is a difference between right from wrong, and the defendants are far more intelligent than anyone who is mentally impaired. I say, ladies and gentlemen, that the only way to right this wrong, is to convict."

Reynolds confidently walked back to her seat and held her nose in the air before sitting. Judge Corby ordered the jury into the conference room to deliberate. They returned four hours later with a verdict of guilty of all charges. Ronald Mullen and Corey Laessig, were sentenced to serve Life in prison.

When the verdict was read, Kay expected to feel a sense of victory. Instead, she looked at the accused and felt sorry for them. She had firsthand knowledge given to her by Stew that Lil' Ron was trying to prevent the rape from happening. She wondered why none of that was mentioned. As Young Corey's frail body inched through the doors leading to the holding cells, Kay shook her head, knowing that he would probably be dead in another year or so.

Thirteen

Disappointment

The autumn snow had frozen and then melted, thanks to the warm temperatures that spring is been known to produce. It had been less than a year since Kay and Pete were married. She went from feeling incomplete, to whole and complete, and now back to feeling incomplete and bored with her life.

As Kay and her husband stood side by side in the elevator of the Neshaminy Interplex ~ amongst other supervisors and secretaries who were bright-eyed and standing ready in their suits and briefcases in hand ~ they smiled, trying to extend normal hospitable manners. However, the anger in their eyebrows betrayed them. The verbal confrontation that they had in the car on their way to work was still on their minds.

Pete was angry and frustrated behind Kay not wanting to have a quick sex session before work, and Kay, once again, was sick with the thought of giving him the pussy ever again. After her spectacular night of finally feeling his manhood inside her, she thought things would be terrific, but she was wrong. Her sex life was close to garbage. She had a husband with the biggest dick a woman could possibly wish for and still grew to hate his touch. Pete simply didn't know how to fuck. In the beginning, Kay tried to bear with him, considering the fact that he was a virgin, but even that didn't work. Even after trying and trying to teach him, he could never stay inside her long enough without a fast orgasm, and when he did, he just couldn't work it right. On top of his sexual handicap, he was pussy-whipped. He became just another man she had managed to cast her spell on.

In actuality, Kay wouldn't have felt so bad about Pete if she didn't have to be around him 24-7 ~ and if she didn't have to give him short, unsatisfying sex in the office, at home, in the car, and any other place he saw suitable for a quickie. It was ridiculous. Each time, just when she would be getting into the groove, he would be finished, and she would be left, wet, horny, and pissed. Besides the first time, on two other occasions she had to slip him a few Ecstasy pills just to get him to fuck her silly, as if it was his first time again. She refused to continue feeding him a drug. She felt that it was bad enough that the women in society were outnumbering men at a ratio of 20 to 1, and she definitely did not want to be one of the twenty women with a man addicted to drugs.

The worst of it all was not the fact that her sex life with Pete has not peaked. It was the fact that suddenly she seemed to be wearing the pants and calling all of the shots without any resistance. Her husband was so pussy-whipped that the spine he once had, has perished and he became softer than a jellyfish. Kay tried doing outrageous things and made out-of-the-ordinary requests to see if he would put his foot down, but Pete would submit to her and call. The requests increased in numbers, aside from the continuous cries for a show of strength. She had even dressed half-naked once and told Pete that she was going out to a club. Her expectations of a husband was for him to halt her at the front door, turn her around, and demand for her to put on less-revealing garments. At one time, he would have done so, but those days were over, and as long as he was feeling the sensation of a quickie, he looked past that.

When Pete entered his office, he sighed at Kay's unfinished interior decorating job. The sight was as if their home had been when she first moved in. Pieces of an unassembled bookshelf lay stacked against the wall in the corner. Three large flowerpots full of dirt were sitting on the floor in front of his pecan-brown desk. The huge square-foot glass window behind his leather chair hadn't been, covered with blinds, drapes, or any sort of shading ~ except for the tall trees of the wooded area that the view presented. Even then, the sun had managed to creep through the passages of leafy branches that the breeze enabled to sway side to side.

Pete stepped over a bucket of opened paint onto a drop cloth to make his way to his desk. It was there, as he sat in his chair, that he was able to find a sense of comfort. The perimeter of the desk was the only thing truly reflecting the fact that he wasn't, disoriented nor an irresponsible person that the mess in his office portrayed him to be.

The scent of Lemon Pledge along the surface of the dust still could be smelled when he turned his head in certain angles. A state-of-the-art Microsoft laptop sat in the right-hand corner. Alongside, working towards the left-hand corner of the desk, was an electric pencil sharpener, a stapler, box of paper clips, and two pictures ~ one of him, Kay, and the kids, and of course, one of him and Kay on their wedding day. Three inches in front of the wedding photo was the phone, and a huge calendar sat in the middle of the desk, showing the month of May.

Again, Pete sighed with thoughts of his heavy workload for the day. He pressed the intercom button on his phone to get Kay's attention.

"Uh, sweetheart, bring me a hot cup of coffee. I have a shitload of work to do. I also need the appointments I have for this morning."

Kay wanted to act as if she had not heard his agitating voice. With her legs crossed and swinging, she continued to flip through the pages of an Ebony magazine until she heard his voice again.

"Uh, sweetheart?"

Kay rolled her eyes and pressed the button on her phone. "I heard you!" she blurted, not caring if Pete had sense the spit in her tone.

He better not had said a word. Even the men in the office cubicles shook their heads, admitting to themselves that it could not have been their wives talking with such a tone. The women were disgusted, admitting that if Pete were their husband, then he wouldn't have to ask for nothing. Everything he could possibly need to do his job would be waiting on his desk, even a quick shot of pussy. They had no idea of Kay's resentment, and she could care less. She lifted her head out of the magazine and looked around the office at them. They hurried to act as if they weren't paying her any mind, but the truth was that even they had began to notice how foul she began to treat Pete. Reluctantly, Kay went to get the coffee, sashaying heavily through the aisles and giving looks that invited the men to stare at her ass.

When she entered Pete's office, she stared him in the face, rolled her eyes, and placed the cup on his desk. Pete was halfway reclined and fumbling an ink pen through his fingers while thinking.

"Thanks, baby," he said, immediately taking a small sip.

"Ummm-huh, no problems," said Kay as she turned, put her nose in the air, and walked out of the office.

Pete remained in deep thought until his phone rang.

"Hello," he answered.

"Hello, Mr. Frazier, this is Doctor Lambert here. We were going over the results of your physical you have taken last week, and we came across an unfortunate matter. Apparently, you have an STD."

Pete leaned forward, threw the ink pen on his desk, and resumed to be more attentive, wondering if he had heard correct. A perturbed face stared at the phone receiver as his clutch tightened while he strained to rid his mind of the reality. He had known that something was wrong with his penis by the way that it constantly discharged, but he still didn't want to believe ~ hoped to death ~ that his wife didn't give him something. How painful it was to his body, the disease was more damaging to his psyche, knowing that Kay had to have cheated on him. The idea of her giving another man that pussy drove him insane.

As the blood temperature in his body boiled, he envisioned his last encounter with his wife: on the kitchen floor, pants dropped to the ankles, and her bending over touching her toes. Twenty or thirty long hard strokes inside of her wetness, and then, splash. He thought of someone else loving her as much as him, and he concluded that if she had given him a chance, then he would have engaged in a fistfight to death simply to prove his masculinity about his property. However, even that was too late. His wife has already allowed someone to pound on something that was supposed to be his. It was no excuse for her actions and his mentality was at zero tolerance.

"What kind of disease is it and can it be cured?" he asked.

"Absolutely, it can be cured!" said the doctor. "I'll just need to give you a shot of penicillin and prescribe you to some pills. The sexual transmitted disease you contracted is Chlamydia. It's nothing I haven't seen before; or something you should be too concerned about, however, in your case, it has not progressed which is very fortunate, furthermore, most people that pass through here with this particular type of disease have different circumstances. My advice is simple, that you stay away from alcohol, sex, and any other forms of narcotics for the next seven to ten days. When can you follow up with me for another appointment?" the doctor asked.

"When is the best time?" Pete shamefully avowed.

"Given the fact that you were here for the physical a week ago, I figured you've been having heavy discharge for a few days now, if not more."

"It's been three days."

"I see. Have you and Mrs. Frazier..."

"Yes, we have," he swiftly interrupted.

"Well, I suggest you bring her in as well. I'll have a nurse scheduled for her arrival. I'm sorry, Mr. Frazier...I sincerely hope that you and your wife can work past this."

"Yeah, so do I."

Pete hung up the phone and sighed. It hurt him to the heart to find out that the woman of his dreams was nothing of the sort. Instead, she was more like his mother, who was nothing more than a cheating alcoholic not worthy, of the love and loyalty that was given to her. He thought of his dead father who had died while working hard, long hours, trying to please his cheating mother. *"Don't tell your father that your uncle had stopped by,"* she would say to him. He later discovered that the men that stopped by weren't his uncles. They were her lovers, and she had used her very own children to deceive their father.

Pete's father was an old-fashioned, set-in-his-way; chauvinistic man who loved his wife more than any man could love a woman. He had found out about his wife's treachery when he walked in on her and another man having sex in their home. Pete had been downstairs while one of his so-called uncles and his mother stayed upstairs. Then fifteen, and knowing the truth about the uncle visits; he had smiled at the sight of his father walking into the front door. He hated that his mother was cheating and just knew that, that day would end everything, but instead, his father, his hero, had slowly walked back down the stairs, sat in his favorite chair, and showed Pete the first time tears, of a hurt man.

Pete shook his head, dispelling the thought of his father. *A weak man never, ever musters the strength, and the nice guys always finish last*, he thought while stepping onto the drop cloth and over the opened bucket of paint. He pulled his office door open in a fury and stood in the entrance, watching the back of Kay's head. His brows wrinkled and his teeth ground his jaw shut. Kay continued reading her Ebony magazine until her name was shouted.

"Kaleen!" Pete yelled.

Kay jumped and turned in anger. "What!"

"Get your things; we're taking the rest of the day off."

"For what? I'm cool." Kay rolled her eyes and resumed reading her article on *'How to Stay Young.'*

Pete looked around and noticed that everyone's eyes were on them. He wasn't the type to put on a show and display his business, so he smiled at everyone, walked closer to Kay, and bent to whisper into her ear.

"Get your fucking ass out of that seat." His lips were touching her ears. His warm peppermint breath traveled in her nostrils and down the side of her neck.

Realizing that it must have been something serious that Pete wanted to talk about, Kay quickly shut the magazine and stood. She brushed the wrinkles out of her tan knee-high skirt, looked at Pet's seriously violent facial expression, and humbly walked past him. Her heart began to beat fast with fear. Something was wrong and she had no idea what was on her husband's mind to make him look like he could kill. What made him so mad to have him unusually curse and shout at her? As crazy as it seemed, she was turned on by his commanding persona. She secretly hoped that he would suggest a quickie.

Kay preserved her humbleness until they were seated inside Pet's car. "Where are we going?" she asked, watching as he buckled his seat belt.

Pete said nothing. He, too, was in a conservative state with the soreness of existing facts written of his face.

"Baby, where are we going?" Kay repeated.

Pete stared a few seconds. "Oh, now it's 'baby,' huh? Did you call that fucking guy baby?"

"What? Come on now, you trippin'."

Kay was starting to worry. Although, she tried desperately to hide it, whatever she may have said wasn't going to weigh as a factor to decrease Pete's agony. He had the doctor, the test, and

Chlamydia tipping the scale and rebutting any lie that Kay would conjure. After a brief moment of silence, Pete began badgering Kay with questions.

"So, how long have you been fucking this guy?"

Again, Kay stayed in a state of denying the truth. "What guy? What guy are you talking about?"

A fake smile appeared on Pete's face, and then a frown. "Stop lying! Where you think we're going! To the doctor's," he yelled.

Kay's body posture transformed from an upright sitting position to a slouch. Her stomach turned with the possibilities of her giving her husband something.

"Look at you... looking guilty! What guy... What guy?" Pete mocked. "Don't give me that shit when you done gave me Chlamydia!" He reached his hand over, placed his palm at the side of her face, and shoved her head. "You are going to give your husband a disease! I should break your fuckin' face right now!"

As mad as Kay felt by him shoving her head, she felt that she deserved it. "Baby," she sorrowfully began.

"I don't want to hear it!" yelled Pete.

Kay shook her head in shame and suddenly heard Jason's voice: *"See, what did I tell you? See, that is what you get for fucking friends anyway. You just like the rest of these hoes out here, married and giving the panties up as soon as you get bored, or feel as though your life is not as exciting as you think it should be. As soon as your little kitty cat gets wet, and you are not around your husband, your values become nothing. You are a fucking nut! You don't know what you want."*

Quietly, Kay cried, allowing Jason's voice to plummet her self-esteem to rock bottom. Once again, she found herself regretting not listening to his voice.

Two weeks prior, she had awakened with Brim in her bed and rushed into the bathroom to regurgitate. The thought of betraying her loyalty to Jason ailed her mental with a sickness that her stomach could not contain. On top of that, she was grieved by the fact that she had cheated on her husband with Cee's man, her best friend kids' father. Time, and time again, she had cursed the other woman for conducting such acts, and though she now sympathized with them, she still couldn't shake her self-accusing spirit.

It was just after 11:00 p.m., when Kay had seen Brim for the first time in over a year. Cee had a birthday party for their son, and eventually, the adults had turned the kiddy-hop birthday party into an adult gathering, leading into the wee hours. They laughed, joked, played cards, and drank shot after shot of top-shelf liquor from the mini-bar in Cee's home.

The longing for a sexual experience with Brim had peaked in opportunity when a sudden malfunction with her car forced Brim to play chauffeur and drive her home. The kids were spending the night at Vita's, and Pete was out on an overnight business retreat. Kay, being drunk, horny, and dissatisfied with the sex in her marriage, had consciously kicked her two-inch sandals off at the door and strutted into her living room. Just as she suspected, Brim stood at the door with his mouth open and his eyes tracing her curves from the back of her neck down to the dip in the small of her back, around the hips, down her thighs, calves, the heels of her feet and back to focus on her ass.

He had secretly lusted for her body when his friend Jason was alive. During that time, he would not dare attempt to pursue his lustful desires. That night, things were different. As much as he held a deep love in his heart for his dead friend, there was only him, Kay, intoxicating drinks, and the devil sitting on his shoulder encouraging the idea of seizing the opportunity to have a woman he always yearned to touch.

Brim intensely watched Kay walk through the double-swinging doors that led into her kitchen. He had always noticed the erotic looks that she would unconsciously give him, but he chose to ignore them. Now, there he was, standing in her doorway, hoping that she would invite him in, knowing that he should have been left.

As Kay walked back through the swinging door with two glasses in her hand, Brim gestured to turn and leave.

"Alright, Kay, I'mma see you. Are you okay?" he asked.

Kay sucked her teeth. "No, I'm not cool. Where are you going? You see me with two glasses here. Have another drink for the road?"

"For the road, shit, any more, and I'll be too drunk to drive."

"Well, then you'll have to stay here and sleep the high off."

Without another word, Brim walked into her home and closed the door. His mind desperately fought to suppress the fact that he shouldn't even be there, but his gut forced him to follow temptation.

Kay filled the glasses halfway with Southern Comfort and handed him one. She watched as he drank, biting her bottom lip and looking into his eyes in a way that he had never experienced ~ it was deep, hypnotizing, intimidating, and even paralyzing. She pulled the glass away from his mouth after four gulps.

"That's enough. Comes on, let's go upstairs," she said, grabbing his hand and leading him up to her bedroom.

As Brim entered her room, he instantly abolished the already thinning traits of loyalty he had to his dead friend Jason, suppressed the newfound love and respect for Cee, and let the longing lust for Kay bombard his mind, only to feed his appetite enough to go all the way.

First, he caressed her soft Oil of Olay skin. Standing before her, he intensely looked into her eyes, watching as her breasts moved in and out with each breath. Her panting was soft and sensual and her eyes were closed, allowing her mind to equate with the feeling she had been missing. His rough, manly ~ yet soft and gentle ~ touch found its way to her warm belly. The butterflies within her pit awakened hormones that had been in a slumber for quite some time. Together they let go of their inhibitions, reached out, and embraced their desires with an aim to break the box spring. An hour and a half later, Kay had nodded off to sleep from exhaustion. In the morning, she found herself in the bathroom vomiting guilt.

As Pete pulled into the mini-parking lot of the clinic, Kay snapped out of her flashback, wondering if her one-night with Brim would become a night that would be, forever etched into her mind as a bad night.

Fourteen

Animosity

The environment at work had not been so tense and stressful since the days she had worked in the cubicles. Kay sat outside of Pet's office at her desk, irritably fumbling through two piles of paperwork that Pete had purposely given her to do. A week had passed since they were in the clinic taking needle shots and receiving a prescription for penicillin pills. Just as the days had passed, Kay thought that Pete's anger would subside, at least enough for him to communicate with her, but it hadn't, and each look into his cold eyes shrank her esteem to the point of having none at all.

How could she have hurt the only man who ever gave her the love she felt was warranted? How could she sacrifice something so pure with a replacement of a disease-infested memory? The questions she asked herself did not have an answer. She thought of Cee and, how meaningful their friendship was. Kay knew that what she and Brim did had to remain a secret if there was a chance of her and Cee remaining friends. It was heartbreaking for her to laugh, joke, and fake like everything was okay whenever they were together, or on the phone, but she knew it was necessary, so she managed.

With his feet propped upon his desk and his datebook in hand while he fumbled through the papers, Pete whistled and unorthodox melody. He noticed that he had an appointment for that very day.

"Shit!" he blurted, quickly leaning forward and putting his feet to the floor. He peeked at his watch and angrily pressed the button to the intercom.

"Kay!"

"Yeah, baby?" Kay attentively responded.

"Get out here."

Immediately, Kay hurried into the office only to face the third degree.

"What's today, Ms. Frazier!" scolded Pete.

"Excuse me? Today is May the thirteenth," she answered.

"Exactly! So why the fuck didn't you tell me about this appointment?" Pete handed Kay his datebook. With her mouth open, she looked at her handwriting on the page marked, *May 13th*. Before she could say a word, Pete snatched the book from her hand.

"Listen, if you don't want to work here, you keep pulling jobs like this." Kay stared while fighting back her tears.

"So is that what this is about? What are you going to do, Pete? You are going to replace me?"

Pete sighed, motioned from behind his desk, and stood face to face with his wife. "You motherfucking right I'll replace your ass!"

"Okay, Pete, this has been going on long enough. We have to talk about us."

"Us!" Pete said with a quizzical look, and continued. "Us, what Us? You fucked Us over when you had sex with another man, and gave me a disease. As we speak, I'm thinking about having divorce papers drew up."

The tears that Kay concentrated on holding back had won their battle to be free from the captivity of her pride. They triumphantly raced down her beautiful face as she began pleading. The pain on her husband's face caused her to rush into him and hug tight.

"I'm sorry," she whispered. "I love you so much. I just didn't know how to tell you that I was not being satisfied in that way."

Pete stood stiff with his arms to his side, harbored by Kay's embrace. The sight of her beauty, smell of her scent, and warmth of her body began to weaken him, but he violently snatched away. "Don't touch me!"

"But, Pete," Kay pleaded, "You can't just do this...you owe it to our..."

"I don't owe you a goddamn thing! I gave you me...all of me! You fucked that up. You gave me your ass to kiss."

Suddenly he thought of his mother and remembered the agony that his father had suffered by the actions of infidelity. He was his father's son, from the work ethic and desire to get ahead to the urge to put his woman on the pedestal, but accepting his wife's adulterous behavior was a trait that he refused to inherit.

Like a form of cancer, Pete's disgust for Kay instantly ate away at his love for her. In a flash, he aggressively pulled his arms loose from her hugging attempt, raised his right hand high into the air, and slapped an opened palm hard, across her caramel cheek. The force of his strength made Kay's body crash to the floor. With her mouth wide from shock, she held her cheek and tried to soothe its stinging pain. As her husband stood looking down upon her, she quickly gathered her mental faculties and wobbled to her feet.

She stared into Pete's eyes, matching his anger as if a twelve-round bout was going to take place. Had it not been for her guilt, she would have hit him back, or at least said something to let him know that the slap would be his first and last time hitting her. Sadly, a part of her felt that she deserved it. To her, accepting the slap was a nonverbal way of saying, *we're even*. She rolled her eyes and stormed out of his office to gather her accessories from her desk, with plans to take the rest of the day off.

While picking up the items from her desk and slamming

them into her pocketbook, she not only noticed that everyone in the office had ceased to work, but she could feel their eyes on her back. The women were happy to see her finally get what she deserved. As for the men, they secretly hoped for her marriage with Pete to finally end, this way, they could manipulate her into their beds.

At first, Kay thought to ignore the stares and leave as quick as possible. However, after hearing a few snickering outbursts, her strong sense of pride willed out embarrassment. She quickly turned and loudly expressed her mind. "All you hating-ass bitches can laugh, but I dare any of you bitches, or dudes, to try and put your hands on me and watch what the fuck is going to happen!"

The coworkers fought hard not to continue laughing as she stomped through the maze-like aisles and out of the building.

As soon as Kay arrived home, she jumped out of her work attire, poured herself a bubble bath, and soaked her body up to the neck in the soothing warmth of the water. Meanwhile, Pete was on the expressway switching lanes, hurrying to get home. He hadn't expected Kay to walk out with so much work left undone, but he rather knew that she wouldn't accept a smack in the face lightly. No matter how she felt about it, he wasn't finished speaking his piece about their sudden discrepancy involving their marriage, and he sought to get it all out. She opened her eyes and listened for a moment.

I know this man did not follow me home, she thought as the juggling of Pete's keys in the lock, followed by the slamming of the front door, answered her question. She sighed and scooped a pile of bubbles out of the water. As Pete's loud and heavy footsteps approached closer to the top of the stairwell, Kay prepared for more torment.

"Kay!" Pete yelled, walking into their bedroom in search of her. He turned around and walked the narrow hall, passed the bathroom, and went into the back room that Kay had yet to finish decorating.

"Kay-Kay! Kaleen!" he continued, growing frustratingly impatient. He turned and again walked the narrow hall. This time he walked swiftly, with his anger conjuring thoughts that he outwardly expressed.

"I know this bitch better be in this damn house. Kay-Kay!"

Finally, he pushed the bathroom door open, stared at his wife's disinterested gestures, and sighed.

"Damn! I guess you didn't hear me calling you, huh?"

Kay never even bothered to look at him. Though she wanted to fly at his neck, dig her claws into his throat, and continuously punch his face with the diamond rock she had on her finger, she maintained the utmost composure.

Furthermore, Kay knew that no matter how much she thought she could hurt him, he was still a man, and she really didn't stand a chance against his angry strength. So instead, she smiled and gently waved her hands side to side in the bath water, continuing to play with the bubbles as if she was, amazed by their existence.

Pete walked to the corner of the bathroom, grabbed the dirty towel hamper, and pulled it to the edge of the tub to sit on.

"Listen here, woman," he began. Kay interrupted before he could say another word.

"Oh, it's *woman now*?" she sassed. "That's funny, because just before you walked in here I was the bitch who had better be in this damn house. And before then, I might as well have been a guy on the street the way you smacked me."

Pete looked at his wife's smooth, pretty complexion and instantly felt guilty. How could he have hit her? Her words were puncturing his inner soul like a sword, slicing into his defensive shell of anger and hurt. He hated the fact that he made her feel the way she felt, but deeply felt that she brought it all on herself. She deserved to feel some kind of pain other than the threat of divorce, which he figured had minimal effect. To him, she wouldn't have cheated in the first place if the threat of divorce meant anything.

"Listen here, woman," he said, again, Kay interrupted.

"Uh-ummmm, noooo, sweetheart, it's *bitch* to you. From now on, you address me as *bitch*. You got a nerve to want a divorce?"

Kay's womanly strength instantly weakened at the utterance of the word "divorce." She persisted, however, to speak her mind, adamantly relaying her opinion and releasing harbored thoughts with tears in her eyes, she pointed her index finger and read him his rights.

"You listen here. I know I was wrong, but what's a bitch to do! Yeah, that's right, *bitch!*" she closed her eyes, and uncontrollably nodded her head up and down, and round and around. "Bitch! Bitch! Bitch! Bitch! Okay, Pete, are you happy? Huh, Pete? Actually, to tell you the truth, I haven't been happy almost throughout this whole marriage."

Pete looked angrily puzzled. "Hold up," he chimed, "What do you mean you haven't been happy! You didn't say that fucking shit when I was showering you with money and gifts! On the other hand, all those times when I sacrificed to watch them badass kids of yours. I provided you with different helicopters and private jets rides. I didn't see a frown on your fuckin' face not once during any of those goddamn times!"

Kay squinted behind the sentences he spit back at her. The nerve of him speaking of her kids in such a way. She sniffled, swallowed, and aimed to be brutally, and aggressively honest.

"Okay, so what...so what! Don't you stand here and say anything about my muthafuckin' children; they don't have shit to do with this. Yes, you did all of that, but don't get it fucked up, I'm Kay-Kay! I could have gotten any good man to do that, believe me; they would have did all of that. Besides, our honeymoon experience wasn't shit. At least another man would have beaten this pussy silly on his honeymoon. No, not Mr. Frazier's stupid ass, he had his wife finger-fucking herself all because he was scared of pussy. You got me hiring investigators, just to find out you a goddamn virgin."

"You had somebody spying on me?"

"You damn right I did! At first, I thought you were a homosexual, the way you would bitch-up whenever I touched you. Matter of fact, you might as well be one because you can't even fuck that good. You had me slipping Ecstasy in your drinks and food just to get you to hit this pussy right. Nigro please!" Kay shouted.

"You drugged me?" he asked, in disbelief.

"Yes, I so certainly did. And..." Kay chuckled at the sight of Pete's pride diminishing, and his self-esteem evaporating. "Yeah, that's right," she continued, "I drugged your non-fucking ass. You sold my house! All that bullshit of yours I had to put up with, and you got a nerve to be talking divorce! Divorce, Pete! This is the only pussy you ever had. Mark these words, you'll never find a woman who'll put up with all that nonsense, and not cheat on your ass! Yes, I was wrong. I cheated. Despite of the disease I got, his dick was smaller, but still better than that worthless dick of yours! God wasted a strong piece of dick when he put it on you."

When Kay finished, she chuckled in Pet's face, knowing she had accomplished her mission. Pete couldn't take anymore. He raised his hand high into the air, making her flinch into a shell. She was bracing herself for another slap, but Pete controlled his impulse. Kay stood up so that she could look him square in the eyes.

"Go ahead, big man! I wish the fuck you would hit me again." Pete stared into her eyes. The rage that she expressed made her look even more beautiful. He felt his heartbeat stutter as the sudden arousal of his penis bulged at the crotch of his suit pants. Her body glistened with wetness, shiny like the glass of a ceramic piece. Her small, yet perky chest stared at him, the nipples hard and pointed like bullets. The scented bubble bath complemented her natural body odor and traveled into his nostrils. The flatness of her stomach, curve of her hips, and the landing strip of hair covering her pussy forced him to succumb to his lustful desires.

Without warning, he grabbed Kay by the waist and wildly darted his sweet tongue into her mouth. They kissed for ten seconds, paused to look into each other's eyes and catch their breath, and then continued. While kissing her, Pete stepped into the tub, totally disregarding his shoes, socks, and pants. Kay peeled her lips away from his and gazed with love while unbuckling his pants and letting them drop into the water.

Her intentions were to pour all of her love, all of her emotional sorrows, and her mental apology into the meanest dick suck ever known to mankind. It was her chance to save her marriage, and failure wasn't an option. The lip-gloss accentuated the beauty of her bright, pink lips as she placed them on the tip of his rod and slowly welcomed him into the warmth of her mouth. Pete's body tensed up. His abs contracted as he watched her amazingly make his rod disappear with each head motion. Slowly and passionately, she sucked, allowing her bottom lip and her chin to meet with his sac.

"Uuuhhh!" he growled, taking a hand and rubbing it with the grain of her slicked-back hairstyle. Kay continued to love his manhood until he buckled in climax.

Normally Pete was a minute man, clearly lacking the ability to stay aroused after having an orgasm, but this episode was different. His eager penis stood tall, long, and hard, ready to punish her womb. He aggressively grabbed Kay by the shoulders and guided her to a standing position. He then snatched one of her legs into the air, strongly held the back of her thigh, and thrust his length into her wet pussy. Kay's eyes opened wide. She took in a deep breath with her mouth open. It was as if she had been the virgin all along. Her womanhood clutched his penis like a baby's hand around an adult's finger.

Pete strolled, making sure that she felt his full length with each plunge. His hips moved in ways that Kay never imagined a man could move them ~ amazingly like a belly dancer and harder with every penetrating thrust. Overwhelmed with emotions, Kay silently cried. She wanted to blurt out *"I'm sorry,"* wanted to yell Pete's name as an affirmation of the work that he was putting down. However, her whimpering simply wouldn't allow it. As tears made their way to trespass down her cheeks, she buried her face into his chest and sustained herself by biting down on the pocket of his dress shirt.

From the tub to the floor of the bathroom, they engaged each other in an hour and a half of sexual bliss. Pete then carried Kay to their bedroom and tucked her in to snuggle into a deep nap. While she slept, he sat on the edge of the other side of their bed with his back facing her and his face buried in his hands. As much as he hated Kay for cheating on him, he still loved her, and he forever sexually craved her body at her very existence. He simply couldn't get enough of her.

His love for her was his weakness, just as his father's love for his mother. The thought of becoming a spitting image of his father began to erode the personal image he once had of himself. Slowly, he raised his head out of the darkness of his hands and turned to look at his wife. As Kay slept peacefully on her back with a leg straight and the other half bent, the sheet covered her body, making her figure appear to be even curvier than it already was, slightly sticking out from under the sheet. He wanted her again. He wanted to pound on top of her until she submitted to his sexual skills. The love-hate emotions that tag teamed in his mind had whirl winded; and, like a tornado, spun his anger to manifest the worst kind of destruction he would have ever imagine himself in.

Lazily, he stood and walked around the bed to the side where Kay slept. He towered over his love and stared as he cried and whimpered, loudly sniffling and finally unembarrassed of his vulnerability. His cries awakened Kay. She moved, repositioned her legs, and slowly opened her eyes while continuously blinking with confusion.

"What's wrong, baby," she asked while stretching and

watching as Pete's weeping eyes transformed into a sudden blank and deranged look.

Before Kay could move another muscle, he opened his eyes wide, clenched his teeth shut, and smashed an iron fist down on the middle of her forehead, temporarily knocking her out. She then awakened by the extremely tight grip that Pete had around both of her ankles. She urgently tried to kick and wiggle her legs loose, but he was too strong. He yanked her off the bed and began dragging her naked body out of the room.

"Pete! Pete! Please no! I'm sorrrrry!" she cried while looking up as the ceiling seemed to move. Her hair roughly combed the carpet and her arms moved in many directions, trying to find something to hold on to. Finally, both hands found their way to grasp the frame of the doorway. As Pete monstrously yanked her ankles, she dug her claws deeper into the wood.

"Oh, you think you're stronger than me!" yelled Pete as he let loose of her ankles and began to hammer his fist into her pretty cheeks. He again, reached for her kinking legs.

"Please, Pete, stop. Don't do this!" Kay cried. "I love you, baby, I swear! I swear!" she informed, frightened and surprised.

"Bitch, you don't know what love is!" he yelled.

After his winning attempt at Kay's ankles, Pete pulled with all of his might, tearing her hands from the doorframe and ripping her fingernails at the cuticles. He dragged her to the top of the stairwell and tried to yank her down the steps, but, again, Kay managed to find herself something to hold. With her naked body lying sideways on the steps, she hugged the wooden leg for dear life, as the steps sharply stuck her in the hips and ribs from the weight of her body.

Realizing that Kay's grip was too tight, Pete began to bash her face.

"Let it go, bitch! Let it go...let it go!" he continuously blurted between each blow. Eventually Kay let go and was dragged down the steps; she cried, begged, and pleaded for the man she loved to stop, but it did not work. As she lay on the surface of the floor, Pete began punching her left rib cage with the strength of a bear.

Before long, the crying and yelling from Kay stopped. She lay paralyzed and out cold from the unbearable pain. Pete hurried into their half bathroom just four yards away and retrieved a small jar of K-Y jelly from the medicine cabinet. He rushed back to his beautiful wife's almost lifeless, beaten body, flipped her on the stomach, lubricated his penis, and rammed it into her ass. He humped hard and fast until he climaxed all over her back. He stood with her body between his legs and his penis in hand, concentrating. Finally, the urine flowed from his manhood on to the side of his wife's face, hair, and back.

Within ten minutes after sexually assaulting Kay, Pete had been in and out of the shower. He put back on the clothes that he wore earlier in the day and ran fast as he could, face first into the wall. He managed to put a gash over the top of his left eye. After putting a compress over the cut, he dialed one of his friends that were a detective in the police force.

"Hello, Detective Kimble," the officer answered.

"Hey, Detective Kimble, It's Pete Frazier."

"Oh, hey, how are you? What can I do for you, Pete?"

"Well…there was an accident and I need you, and only you, to get out here."

"Is everything okay?" asked the detective.

"N-n-no. I had a couple of fraternity friends over and things got out of hand with this stripper," Pete lied.

"Is the stripper okay?" The officer wondered.

"I don't know, but I think I should call the ambulance."

"The ambulance! Geesh! Hold on, I'm on my way!"

Pete hung up the phone feeling ashamed, and he hoped that he didn't hurt his wife badly. He loved Kay and simply didn't know what came over him to make him do such a thing.

Fifteen

The Murder

Detective Kimble ~ a short, bald headed, dark-skinned man with a Napoleon's complex ~ stood in the hospital room with his chest poked out. He watched as Cee sat by Kay's bedside while holding her hand and crying. Cee had gotten the call from Pete about the unfortunate incident that occurred in his and Kay's home. Though Kay, suffered from the pain of three broken ribs, two black eyes, a mild concussion, a dislocated jaw, and an inch-split rectum, Cee worried more about what the incident would do to Kay mentally.

As Kay started to regain her consciousness, she turned her head, looked at Cee, and smiled while tightening her hold on Cee's hands. Cee smiled back.

"Hey, girl!" she said, trying hard to think of what to say next. "Girl, when you get better, I'm going to fight you. You know I have to postpone my engagement party now," Cee informed. She held up her hand and showed Kay an engagement ring. "Yes, girl, Brim gave it to me last night. Isn't that something? He got me ready to stop hoeing. I will devote this pussy." Kay was smiling. She loved to see Cee still in the same spirits.

When Kay finally tried to talk, she realized that her jaws were temporarily wired shut. She couldn't even make the slightest move without her body feeling pain; however, she managed to mumble Vita's name after three attempts, Cee, sucked her teeth.

"Girl, fuck Vita! I'm here. That bitch acted like her stank-ass business meeting was more important. Well, look, I won't get into all that, but if it weren't for you, I would have kicked her ass a long time ago. But anyway, I'm about to be like you and Pete." Cee, held up her hand, displaying her ring and smiling again.

Kay squinted, wondering what Cee, had meant by being like her and Pete. If she was talking about their so-called marriage, the fact that she was lying in the hospital should have dispelled that perfect picture. When Kay let her eyes roam, she noticed Detective Kimble standing in the corner. He motioned toward her bed and stood in front of it.

"How are you feeling, Mrs. Frazier?" he asked. "I'm Detective Kimble. Your husband called after finding you. It's a good thing that he arrived when he did, or who knows how things would have turned out. I'll tell you, you're lucky to have a husband like that. He is a good man. I've seen cases where a husband sat back and watched his wife assaulted by robbers. I know that you need to rest up, but a woman detective from the Philadelphia Special Victims Unit will be in to see you sometime within the next hour or so. You have a good recovery. Your husband and children are outside waiting to see you."

As Kimble walked out of the room and Kay watched as Pete entered the room with the kids; in his hand, were get-well balloons and a bouquet of flowers. The kids raced to her bedside and stared with sadness in their eyes. Kay was happy to see her children. Her eyes immediately scanned the surface of their bodies, checking for any unusual bruises and blemishes that her husband's rage could have forced him to commit. She deeply exhaled at the sight of them being okay. Pete positioned the flowers on the nightstand next to Kay's bed and released the balloons in the corner, allowing the helium to keep them glued to the ceiling. He excused himself past Cee, stood at the bedside, and gazed into Kay's face before bending over to kiss her forehead.

"I'm so sorry," he whispered.

Her friend smiled with tears in her eyes. She realized that it had suddenly become a moment for family, so she stood to let Pete take her chair beside the bed.

The kids were in their own world entertaining each other with unimportant chitchat while struggling in a game of seeing who could be the only one to occupy the hospital visiting chair. Kay's attention was drawn to them. She would have told them to stop playing, but Pete beat her to the punch.

"You kids go on and keep still now," he said before taking his hand and placing it into Kay's hand. "Baby, I am really, really sorry. I don't know what got into me. I love you. You are my queen."

Kay gathered a blob of saliva in her mouth and swallowed before speaking through her wired-shut jaws.

"Look what you did to me," she muffled.

"I know. I know, baby," said Pete. "I swear to you that it will never happen again. You are my life. You and the kids are the best thing that could have happened to me."

Kay burst into whining tears. "I was all yours and you raped me. Why you do this to me? You told them that I was raped by robbers!"

Pete quickly looked around, put his index finger to his lips, and shushed Kay.

"Baby, I had to, or I would have gone to jail. Do you want to see me in jail? I know I was wrong, but do you hate me that much? You cheated on me baby, so we both did wrong things. I love you. Let me make this right. Let me take care of you. Let me love you like you supposed to be loved. Do you still love me?" he asked.

Kay looked into his sincere eyes and began to melt. Indeed, she still deeply loved him. As Pete tightened his grip on her hands, she pulled his hand to her lips and kissed them.

"I still love you. I love you so much, but you hurt me, Pete. How do I know you're not going to do this again?" questioned, Kay.

"Because this is not who I am, you know me, Kay. I'm no woman beater. I love you and it will never happen again…I promise, okay?"

Kay nodded her head *yes* while the tears streamed from her eyes and trickled into her ears.

She just wanted things to be as they once were. All of her belief in Pete told her that she was doing the right thing. Her self-accusing spirit consistently told her that she was part of the blame for the beating. The words that she had conjured to say to Pete were like poisonous venom. She knew that no man could ever stand such a tongue-lashing from his wife after she had cheated on him. As long as the thought of her perfect life was still tangible, forgiving Pete would be easy. She later found that forgiving him was the wrong thing to do.

As the weeks had passed, Kay looked up and saw herself trapped in a marriage. Pet's abuse hadn't stopped, in fact, his anger would surface more, and more, frequently. Although the beatings continued, they weren't nowhere near close to the first one; however, they were no less painful either. He had literally beat fear into his wife. Kay became afraid to hold her head up and walk with the confidence that she once displayed. The shame that she faced when she looked into the mirror had even driven her to suicidal thoughts. Had it not been for the kids, Kay would have taken a thousand pills to escape her life.

Yes, her kids, they were her rock, her strength at times when she needed love the most. Somehow, she drew a sense of bravery when with them. Maybe it was because Pete's attitude toward them hadn't changed. He was a good-for-nothing woman beater when the kids weren't around, but when they were home he was always on his best behavior. To them, he was the greatest step daddy ever.

Time and time, again, Kay selfishly kept them home from

summer camp, and even their first days of school, just to be certain that Pete wouldn't suddenly arrive home from work with his *Ike Turner* mentality.

Pete unexpectedly caught on to Kay's stunts when he received a call from a doctor letting him know that he could pick the kids up. Kay was being admitted into the hospital for twenty-four hours for tests. The night prior to that call, Pete had slammed yet another fist into Kay's eye. The doctors suspected that she ruptured a blood vessel, and the last thing she wanted to do was let her husband know that she had been seeing multiple doctors. With doctors, comes many questions, with questions, come police, and with police, comes a possible arrest. Kay had been to three other hospitals for treatment. Whenever the women from the Special Victims Unit came to talk to her, she would always tell them a wild lie about being drunk, or falling down the steps.

Of course, after a while, Kay had broken down and told Cee about the abuse. She would have told Vita, however, she did not want to be looked down on. Vita would have consistently told her how stupid she was for staying in an abusive marriage, and how she should not keep the kids around that kind of environment. Vita did not understand that the environment was an excellent one for the kids, which is one of the reasons why Kay, was still hanging in there. She had long ago realized that her chances to meet a man, such as, Pete may never come again, and the kids needed to experience having the closest thing to a father in their lives.

Cee, on the other hand was more understanding to Kay's situation, as to Vita's assumptions, so, she made it her business to support Kay's every decision.

"As soon as your ready to leave his ass, just call me, girl," Cee, would say.

Kay knew Cee was sincere, and fought hard with the decision to call her after each beating. Kay still loved something about her husband, and she believed that if she stuck in there, then he would return to the loving, charming person she married. Throughout the degrading, abusive experience, the voice she mostly fought against was that of Jason's.

"Let that guy go!" he would say, haunting Kay's thoughts with every painful, aching movement she made resulting from Pete's abuse. *"As long as you're happy, the kids will be happy, but if you stay with that man, you're going to be dead one day, and then the kids won't have anybody...what the fuck is wrong with you?"*

Jason's voice always left her in regret. She knew that when he was alive, he would never tell her anything wrong. Sadly, it was just a voice in her head, and she refused to cater to the silly suggestions of a person who no longer was on Earth. Therefore, she bombarded her mind with thoughts of a good life and prayed for the death of Pet's *Doctor Jekyll/Mr. Hyde,* transformations.

For a minute, it seemed as if Kay's prayers were to be, answered. For sixty beautiful days, Kay lived in paradise. Her house had become a happy home, and the beatings had completely stopped. In a split second, the confidence she had once displayed was starting to restore. She allowed herself to embrace the beatings as a learning experience, and vowed never to be a victim in such a manner ever again. Little did she know that the sincere oath, that adamant mentality of wanting to exhibit her strength as a woman, would soon face its true moment.

No soon thereafter, Kay, Pete, and the kids were putting the cap on a family day. The children were, tucked-in to bed after their baths. Kay and Pete snuggled close on the couch to watch a movie when suddenly a call came in from Vita, and Cee. It was 9:00 p.m., the night was young, and there was plenty of places to go and things to do. Vita wasted no time proposing for Kay to join them. Kay looked at her husband, then to the floor, and sighed before speaking into the phone.

"Girl, I don't know."

"What do you mean you don't know?" asked Vita. "I haven't had a chance to spend time with you in ages."

"I know. You're the one always busy."

Cee snatched the phone from Vita's hands. "Hello!"

"I'm here. Look Vita, I don't know," Kay explained.

"This is not Vita."

"Well, who is this…Cee?"

"Yes, Kay!" Cee, sucked her teeth. "What are you tripping for? Are you with Pete?"

"Uh-humm."

"Oh okay" responded Cee.

Kay and Cee, shared a chuckle before Cee, announced that they were on their way, and hung up the phone. Kay looked at Pete with puppy dog eyes, hesitant to come out with the news that she wanted to interrupt their cozy night of bonding for a wild night of bonding with her girls.

Pete snickered. His eyes fixed on the television, but he made himself cognizant of Kay's facial expression. He knew that she wanted to go out, and he really had no objection.

"So you want to go out, huh?" he asked.

Kay burst into an embarrassing chuckle. She felt relieved that she didn't have to present her question to him.

"Just for a little while," she answered.

Pete stared, looked into her eyes, and shook his head.

"You are a piece of work, you know that? Go right ahead. I'll take care of the children. We'll be alright."

Kay excitedly jumped up from the couch, kissed Pete's still smiling cheek, and raced upstairs to get herself together. Twenty minutes into her personal makeover, Vita and Cee, arrived at the doorstep.

"Baby, they're here!" yelled Pete as he held the door open, staggering with a glass of red wine in hand. When Kay's body came into view as she descended the stairs, Pete's bottom jaw dropped. He had not seen her so beautiful since they first married.

Her hair let down, slightly touching the top of her shoulders, and her eyebrows arched. The blouse she wore crisscrossed at the base of her chest, acting as a bra. Its jet-black color fairly complemented her olive-green, tightly fitted cargo pants matching her jet-black, canvas-like, strapped sandals that crisscrossed at the toes; and tied in the back, just below the drawstring of her pants.

Pete looked at his wife's pretty feet as she met with the bottom of the stairwell and walked toward him with the strut that he had not seen in quite some time. The fit of Kay's pants hugged her thighs, hips, buttocks, and showed a nice print of her womanhood when she moved in particular ways. Instantly, Pete felt a strong sense of jealousy. Her beauty reminded him of how much of an asshole he had been. No doubt about it, wherever they were going, there was bound to be man after man approaching her to get her to see them in a light that would make her label them a possibility. That, above anything else, was what he couldn't stand, so he shut the front door after inviting Cee, and Vita inside, grabbed Kay's hand, and guided her into the kitchen to talk in private.

Kay leaned her back against the huge stainless-steel refrigerator. "What's up, baby?" she asked.

Pete sat his glass of wine on the counter and staggered toward her. His voice was intoxicatingly muffled, and staggered like his walk.

"What's up?" he shot back sarcastically, letting his breath travel into Kay's nostrils.

Kay was alarmed. She mentally prayed that he wasn't about to act a fool.

"Yeah, what's wrong, baby," she said, trying to soothe his apparent anger with her sexy, gentle voice, and propping her hands upon his chest.

"You know what's wrong! Look at how you're dressed! I changed my mind, you can't go out!" Pet yelled,

Kay was furious. She stared with disbelief, swallowed, and angrily voiced her opinion.

"Uh-ummm, Pete! I am not in the mood for this nonsense.

Now Vita, and Cee, is waiting on me. I haven't been out in God knows how long. They came out here to get me, and I'm going out." She turned to walk away and all hell broke loose.

Pete grabbed her by the hair and pulled, yanking her body to the floor in a hard thump. "Bitch, I said you're not going out! Now get up!"

Kay quickly stood, and was met with a chokehold. She struggled and gasped for air while reaching for his eyes to poke.

"Bitch, I'll kill your fucking ass!" Pete blurted.

Suddenly, Kay's knees rammed into his crotch, making him loosen his clutch around her neck and allowing her to finally yell and scream.

She was scared. Pete continued blurting obscenities while slinging her around and arching her face back into the sink. Quickly, he turned the faucet on and left the water run into her face as if he wanted to drown her. He watched her struggle, breathing with the water showering her face. Suddenly, he felt Cee's arms around his neck.

"Get your fucking hands off of her!" she yelled before Pete slung her off his back and onto the floor.

"Oh, you want some too, bitch!" He yelled as he stood over top of her and began punching and bashing her face as if she was a man. Cee, hollered with each blow.

Kay went into a functional shock. She grabbed a butcher knife from the knife rack and repeatedly slammed it into his back. Visions flooded her mind; her wedding, the house of hers that he sold, the Century 21 sign, the flowers, and get-well balloons. The aches and pains of his multiple beatings, the unbelieving faces that the ladies from the Special Victims Unit showed, the hating-ass bitches at the job snickering when he first had put his hands on her, and the first time she actually gave him her phone number years ago....

"Ummm! Ummm! Ummm! Ummm! Ummm!" she yelled, while crying in frenzy. She stabbed him until her arm felt like it was going to fall off; until she was certain that he wouldn't get up, and hit her again. It took her thirty-six stabs to stop. Cee, quickly threw Pete's heavy, lifeless, bloody body off her and attended to Kay, who stands now with her back against the kitchen sink shockingly looking at the bloody knife that lay before her. Vita stood at the entrance of the kitchen with her mouth open and speechless. That night, their lives changed.

Cee, stood and looked down at Pete's dead body, then over to Kay, whose eyes were wide, staring into a blank world and trembling with fear.

"Vita, can you grab a mop or something!" Cee, yelled as she ran over to Kay, kneeled, and hugged her. "It's okay. It's okay. It's okay," she repeated while rocking Kay to, and fro.

Finally, Kay bellowed a loud scream. She twisted, turned, and fought against the embrace. Cee, tried to reassure her that she was safe. "It's okay. It's me, remember? It's me. It's your girl Cee."

When Kay stopped pushing and fighting against Cee's embrace, she wrapped her arms around Cee's neck as tight as she could.

"I killed him. I killed my husband, Cee, he's not dead, is he? Please tell me he's not dead? Please tell me he's alive," she cried.

Cee's mind was racing like a sports car moving in and out of lanes as she thought of what to do next. She noticed that the blood from Pete's body had spilled into a dark, red puddle. "Vita! Get a mop or something!" she yelled.

Vita continues to stand frozen, shaking her head in disbelief, watching as the blood poured from the corpse.

"Uh–ummm," she said, pulling her cell phone from her pocketbook. "I'm calling the cops." She began dialing numbers when suddenly Cee, raced towards her and snatched the phone.

"What the fuck is you doin'?"

"Cee, we have to call the cops," cried Vita. "We have to call them. She killed him. He's dead." Vita, was as much of a wreck as Kay.

Cee, placed both palms on her head, clutched a bunch of hair, and slightly pulled to see if she was dreaming, or if things were real.

"We're not calling the cops!" she explained, while walking in the corner, grabbing a mop and bucket. She began mopping and continuing to explain her theory. "If we call the cops, we're going to jail!" She pointed to Pete's body. "Look! This no good muthafucka, is dead!"

"But we just have to tell them it was an accident," exclaimed Vita.

Cee, placed the mop inside of the ringer and squeezed blood from the strings. She looked at Kay, then to Vita, and spoke softly, trying her best to appeal to their listening.

"The cops won't really understand what has happened here. They can clearly see that this wasn't any kind of accident. All they'll see is three angry black women, and a dead black man with money. And make no mistakes about it," she looked deeply at Vita, "Kay, if not all of us, will spend the rest of our lives in prison. When the district attorney finishes making up his own story, we'll never see the streets again."

Vita wiped her tears. "But what are we going to do?"

"We're going to bury this muthafucka!" Cee assured.

"Cee, what are you saying. We're going to get caught. You're not thinking right."

"Okay! Then here's the telephone. Call the cops!" Just don't express how much you love Kay when they're dragging her children off to some foster camp. So, go ahead. Call the cops, Vita!" Cee ordered.

Vita, looked at the phone, then to Kay, and sighed.

"Yeah, I thought so. Now hurry up and help me clean this shit up," Cee, told her.

Vita tiptoed her feet into the puddle of blood, feeling nauseous and afraid. She hugged herself and watched in amazement as Cee, slopped the thick, dark blood with the mop. As Cee's manicured hands pushed down on the handle of the ringer to strain more blood from the mop strings, Vita, fought to hold down her vomit.

"Look, what is you two standing around for?" said Cee, stopping her cleaning motion and angrily looking at Vita and Kay. "Kay, girlfriend, I know you fucked up, but we have to do this. You know I can't do this without y'all."

Kay looked at Cee, and then to Vita. She slowly stood and hurried into the walk-in pantry to retrieve a huge plastic tarp.

"Ooooh yeah, we can use this!" said Cee, snatching the tarp from Kay's hands excitedly. "Alright y'all, come on."

They laid the tarp down and spread it away from Pete's body, and then each grabbed a hold onto him and struggled to move him onto the tarp. Kay, and Vita grabbed his legs, and Cee's cupped her arms under his pits. The blood from his body dripped like a runny nose, creating a red trail on the white, vinyl tile floor. After placing him on the tarp, they stared at each other, not a word mumbled. At that moment, they were on the same page. They were scared and uncertain. For the rest of their lives they would know that a specific bond was birthed by the death of a man ~ Pete.

Vita began wrapping his body when Kay interrupted. "No, wait," she said with a low and timed voice, "don't we have to burn the clothes, or something?"

"Damn, you're right!" chimed in Cee, in an equally low whisper. "Because the bones and stuff will decompose, but the clothes won't. Hurry up, grab me a knife."

Kay grabbed the murder weapon and began cutting into Pete's blood-soaked sweatpants. She stripped the lower half of his body naked and quickly cut his t-shirt off.

"Alright, come on, let's wrap him up," Vita encouraged.

"No, wait!" said Cee. "One more thing, we got to wrap the body in saran wrap with cat-litter in it, so it won't stink," Cee added, assuming this will work from watching one of her mystery killing television shows.

Again, Kay hurried into the walk-in pantry, and this time retrieved two huge rolls of saran wrap. The cat litter wasn't available. They started with his face and continued wrapping Pete's body until he's wrapped like a mummy. Then they wrapped him in the tarp and tightly duct taped him, again like a mummy.

The girls dragged the body into the corner, got on their hands and knees, and mimicked Cinderella's cleaning tactics. Blood was everywhere, as if that particular section of Kay's kitchen had become a slaughterhouse, or even something similar to the crime scene surrounding the O.J. Simpson murder trial.

At least, after cleaning with bleach and ammonia, the girls changed into different clothing, provided by Kay, and struggled to carry Pete's body out of the house and put it into the trunk of Vita's Jaguar. Upon Kay's suggestions, they drove to the Neshaminy Interplex, dragged the corpse deep into the wooded area behind Pete's office view, and scoped out a suitable burial ground.

It was 2:30 a.m., with the cracking light of dawn being just a few hours away, they raced against time with their digging. Hearing each other's shovels spear into the dirt was the most, unbelieving reality of their whole night. The grunts that came with lifting each heavy pile of dirt, and the exhales from the lightened shovel after each toss truly reminded them that they were actually burying a body. Not just anybody; it was Pete, Kay's husband. Throughout the digging, one of the women would pause to either regurgitate, or cry while the other two would continue to dig, ignoring their lower back pain, tiring arms, shoulders, and developing blisters on their hands. They just wanted to get it over with.

When they threw the last pile of dirt Kay, Vita, and Cee, gave a few hammer pats with the back of their shovels, and stooped over top of the grave in order to pack the dirt tight.

"Here, give me the shovels," said Cee, remembering that there was one last thing they had to do. Kay and Vita watched her as she went into the trunk, laid the shovels inside, and grabbed the trash bag full of bloody clothes, rags, towels, and mop strings. She carried the bag over to the grave, laid it on top, doused it with lighter fluid, and threw a match on it.

"Alright Y'all, let's get outta here," she said, anxiously noticing from the one or two periodical bird chirps ~ and her experience in pulling all-nighters ~ that the crack of dawn would be arriving in less than an hour. Kay agreed with her suggestion and got into the car, desperately wanting to get away from Pete's already haunting spirit, and hoping she could put everything behind her. Vita never moved a muscle. She stared at the dwindling flames while hugging herself, whimpering and shaking her head with second thoughts. Cee, looked out of the window from the driver's seat.

"Vita! Come on before we get caught out here!" Cee yelled in a whisper.

Vita ignored her, still shaking her head and crying. "I was at their wedding," she cried. "We can't do this y'all. It's not too late. Let's just call the cops."

Cee, angrily took a deep breath and got out the car. Kay followed and looked on as Cee, stormed over to Vita, and smacked her hard across the face. She grabbed her and said. "Look, bitch, either you're going to get in the fucking car, or we're leaving your ass. It's about to be daylight! I don't have time for this stupid shit, Vita! Now is not the time for this goody-goody shit.

"But he…"

"But what…but what? Vita girl, he had his foot all up in Kay's ass! See, you would have known that if you weren't too fucking busy. Besides, he probably would have killed her one day. He was alright with me too. This was an accident, no doubt, but you tell me how we're going to explain him getting stabbed all them times were an accident. This is an accident, I will not be going to jail for," Cee screamed.

When Vita looked at Kay's facial expression, she felt overwhelmed with both the moral responsibility to protect her friend and the guilt for not being aware of the abuse that Kay had been living with. It used to be a time when she knew everything about her, now all she knew was that Kay needed her. Kay's eyes filled with tears, but her cheeks were dry. She looked tired, weary, and pitifully scared, as if Vita had become the judge and jury, as if her whole life depended on Vita's decision ~ and it did. Although Vita was scared, she suppressed her fears and walked over to Kay with her arms out for an embrace. She sobbed on Kay's shoulder while hugging tight.

When they arrived back at Kay's home, Kay raced up the stairs to check on her kids. She was deeply disturbed about leaving them in the house alone, but at the time, she had no choice. She was just glad that they hadn't awoken in the middle of the night only to find that she wasn't there. After finding that the kids were alright, Kay grabbed some bloody towels, their soiled clothes, and watched them spin in the washing machine. They were tired, sore, and needed rest. Within an hour, they were all in silence, lying stretched out on Kay's long extended couch until they fell asleep.

The Sacrifice

Thanks to the unruffled quietness, the afternoon easily approached. Everyone in the house remained in a state of slumber. Even the kids had strangely overslept, as if they were up all night as well. Kay tossed and turned. In her dream, she sat before Jason, confessing her sins. It felt as if he was finally calling her to account for the irrational decisions she had been making in the absence of his presence.

He looked the same: brown-skinned, about 150 pounds, slim, with thick eyebrows hanging over his light-brown poppy eyes. Kay looked around and wondered if the place was a ghetto version of heaven. It was peaceful. Jason displayed the humility of an angel; yet in the background, standing as high as Kay could look, was a brick wall full of graffiti tags. For a moment, she looked past Jason, squinting and focusing on a writing that surprisingly read "R.I.P. Peter Frazier." She readjusted her focus to Jason, and like a child who had to face their father for chastisement, she sorrowfully bowed her head low, and looked to the floor in shame.

Jason started. *"Kay, why do you always seem to make decisions that you live to regret? When is it going to end? You are now a killer. I mean, I can't say that I blame you, but how did you allow your girlfriends to talk you into burying the body? Now, you have to play it all the way out. You cannot tell anyone what has happened; however, I suggest you watch out for Vita. She's one question away from giving everyone up. You know you should have left him the moment he put his hands on you the very first time, but, I do understand. You were in love huh?"*

As Jason's voice echoed, her vision of him became blurry until she was no longer looking at him, but at the brick wall with Pete's name on it.

"Kay...Kay...Kay," the voice continued, when suddenly, she had awoken to the shakes of Vita.

"Kay...Kay! Girl, we're about to leave. Is you alright?"

Kay delayed her response. She lay on her side, looking into Cee's, and Vita's faces. She then realized that she had been dreaming, and the only truth of the dream was that she had killed her husband. She exhaled and brought herself to a sitting position, still half-asleep, but quickly coming around.

"Is you cool or what, girl!" Cee asked, apparently anxious to leave.

"Fuck no! No, I am not cool! Where are you guys going?" Kay's face resembled a mixture of disappointment, anger, and fright. "What I am I supposed to do? How y'all going to leave, like that! That's really horrible."

"Uh-ummm, Kay, don't even try it," started Vita. "You're the one who killed him. Don't be trying to make us feel all guilty... because we wouldn't even be in this situation if it weren't for you. I mean, damn, we already accomplices in a murder...our hands are dirty enough. What more do you want from us?"

"What I want? I want my friends to stay with me, I am afraid."

"Look, you'll be okay. I mean, do you want us to move in. Hell, Cee, you can stay, but I'm out of here."

Cee, listened for a while, running all of the logical alternatives in her mind before she spoke. "Listen, girls we can't let this situation tear us apart. If we're acting like this now, just imagine how things will be when the detectives start coming around with questions.

"The Detectives!" Kay and Vita said simultaneously.

"Yes, the detectives. A man is dead. What you two don't think the detectives will not get involved in a questionable missing person, or murder investigation. Come on, I now you two aren't that naïve. They are coming...I don't know when, but they are, and we got to have our story tight," Cee explained.

"Oh my God, we should've called the cops," said Kay, bursting into tears and triggering Vita's emotions. Cee, shook her head, again wondering what she had gotten herself into. Her life with Brim was just about to begin, and now it could be over if she didn't find some way to keep Kay and Vita strong. She grabbed Vita and Kay's hands, and squeezed them both while gently explaining the rules, as if she had suddenly become a kindergarten teacher.

"This is what we have to do. We never, ever, I mean ever, mention faults. We in this together, and that's all the cops will see. Now, Kay sweetheart, I hate to say it, but Vita is right. We can't move in, it's too suspicious. We have to continue life as we live it."

"But how am I supposed to do that without Pete?" Kay whimpered.

Cee, looked into her eyes and hypnotized her soul. "I saaaaid... we're going to live life as we been living it. We went together, and when we came back at 2:30 a.m., Pete said he was going to the store, and never came back. Now everybody say it.

She made Kay and Vita repeat the story until the words fluently flowed from their mouths. After the women embraced Kay tightly, Cee and Vita both left, assuring Kay that they'll both be calling her within the hour. For the rest of the day, Kay indulged her time with the kids and fought against Jason's voices, which reminded her of the life she had destroyed. Somehow, she just knew that the act of covering up the murder would smack her deep in the face, and it did.

Two weeks after Kay had killed Pete, things began to heat up. A woman ~ a miserable, good-for-nothing, hating-ass woman ~ had become suspicious of Pete's sudden disappearance, so, she questioned Kay's story more and more, of him never coming back from the store. She not only used to have a relationship with the love of Kay's life, Jason, but she was working in the same company as Pete, and often flirted with him. Kay however, was the one who managed to get papers on him. To her, Kay's story raised a red flag, and now that she had not seen Pete in an unusual two weeks, the vibe she received when seeing Kay was confirmation that something was definitely wrong.

On the fifteenth day of Pete's disappearance, the short, compacted, 173-pound, dark-skinned woman wobbled into the police station to file a "Missing persons" report. The heels of her shoes clicked loudly as she heavily stepped, huffing and puffing her way to the counter. The police officer looked into her angry, full face, and tried to assist her.

"Can I help you, ma'am?"

"Yes, I believe you can. I have a friend who is missing." The woman placed her hands on her hips and waited for an answer with her brows raised. She continued. "I need someone to do something about this," she demanded.

"Uh…okay ma'am. When exactly was the last time you saw this person?"

"I don't know, about two weeks or so ago at work," she replied.

"Oh, so we're talking about an adult?"

"Well, I just can't be talking about a child, now can I?"

The officer raised his head from his scribbled notepad and gave an uneasy look before speaking again. "What did this person have on? Is it a he or she, and what's the relation to you?"

The woman stepped closer to the counter. "Well, his name is Peter Frazier. He's my boss, and I truly couldn't tell you what he had on last. You will have to ask his wife about that…with her sneaky ass. I'm telling you," she pointed her index finger, "I know she's hiding something."

"Ma'am, are you telling me that you suspect foul play?"

The woman threw her hands in the air, looked to the ceiling, and rolled her eyes. "What do you think I'm telling you for?"

"Ma'am, you need to just calm down. I'm trying to help you out here. Please wait just one moment," the male officer stated, while walking away.

The officer went into an office for five minutes and returned with a detective. The woman patted her feet on the floor and rested her hands on her hips as she watched the two officers approach the counter. The detective introduced himself while extending his hand for a shake.

"Grayson Kimble," he said.

The woman suspiciously looked at his hand before slowly giving him her hand to grasp. "Casey Allen. Now, can I get some assistance here?"

"Yes you can. Mrs. Allen, I do apologize, this is officer Pile. He's just four months into the job, so be easy on him."

"Uh-hummm, it figures. Now, can I please just get some assistance! Where is the chief or some damn body! I do not have time for the games.

"Ma'am, I understand, just..."

"And stop calling me ma'am! I isn't anybody's damn ma'am!"

"Okay, Mrs. Allen, who are we talking about?" asked the detective.

"I'm talking about Kaleen Frazier."

Kimble looked at her strangely. "Is her husband, by any chance, named Peter Frazier?"

"Yes it is."

"And you're saying Pete...I mean, Mr. Frazier is missing?"

"That's what I'm telling you. He's been gone for two weeks or so, and his nonchalant wife just keeps saying that he never returned from the store. Now you tell me if that doesn't sound like the strangest cover-up if you've ever saw one.

Mrs. Allen's comment enabled everyone to smile and chuckle at the humor, despite the seriousness of the issue. Detective Kimble finished listening to her, and within thirty minutes, he found himself on his way to the Neshaminy Interplex, trailing behind Casey's car. The first line of questioning would begin at the place where Pete earned his keep.

As usual, the office floor was busy with phones ringing, the sound of fingers tapping against computer keyboards, and men and women dressed in corporate attire, as they scurried about in the interest of their work loads. Kimble walked through the maze of cubicles with his badge on a chain swinging from his neck, his presence brought a sort of calm to the atmosphere. Although people continued to work, however, their interest in him became their distraction. His dominant swagger raised curiosity, but was intimidating, nevertheless.

With his short legs moving nowhere fast, and his arms swinging back and forth, Kimble approached Kay's desk with Casey on his heels. Before he could say a word, she blurted her concerns.

"Now, you bitch! You tell him what you've been telling us!" she yelled, pushing pass the officer.

Kay looked up from an update report that she had spent three hours on typing the same line. She looked at the badge hanging from Kimble's neck, and for a second, stared into his eyes. The strongest feeling of shame, seemingly, conquered her emotions. She looked at Casey and exploded into tears.

"He hasn't come home in fifteen days. Please tell me he's okay!" Kay stated.

"Lock her lying ass up!" Casey yelled. "That bitch is hiding something."

Kimble turned and placed his hands on Casey's shoulder. "Okay, okay, Mrs. Allen. I can handle this from here."

"Lock her ass up!" The women screamed, looking pass the detective, directly at Kay.

"Please, please, let the professionals handle this," he pleaded, slowly forcing her backwards, away from striking reach of Kay. Kimble strolled back over to Kay's desk and watched her sob over the disappearance of her husband. He examined for possible traits of fraud, directly noticing that the tears that fell from her eyes hadn't amounted to the loud sobs.

"Here you are, Mrs. Frazier," he said, reaching into a pocket and retrieving a napkin. "I know this must be hard for you, your husband is a very good friend of mines. You may not remember, but you and I met some months back when that accident occurred in your home."

"I remember," Kay responded.

"Yeah, like I said, your husband is a good friend, and I'll get right on the case. If there's any foul play involved, I'll get to the bottom of it, now, when did you last see him?" Kimble asked.

Kay dabbed her eyes with the napkin and exhaled. "Well, when my girls and I went home, it was around 2:00 a.m., and Pete decided that he wanted to going to the store, and he never came back."

Kimble stared intensely. "He went to the store! Huh? Do you know what store?"

"No. I think it was Seven-Eleven, or something."

Kimble jotted notes on a small notepad; he nodded his head and entertained the fact that Kay was possibly being deceptive.

"Can you tell me what he had on?"

Kay thought for a moment. Visions of cutting Pete's blood-soaked sweats, popped into her mind. Her eyes moved about, showing the condition of nervousness that she severely tried to hide. Her palms were moist, her stomach bubbled, and her heart directly pumped blood into her brain causing an instant headache. "Um...I think he had on gray sweatpants."

"And you say you were with your daughters, right?" Kimble asked, in hopes of tricking her up.

"Oh, I'm sorry. I was talking about my two girlfriends, Vita and Cee. We went out to a club that night," Kay responded looking down at the floor.

After giving the officer Vita's, and Cee's real names and addresses, the questioning was over. Kay tried to call and alert them, but for some reason, neither Vita, nor Cee had answered their cell phones. She hoped that the detective wouldn't take them by too much of a surprise. She had been anticipating the interrogation ever since the night of the murder, and she got through it with little to spare. She knew that if there was to be a next time, then she would surely do a better job, but she worried about Vita.

Seventeen

The Investigation

T hings were looking shady, which gave Detective Kimble more reason to believe foul play, as Mrs. Allen had suspected. He had paid a visit to Fidelity Bank, where Pete had the bulk of his money ~ to see if any money had been recently, withdrawn ~ no funds had been touched, and Kimble was now on his way to speak to Vita.

He coasted behind the wheel of his Grand Marquis, slowly turning the corners of the familiar streets of North Philadelphia. These streets, is where he had made a name for himself on the force, making it to detective. Back then, things in the city were different to the point that even as a cop, a black man could take pride at the sight of the many programs established to cultivate, educate, and encourage poverty-stricken black folks. He had taken pride, despite knowing that some of the funding came from illegal activity.

As Kimble pulled into the front of Vita's Lehigh Avenue home, he shook his head in disgust at what that particular neighborhood had become. Nothing but crack-addicts, dope fiends, men and women of all ages still conducting illegal activities to get by. From the outside of Vita's home, it appeared that somehow she had found a way to keep her head up and successfully became financially stable.

The shiny black gates bolted into the concrete in front of each window had cost ~ he estimated ~ thirty-five hundred dollars; not to mention, the beautiful brownish, tinted windows with brown fixtures, that made the other houses look like crap. A night lamp sat above the heave-duty, black screen door, along with a picture of a hand holding a gun, which read, *"Beware of Owner,"* on the lower left corner of the first floor windows.

Kimble exited his car and motioned toward the house, still admiring the beauty compared to the others, he then started wondering if all of the money she had spent to live comfortably would be the curse that attracts crooks to her abode. Vita, was exiting her front door dragging a suitcase on its wheels, and balancing herself in Prada sandals.

"Are you going somewhere, Ms.?" Kimble asked while holding the screen door open for her.

Vita gave a discriminate smile. "Thank you for the help, but it's none of your business where I'm going." Her face had transformed into anger. She definitely was not in the mood for any weak-ass pickup lines.

After the steps, Vita reluctantly thanked the detective again while surveying his body. She noticed that the bulge on the side of his hip distinctly resembled the form of a gun, and his shirt just barely concealed it from plain-eye view. As she continued to run her eyes across his apparel, she observed his badge dangling from a chain on his neck. For a brief moment, she forgot about the murder, forgot that she had played and intricate part in a murder cover-up, and if caught, the story could be made into an A&E *"America Justice"* television program.

"Excuse me, Ms., but I believe it is my business when a friend of yours tells me that she was with you when her husband just mysteriously disappears. I'm Detective Kimble, by the way."

"Uh-huh. Yeah, she was with me," Vita responded.

"She was, huh?" He asked.

"Yeah, she was with me. We came back from the club at 2:00 a.m., and Pete said something about going to get something from the store. From what I recall, he didn't come back."

Kimble gave a chuckle while writing on his notepad. "Okay, Ms...uh..."

"Just call me Vita," she said, cutting him off.

"Okay, well Vita, one last question. Do you have a lot of friends?"

"Do I have a lot of friends? What does that have to do with anything?"

"Please, Ms. ~ I mean Vita. Do you have a lot of friends?" he asked again.

"Yeah...and?" she sassed.

"I'm just wondering how, did you know which one of your friends I was talking about. I never told you a name, but I see I don't have to tell you I was talking about Kaleen, huh?" Kimble squinted, and from the corner of his eyes, he carefully watched Vita tuck her chin. She was hiding something and he knew it. As he turned to walk back to his car, he realized that he would definitely be visiting her again.

"And, uh...Ms..." he stated, turning to get in his car.

"Vita!" she quickly responded.

"Oh yes, Vita. I'm sorry, but I suggest that you don't leave town so early." Kimble pulled his car door shut and gave a fake smile.

Vita remained paralyzed as she watched Kimble's car get further away. She loosened her grip on the luggage with wheels and sat it upright. In her mind, she still thought of skipping town, just locking everything up, emptying her bank accounts, and hiding out in a small town with a population of only twelve hundred. Knowing that disappearing would make matters worse, she sighed and called Cee. Her fingers trembled while dialing the numbers, and her body temperature began rising at a level that would soon have her linen blouse soiled in sweat. She was afraid and remorseful. Out of all the decisions in life she had made, she knew that being a part of the whole murder situation was a decision not truly made on her own, but it was coercion on Cee, and Kay's part.

When Cee received the call, the unusual company of her so-called friends Shelly and Liz was entertaining her. It had been over a year since she had swung with them. Had it not been for them bumping into one another at the grocery store, she probably would not have given them the time of day. However, here they were in her home, surprisingly, having a merry time.

"Hello," Vita whispered. "They're coming!"

Cee, pulled the phone from her ear and looked at it strangely before placing it back against her ear. "Who is this? Who is coming?"

"Sssshh! It's me, your girl, Vita."

"Vita?" Cee asked looking around curiously.

"Yes!"

"Girl, why are you whispering? Are you high or something?"

"Fuck no I am not high! I'm talking about the cops. They just left here."

"Okay. And?"

"And? He's on his way there, I think."

"Who is *he,* and what did you tell him?"

"The detective…I did not tell him anything. Only what we rehearsed."

"Alright, just be cool then. It's just his job. I got this on my end," confirmed Cee.

Shelly and Liz were looking at Cee in wonder of the sudden buddy-buddy relationship of her and Vita.

"That was Vita?" Shelly asked.

"Damn, why you all in my business," Cee, asked her, turning her noise up.

"Well, it wasn't like you were whispering," added Liz.

Cee, stared. "You too, huh? Yeah, that was Vita if the both of you need to know. She asked me to handle something for her."

Shelly and Liz looked at each other and jokingly smirked.

"Whatever, Cee," said Liz.

"Uh-hummm, Y'all two are definitely up to something. Let us find out that you two like each other a little too much," said Shelly.

Cee, sucked her teeth. "Really, is that the best you two could come up with? Anyway, ladies, it's time for you guys to go. I have something very important I need to take care of."

Cee's announcement of business was the entire cue that her company needed to gather their things, and begin to leave. As she walked them to her door, she noticed that Liz purposely slowed down her walk to allow Shelly to distance herself. She engaged Cee in a brief conversation about what she has been hearing in the neighborhood, although she ended the talk before Shelly could imagine it took place.

Quickly, Cee scurried about, trying to make her place look presentable. She started with her kids' toys that is, scattered about in the living room; then to the ashtrays, empty weed bags, and blunt paraphernalia, and ended with saturating the air with a mist of Lysol disinfectant spray. Shortly afterward, Kimble knocked on her door with enough force that made the sound echo throughout the house.

Cee instantly went into a fit. "*Who is knocking on my door so hard?*" she questioned, walking to answer the door, forgetting all about the cops arrival.

"It's Detective Kimble. May I have a word with you?"

Butterflies flew loops in Cee's stomach. She sighed and mentally talked herself to a state of calmness before opening the door. "Hello Detective. How may I help you?" She asked, with a small smile on her face.

As she opened the door and stood before Kimble, resting her hand on the knob, Kimble couldn't help but admire her physique.

Her breast, posing firmly in her black sports bra snatched the attention of his eyes first. From there, they raced across her flat stomach following the light, thin strip of hair that led into the band of black thong panties. She wore a pair of light-blue, tight short-shorts on her bottom that were totally unbuttoned, bearing parts of her front hip and drawing attention to her pussy. Cee, exhibited a devilish smirk, knowing that her display had taken Kimble by surprise.

"Well, can I help you? Is everything okay?" she wondered.

Finally, Kimble snapped out of his lustful desires and back into detective character. "My name is…"

"Kimble…yes, I got that part," she interrupted.

"I need to question you about the disappearance of Peter Frazier. He's been missing for two weeks or so, and it looks like foul play. Now, were you with Kaleen Frazier, on the night that her husband disappeared?"

"I was with Kaleen Frazier a lot of nights."

"Well, your friend Vita and Kaleen said that you were with them when Pete disappeared. Were you?"

Cee, eluded the question just to disturb him a little. "I remember you. You're that detective that was in the hospital that day when Kay was raped."

"Yes, that was me," he affirmed, noticing her deviating from the question.

"So, Pete was your friend, right?"

"That is also correct. Listen, uh…your name is?"

"Ciara Collins," Cee, responded.

"Okay, Mrs. Collins, here's the deal. I'll be asking you the questions okay. Now, were you, or were you not with Kaleen Frazier the night her husband went missing?" he asked, voice now becoming more demanding.

Cee chuckled, and then apologized. "Forgive me officer. Yes, I was with them both."

"Thank you…let me guess, you three came from the club

around 2:00 a.m., and Pete decided that he wanted to go to the store soon as you three arrived.

"Yes, that is exactly what happened!" Cee, responded quick and loud.

Kimble angrily pulled a card from his pocket and placed it on the coffee table.

"It's only a matter of time. You know how it goes Mrs. Collins. The first one who talks gets the best deal. Oh yeah, there is no such thing as a perfect crime," he said, as he stormed off in disbelief.

Cee, became silent. She walked the detective to the front door, and let him out of her home, afterwards, she hurried into her living room to glop onto her couch. Thoughts of Pete and Kay dancing romantically rampaged through her mind. Cee relaxed on the sofa until she fell asleep.

Meanwhile, later that evening, Vita found herself snuggled in her bed watching a movie while throwing back kernel after kernel of buttered popcorn. Her nerves were returning to normal. She began to feel a sort of confidence that the plan she and the girls had agreed upon would work. Unfortunately, no soon, as her mind forced her body into total ease, Kimble revisited her to lay down a more intense line of questioning.

His knock on Vita's door was subtle yet, it traveled, bouncing off the thin walls of Sheetrock into the midst of the serenity, and touching the core of her eardrums. Kimble stood at the top of the front steps, patiently waiting for her to answer his knock. When she finally opened the door to the sight of his face, her heart skipped. *Shit! Not this motherfucker again*, she thought as he gave a fake smile. "Hello again, I see your back so soon, huh?" she said, sarcastically.

"Yes, and I do apologize for disturbing you again, at such an hour," Kimble said, not honestly caring about disrupting her at all.

"Well, it's okay, besides, it's not really that late. I only ask next time that you call me first."

"Yes, I understand, however, I just have a few more questions, about the disappearance. May I come in?"

Vita held her door open and rolled her eyes as Kimble walked into her home. He stood in her living room with his small notepad in hand, taking a glimpse at the number of certificates framed on the wall. As he took further notice of the layout of her home, he realized that she probably lived alone. Nothing about the decorations suggested the slightest touch of masculinity.

So, I'll get right into it. You stated that you guys had come back from the club around 2:00 a.m.?"

"Uh-humm. Would you like something to drink? Some coffee, or water?" she offered, hoping to keep her nerves together.

Kimble thought for a second. "No, No thank you. You know that you're going to jail right?"

"What! Jail! For what? What did I do!" yelled Vita.

"You see, when I talked to your friend Ciara, she told me all about what you guys did," he lied.

Vita's uneasiness began to exude. Kimble carefully watched and smiled on the inside, knowing that if he turned it up a notch, she would reveal anything he needed to know.

"Yes, that's right," he continues. "All I want to know is why. You might as well help yourself out. Here is your chance. Your girls are sitting down the precinct as we speak. Would you like to tell us what hand you had in it?"

Vita's conscious had been tearing away at her for days. The thought of harboring such a dark secret for the rest of her life was too cold-hearted for her to handle. Finally, with tears in her eyes, she spilled the beans and told Kimble the whole story. Within minutes, Kimble was on the phone calling in a warrant from the magistrate judge. He took Vita into custody, and then proceeded to serve the warrants for the bodies of Kaleen Frazier and Ciara Collins.

Eighteen

The Arrests

Sirens wailed and engines roared from the fleet of police cars en route to Kay's home. At the same time, equal amount of cars were en route to Cee's home. As he sat passenger in the lead vehicle, Kimble's voice squawked over the radio.

"We're just a minute away from Frazier's. How are you guys looking?"

"We're pulling in front of the Collins residence now," a voice responded.

"Okay, proceed with the warrant and be careful. I'll see you back at the precinct. Over…"

"Roger that. Over…"

Kay heard the sirens from a distance. In her mind, she questioned if they were for her, but not wanting to be a pessimist, she tried to bury the possibility with a happier and more pleasant thought. She could not. The sound of the car doors slamming shut was like thunder to her ears. She stood in her kitchen in a trance at the sink, and stared at a plate, rubbing a soapy dishrag across it. She listened and listened, hoping that she would not get an unusual knock at her door, but noticing that the voices were growing louder. Suddenly, she lifted her head from the dish and peeped through the kitchen window to see a herd of police dressed in S.W.A.T. (Special Weapons and Tactics), gear.

Quickly, she raced through her kitchen door and up the steps into her bedroom where Cashmere, Asr, and Charity happened to be sleeping.

"Wake up babies," she whimpered, shaking their little legs and snatching Charity into her arms.

Half-asleep and unbalanced, the kids moved about in a frenzy, not knowing whether to start with shoes, socks, or pants.

"Come here, y'all. Come sit with mommy," said Kay.

They huddled around her, each hugging an arm. At once, the front door crashed open, startling the kids into tears. Their already trembling embrace of Kay's arm tightened. Their faces buried into her shoulders with their minds hoping that the sound of the imposters' footsteps would contradict what would happen to their lives.

"Move! Move! Move! Move! Clear!" the voices repeated as the Homicide Task Force checked every room in the house before entering Kay's bedroom. The moment her door opened, the yelling matched the aggression that they used to subdue her.

"GET DOWN! GET DOWN! Let me see your hands!" They yelled.

"Please don't hurt my children. Don't hurt my kids!" cried Kay as she threw her hands into the air and allowed the officers to snatch her from the kids' embrace.

The children cried at the top of their lungs and stretched out their little arms, reaching for their mother. Their hands clutched the air into their fist, a disappointment for failing to grasp at least a part of her limbs. The three snatched into the arms of different S.W.A.T. members. As she lay on her stomach with her chest pressed against the floor, her hands cuffed behind, and a knee in her back, Kay managed to look into her kids' eyes. She felt extreme shame and sorrow to see them kick and scream. Their tears of uncertainty sent her into a rage.

"Get your fucking hands off of my babies. Get off them! Where are you taking them?" she continued to scream.

Of course, none of the nine officers answered her. The children's facial expressions pleaded for help and asked the question: *Why is this happening?* In Kay's mind, she asked the same question, sadly, she knew that Pete was the answer.

....

On the other side of town, the Homicide Task Force strategically covered the front and back of Cee's home, eliminating all possible exits for escape. Very oblivious to their existence, Cee indulged in the comfort of being in the company of her four kids and husband-to-be, Brim. As she put a few more dashes of spices into her dinner that cooked on the stove, she blurted obscenities at her kids to get them to behave. Suddenly, the phone rang.

"I got it!" yelled Brim from inside of the living room.

Within seconds, Cee heard him race up the steps and fumble about in the room above the kitchen. She strangely looked to the ceiling.

"Brim, what's going on? Do not say that one of your friends got into something and you are on your way to their aid!" she stated, disapprovingly.

"They coming!" he yelled.

Before Cee could fully interpret what he had said, the Task Force crashed into both the front and back doors of the home.

"GET DOWN! GET DOWN! Let me see your hands!" they yelled. Cee, was startled. Her experience in the streets compelled her to respond by throwing the hot pot of hamburger helper into their direction as fellow members slammed her to the floor, cuffed her, and began kicking her head. Surprisingly, she did not scream, nor yell. They yanked her to her feet, almost breaking her arms, and ran her through the living room.

With the barrels of guns pointed in his face, Brim yelled at Cee, asking for answers. "What you do! What happened?"

Cee, looked him in the eyes and bowed her head. "Just take care of the kids," she told him, her voice low, fighting the change in tone precipitated by the emotional pain.

She hated the fact that it had been the fourth time that her kids had experienced such an atrocity. The guns, men in masks yelling and screaming, and the sight of their mother being mistreated would probably haunt them, let alone plant a negative image of the police in their heads. As their mother was being, carried out the door, the kids stared at her back. Although their emotions were running rampant, they felt empathy for their mother's pain, not one of them cried. The experience of seeing such activity in their home has taught them to be numb. In their minds, they hoped that their mother would be okay.

The police station was not the least bit of a frightening episode for Cee. She had visited once before for boosting, retail theft, once for an assault with a switchblade, and twice for possession with the intent to deliver a controlled substance. The homicide charge that she presently faced was a charge that would surely keep her behind bars. The chance of bail was slim to none; and even if ~ by the grace of God ~ she was given bail, there was no money to pay a million-dollar bail, even if it was only ten percent.

After being, fingerprinted and thoroughly processed, the officers placed Cee, in a holding cell where she had to endure the stench of urine and the cries of drunken prisoners, demanding medical attention, furthermore, it was dark and moist, and the slightest whisper could be heard in the eight-cell corridor. Cee looked around and sighed, wondering what Kay and Vita had revealed about the murder. She knew that they were in the precinct somewhere, but worried that the cops would keep them apart.

Somewhere in another part of the police station, Vita and Kay had been, separated, fingerprinted, and placed in their own cells, with the feeling of uncertainly, making its mark by enhancing their fears. They sobbed until they fell asleep. When they awoke, the precinct had sheriffs escort them to a van where they met with Cee, and began a trip to the county prison.

Despite prison being something they didn't want, their faces lit up as they entered the van one by one, and saw that they would be taking the trip together.

"Are we going to be in the same jail?" Kay asked, her voice whimpering as the door slammed shut and the engine started.

Cee sat in the last row. She stared at Kay and Vita, and then rolled her eyes. "Which one of you bitches said something?" she asked angrily.

A minute of silence occurred before Vita spoke. "Well, you two told that Detective Kimble guy some stuff," she offered.

"What! Vita, please tell me you didn't let him pull that over your head," Cee stated in disbelief.

"But, Cee, he said that y'all were locked up already. He said that you two swore I was part of the whole thing." Suddenly, her personality switched from a weak and afraid woman to an aggressive, angry woman, but still very much afraid. "Don't get upset with me. I said we should've called the cops in the first place."

Again, Cee sighed, and then shook her head in disgust. Had it not been for the fact that Pete was beating on her when Kay had stabbed him, then she probably would have disowned the whole incident, however, it was too late. Her hands were already dirty, and she had to make Vita, and Kay understand that they still had to stick to the same story.

"Are we all going to the same jail?" Kay asked again.

The more Cee looked into Kay's eyes, the more sadness she felt toward her situation. To her, Kay's eyes resembled one of her kids', a child in desperate need of a hero. She never imagined herself to be none of the sort, but someone had to orchestrate a code of speech in the trial to come.

"I don't know Kay, if we'll ever see each other again, until our court hearing; therefore, we should to keep the same story, y'all. Vita, how much did you actually tell him?" Cee wondered.

Vita's face showed silent tears. She bowed her head and in a low pitch said, "Everything."

"We'll be alright. We just have to wait until our hearing to see if they got all of the evidence," Cee informed.

"Well, when is the hearing?" Key asked.

"I don't know, maybe in a few days. But until then, don't talk to nobody." Cee, looked at Vita, and rolled her eyes. "Yeah, Kay, we'll see what kind of evidence they're going to use when we get at the hearing.

The girls were quiet for the rest of the ride. Kay and Cee were both thinking of their kids; in addition to thoughts of her kids, Cee wondered how long she was going to have to fake it as if she believed everything was okay. As the van pulled in front of the Women's County Prison, Vita's thoughts were on calling her lawyer the first chance she got.

The three remained confined for a period of twelve months before a motion for a speedy trial has been, granted on Cee, and Kay's behalf.

During their year of confinement, a number of troubling events had occurred that made the girls look at each other differently. The District Attorney had struck a deal with Vita, for immunity in exchange for her testimony against Cee, and Kay. Shortly after two months of their arrival at the prison, she was, transferred to another place. With the money in her account, and the advice from Sasha, a jailhouse lawyer, Kay hired a lawyer to represent both, her and Cee.

Strangely enough, Reynolds was the district attorney on the case. Since she was the same D.A. that handled Kay's cousin Stew's case, Kay figured it would be anyone but her. She felt betrayed by Reynolds, even though her love for Stew obliged her to show up for court. Back then, it was more than that. It was also the strong sense of admiration for Reynolds by thinking that she cared. Now, there she was, extending the same care towards her, which Kay realized was false. Her eyes began to open wide to the intricacies of the system. She formally became a resident on the other side of the law, and consciously grew to hate law and order.

Key knew Reynolds was a good attorney. Watching her dazzle the entire courtroom at Stew's rape trial was like watching the best, if ever anyone was deserving of the title. The only way she thought she could get a chance at beating, the case was to hire Angelino, who was the only lawyer to give Reynolds a run for her money.

Key called Mr. Marshall and hired him to handle the investigating procedures. Because she claimed the murder was along the lines of self-defense, he managed to solicit the cooperation of expert witnesses who worked closely with *"Women, Against Beatings,"* a grass-roots organization established in Philadelphia for support against domestic abuse. He also promised her a secret weapon.

While things were working in her favor outside of the prison house, inside, she was, faced with a dilemma. All of her life, one way or another, her presentation of self, though always the same, had been the core of both negative and positive experiences. Her natural beauty and enticing strut was something attractive to not only men, but it was alluring to women as well. Over the past few months, she had respectfully established her womanhood with a few verbal matches and fisticuffs scrimmages. However, Sasha challenged her womanhood, but not by violent verbal threats or physical force. Sasha simply asked Kay for some special time alone with her.

Two days prior to trial proceedings, Cee and Kay were in Kay's cell. Cee had just begun telling her about how much she missed Brim.

"Girl, I'm telling you," she rambled, sitting in a chair, swinging her knees in and out. "I'm horny as shit! Right about now, it ain't even got to be Brim. I'll put this pussy on any available man. Earrrrly!"

She gazed into an open-eyed dream of lowering her body

onto a penis and working her hips. She was serious. Jail had begun attacking her will to restrain from sexual thoughts. The more she thought of sex, the more she talked about it. The more she talked about it, the more she openly expressed how much she wanted it. The entire nature of that kind of conversation, in that kind of environment made Kay, uncomfortable.

A knock on the door caught their attention. Kay looked through the rectangular window of the door and waved her hand.

"Come in!" she yelled.

In walked the six-foot, 160-pound, red-bond Sasha. Her hair and nails were done as if she was about to attend a party or banquet of some sort. The blue county-issued khaki pants fitted like spandex, and her sky blue county-issued shirt was, tailored to fit with a sleeve hanging off her shoulder. In her hand were copies of legal materials. She handed them to Kay.

"Here you go, pretty lady."

Kay smiled. "Thanks Sash."

"Girl, you know it's no problem. I do want to know, have you thought about what I asked you?" Sasha asked.

Kay continued smiling, trying to hide her insecurities. She never considered having a relationship with the same sex. *Would it be wrong to deny her?* Kay wondered. Had it not been for Sasha, she would not have been in a position that established a greater percentage for her to win her case. She would not even have known the first thing about the law, or probably would not have made it past one day without breaking down. Of course, Cee was there and had her back, but Sasha was the one who gave her the understanding of how the system truly works.

"Well," she started, looking at Sasha's beauty, trying to draw a sense of attraction, "I'll get back with you in like a half."

Sasha nodded and eased out of the cell. Kay stared at her back, watching as the cell door shut.

Damn! She thought as her mind bunched with thoughts over top of thoughts. *Why didn't I just tell her I don't get down like that?*

She has been looking out for me at least, I can let her taste the coochie. I mean, what's a little taste? But naw, I can't go out like that.

As her thoughts ricocheted like a pinball, they began to take on a stronger personality ~ that of Jason.

Fuck Sasha! Why are you stressing? She probably was doing all that stuff for you just so she can eat the pussy. You think she was doing it because she's sincere. You are in jail! Sincerity is far-gone. Just get Cee to take care of her. She's always talking to you crazy, and freaky like she's leaning that way. Put Sasha on her. Kay shook her head and pinched the bridge of her nose between her eyes. She looked at Cee, who remained seated in the chair, again, swinging her knees in and out, trying to soothe the tingling between her legs. Kay knew that if she asked such a favor, then Cee would do it, even if she truly weren't leaning toward an act of lesbianism. For the loyalty of friendship, Cee was one who would easily sacrifice herself.

Kay wondered what had become of herself. It seemed as if the events that occurred in her life had formed into a cumulative cloud, shaping her mentality to the point of being exceedingly self-centered. The jail life hadn't done anything but contribute to a personality that she grew to dislike, however she felt about it, Jason had already helped her to make a decision.

She cleared her throat. "Cee, I need a favor."

Cee instantly became attentive. "What do you need Kay?"

Kay chuckled. "Girl, it's deep. You know all the work Sasha been doing for us?"

"Uh-hummm. What about it?"

"Well she asked me if she can suck my pussy."

Cee's, mouth opened from shock. "Are you serious?"

"I am dead serious," Kay said.

"She gets down like that? I didn't even know," Cee answered, smiling.

"I didn't know either, but apparently she do. And she's coming back in a minute."

Finally, Cee caught on to the nature of Kay's favor. "Uh-ummm! Girl, I know you not. Why are you telling me?"

"Please Cee," Kay pleaded.

"Um-ummm, girl you're really asking for a big favor. I mean, I am horny, but damn! Don't get it misunderstood; I have two fresh cucumbers in my cell, and I'll push them motherfuckers up in this pussy as far as they can go.

"Please Cee," Kay continue to ask grabbing her arm.

"No! What's wrong with you?" Cee, wondered with a stern face.

"Cee, you know I don't even play that way."

"But I do, huh?" Cee shook her head with skepticism.

A brief moment of silence took over the room. The friends stared at each other. Cee's face resembled disappointment and Kay looked as if she had asked her big sister to save her life. Her eyes filled with such helplessness, matching the strain of all her life experiences. Cee felt sorry for her, and though she was far from a lesbian, she sighed and reluctantly agreed.

When Sasha returned to Kay's cell, Kay explained the deal to her. She wanted to taste Kay badly, but Cee was just as good. Other women in the prison had been keeping their eyes on Cee, however, she was known to go crazy. After having four women walk around severely beaten and bruised, no one dared to try her or her little sister Kay.

As Kay left out of her cell, a tear dropped from each eye. She knew that she had just put a stain on their relationship. A little over three minutes passed by when she heard a loud crash. Quickly, she turned to look through the rectangular window on the door. Surprisingly, she witnessed Cee in the cell beating Sasha's topless body with a milk crate. She slammed the hard, orange plastic against Sasha's body, kicked, and yelled admonishing language at Sasha, for having the nerve to ask such a request.

Nineteen

Troubled Times

The smell of mist was in the air. Those who had experienced broken bones or other injuries affecting the limbs were predicting rain. As the sheriffs began pulling into the garage of the courthouse, Kay looked out of the window into the gray sky and silently agreed with the self-proclaimed psychics that precipitation was in the forecast. Although the dreary, dull atmosphere tried to squeeze out what little spunk she had left, she held on. All the while, thinking of positive things to help her along.

Not only was she being strong for herself, but also for Cee. Cee, had in her mind that they were going to lose the case, but Kay was persistent in efforts to help Cee, imagine otherwise. As they, were taken into the courtroom handcuffed to each other, Kay smiled and held her head high. The one thing she learned from Sasha was, never let them see you sweat. Even if she thought that things were going to go bad, she would force herself to see herself winning. It had brought her through over 365 days of waiting, and she didn't expect her methods to fail her now.

Proceedings were underway immediately. Watching Reynolds parade before the jury in her expensive two-piece suit, insinuating and accusing Kay of never loving Pete, was the hardest part to hear, even for Cee. If no one else knew, she was well aware of what Kay had gone through in loving Pete. As Reynolds continued, Cee could tell that the prosecutor's words were entering Kay's ears and molesting her heart.

The picture was painted. The faces of the jurors had depressingly showed what visions of a horrific act they thought the crime to be. Defense attorney Angelino, had his work cut out for him. If he wanted Cee, and Kay to go free, he had to tear down the already painted visions of them being equated to some of the most heinous serial killers know to America. He started with calling a psychiatric doctor to the stand.

"The defense calls Kimberly Jennings!"

As the doctor entered the courtroom, the heads of the viewers sitting in the rows followed her motion. She walked upright like a marine or some sort of soldier in the armed forces. Her pants neatly starched, showing three pleats and hanging just below the ankle, but above her plain-looking, black Stacy Adams. She took the stand and raised her hand to be, sworn in.

The case was more than just a case to Angelino. Finally, it was about him putting an end to the negative stigma that hung over his head, the feeling of being inferior to Reynolds in the courtroom. As usual, he stood, gave a smile, and began walking toward his witness.

"Good morning, Mrs. Jennings. For the record, can you tell the court exactly where it is you work?"

"I…" she cleared her throat, "I work at Einstein Hospital."

"What exactly is your job there at Einstein Hospital?"

"I do psychiatric evaluations on victims of domestic abuse and rape to determine if any mental damage has occurred."

"Do you know my clients?" he asked.

"Yes, I know that one right there," looking directly at Kay.

"Your Honor, for the record, the witness has pointed to my client Kaleen Frazier," Angelino informed.

The judge nodded his head in affirmation, "so recorded. You may proceed with questioning," he advised.

Slowly, Angelino motioned in front of the jury before continuing. "How do you know my client?"

"I…" Again, the witness cleared her throat. "I treated her when she visited the hospital."

"And what treatment did you give her?"

"I could only prescribe her to Valiums because she refused therapy, but she really needed it. She tried to say that she fell down the steps, as they all do, but I know the beatings of a man when I see it."

"Objection!" yelled Reynolds. "Your Honor, there is no record of spousal abuse!"

"Your Honor, this is a woman's life," Angelino responded. "The doctor is a professional who has seen hundreds of cases. I think she earned the right to conclude foul play when she sees it, it's her job."

"Overruled. Please continue," said the judge.

"Thank you, Your Honor. How many times has my client, Kaleen Frazier, visited the hospital, Mrs. Jennings?"

"On several different occasions," she replied.

"Thank you. No further questions."

Angelino introduced two other doctors from separate hospitals to account for the same treatment. He began winning the jury over through the basic human trait of empathy and by discrediting the Commonwealth's key witness, *Vita Daley*.

When Vita took the stand on re-cross, the shame of betrayal had run so deep that she kept her head bowed throughout the whole questioning.

"Mrs. Daley, can you please tell us why your girlfriend Kaleen Frazier stabbed her beloved husband so many times?"

Vita sat on the stand, looked Angelino in the eyes and lied her face off, just to get a deal for immunity. Since she had been in the dark about the beatings until the murder, her reason for Kay killing Pete had coincided with the Commonwealth's speculations: Kay wanted Pete's money. The trial was leading into ten long hours, but it was worth the wait for Kay to hear the testimony of the weapons investigator Marshall had promised.

The tired and weary Angelino kept his composure. He could smell his first victory against Reynolds and was determined to see it through with intensity from the beginning to the end.

"The defense calls Detective Grayson Kimble to the stand."

"Objection! Your Honor, he's not on the list!" Reynolds blurted, desperately wondering what was to become of her case.

Angelino smiled, "Your Honor, surely the Commonwealth doesn't expect the defense not to question the arresting officer."

"Overruled!" said the judge.

Kimble took the stand and stated his name and badge number. Angelino continued to parade before the jurors. The courtroom was quiet. Everyone in the room watched and listened to the heels of his shoes tap and scratched the floor from his heavy steps, and dragging of his feet. His head was bowed yet the smile remained on his face, which gave the jury and impression of confidence about the witness testimony.

"Mr. Kimble, you were the lead detective on this case, am I correct?"

"Yes, that is correct. I learned of Pete's disappearance through an employee of his, and immediately started investigating."

"I noticed that you called the deceased Pete. Could you elaborate?"

"Well, the deceased, Pete, and I were in college together. I was on my last year and he had just arrived, but he was an alright guy."

"Back then, when you were in college, did he exhibit any violent characteristics?"

"No, he did not. It's not like we frequented each other, but he had acted strange on one occasion."

"Strange...can you explain to the court, that strange behavior you're talking about?"

"Around two years ago, I received a call from Pete. He asked me to drive over to his house because of an accident that occurred with a few of his old frat friends, and a stripper."

"And what did you think of the accident?" asked Angelino.

"At first I didn't think anything. I mean nothing serious. But that's when he told me."

"What did he tell you?"

"He said that he needed an ambulance."

"What did you do?" asked Angelino, looking around the courtroom.

"I drove out to his home and that's when I saw her."

"Who did you see?"

"I saw Kaleen Frazier lying on the floor naked and beaten."

"Did you know who Mrs. Frazier was?"

"No. As I said, we really didn't frequent each other, but I did consider him a friend. He told me he needed me to help him. He paid me a quarter of a million dollars." The courtroom erupted into commotion. The look of shock now stamped on the jurors faces.

Reynolds angrily shouted, "Objection! Your Honor, this is insane. There is no record of such activity, or even proof that the detective even knows the deceased. The deceased clearly isn't in any position to dispute, how convenient."

Angelino quickly responded. "Your Honor," he said, opening a folder and grabbing two pieces of evidence. "Here are photos of the detective and the deceased on a fishing trip. Clearly, they were friends. Again, Your Honor, with all due respect, but a woman's life is at stake here. What, or should I say who, is more capable to tell us about the deceased than a friend of his?"

The judge thought while studying the photos for authenticity. "Objection is overruled. You may continue," said the judge.

Angelino cheered on the inside; however, he managed to keep his cool.

"What did you do after your friend gave you the money?"

"I simply called an ambulance and had the woman taken to the hospital. Instead of filing a report, I made sure that no mention of it gets to the precinct."

"Mr. Kimble, when did you realize that the woman was not a stripper, but in fact, Peter Frazier's wife?"

"The next day he called me, and confessed." Kimble added.

"Confessed to what? What did he tell you?"

"He said he lost control of his anger. That he was not going to let a ghetto whore, run all over his life. Afterwards, I showed up at the hospital when Mrs. Frazier regained consciousness. I was going to take a statement from her, and charge Mr. Frazier, but I had already taken the money, and he promised that it'll never happen again."

"Thank you, Mr. Kimble. One last question before you go, how did you obtain the arrest warrants for my clients?"

"Well, after taking the statement from Mrs. Vita Daley, I called in my information and communicated with a magistrate judge."

"Did you verbally express to Mrs. Daley that she was a suspect?"

"No, but I did inform her not to leave town."

"So far all you knew was that Mrs. Vita Delay could have been lying?"

"She wasn't lying," he quickly responded.

"How do you know?" Angelino asked.

"The decomposing body was discovered exactly where she stated it will be!"

"The question was how you know that my clients did anything? Isn't it possible that she could have been lying?"

As the questioning continued, the detective began to grow agitated. He was there to help, to make right of the wrong he had done, but somehow Angelino, turned this on him. Angelino glanced at the district attorney, who had her face buried in her hand, in embarrassment. The sight made him stand even taller in confidence. He became a scavenger, a buzzard soaring high, with the Commonwealth being the wounded prey for him to stalk its last breath. Kay and Cee looked on as he swooped in to finish things off.

"Mr. Kimble, did you file a complaint?"

Kimble looked confused in fear, not exactly knowing how to respond. He spoke softly. "Excuse me? A complaint?"

"Yes, I don't seem to have one here. A complaint is the documentation that states a person has committed a crime in a certain region. It is the initial documentation stating the charges, which goes against the peace, and dignity of the Commonwealth. Furthermore, the complaint is the only documentation that institutes criminal proceedings."

"Objection, Your Honor, is we in closing argument here?" bellowed Reynolds.

"Your Honor, I simply asked the man did he file a complaint. I am explaining what a complaint is because it seems as if he doesn't know. In fact, Your Honor, I challenge Mrs. Reynolds to produce a complaint if there is one. I personally don't have one in my files."

The judge looked at Reynolds, with his brows raised. "Mrs. Reynolds?"

"Yes, Your Honor, just a minute," she responded while shuffling through her papers nervous and ashamed to come to court not being on top of her game. She spoke again, while still looking down. "Your Honor, I must have misplaced it."

Angelino: "Your Honor, I move for an immediate dismissal on the grounds that without a criminal complaint to institute proceedings, then this court has no jurisdiction to try this case."

The judge stared at Reynolds. "Mrs. Reynolds? You have to produce the complaint now, at this very moment. It seems quite strange that you have a complaint, but neither you nor the defense has a copy of it, when it is supposed to be disclosed with the full discovery. I'm sorry, Mrs. Reynolds, but the motion is granted, and the defendants are free to go."

For the second time, the courtroom sounded as if a circus was underway. Folks cheered, cursed, laughed, and cried. Angelino took in a deep breath and exhaled. He placed his palm on Kay's shoulder and smiled.

Still seated, Kay looked up at him with her mouth open and unbelieving eyes. Cee leaned back in her chair, looking to the ceiling while feeling the hands of congratulating pats from the supporters who sat behind them.

Cee turned and faced Angelino. "So you saying, just like that, it's over?"

"Yup, just like that," he responded.

Cee began pointing. "So I can walk right out of here without any of them cops trying to shoot me?"

"Yup," he said while smiling.

After staring intensely for ten seconds, Cee sucked her teeth, poked her lips out, and put her nose in the air as she stormed out of the courthouse. Kay followed.

Surprisingly, the press was limited. The women stormed past them and got into a van that belonged to the Department of Human Services, where Kay had to meet with her kids. As the van reached full motion, they looked out of the window and could see Vita being, arrested. The deal she had made with Reynolds was only contingent upon a conviction of Cee and Kay. Since, they were released Vita had no more deal. There was a confession, and Reynolds was determined to make someone pay for Pete's death. This time she was sure to follow the correct procedures. A complaint stamped with Vita Daley, was in the making.

Twenty

The Truth

TWO WEEKS LATER:

The kids were in school. Instead of taking advantage of the free time to do her wedding planning, Cee sat on the couch in her living room and cried. Something had been troubling her that wouldn't leave her alone. It wouldn't ease itself out of her mind, and time definitely wouldn't be able to heal her heart. She poured herself another glass of wine and increased the stereo volume with a remote, when suddenly the phone rang.

"Hello," she answered.

"Hello Girl, you do not even sound right answering the phone all proper. What's up with you?"

"Who is this, Kay?

"Whatever. Cee you know it's me. What's up?" Kay, asked excitedly.

"Nothing, I miss you. I am so happy we're home," Cee responded overwhelmed.

"I know that's right. I feel like you've been upset with me though, because of what I asked of you in there. I am truly sorry. I should've never asked you to do something like that Cee."

"No, you shouldn't have. But all is forgiven on that."

"Is everything okay besides that?" asked Kay.

"I do need to see you in person. Something has been on my mind. Can you come over?"

"Okay," Kay stated while hanging up the telephone, before Cee, could get in another word. Kay was happy to be seeing her friend beyond them prison walls.

Cee, thought about the conversation she had with Liz over a year ago. She thought about life and the purpose of love; more so, about the things Brim has said to her, how his face seemed to be smirking when he said it. She had been the only real woman in his life, bailing him out of jail, keeping him fed and out of the streets when he needed to be. To realize that none of it meant anything killed her spirit. She knew that she had many lovers in her life, but Brim had her heart. *Why couldn't he just see that?*

Just as she finished her wine, Kay knocked on the door. "Cee, its Kay, let me up."

Cee, looked at the door, sighed, and lazily walked to unlock it. She left it wide for Kay's entrance. She headed up the steps in mild tears, mad, and feeling weakened by Kay's presence.

Kay had never seen Cee, in such a state. Cee had been the rock for Kay on so many occasions, now it was her turn.

"Uh-ummm, girl what have Brim done now?" Kay asked, voice strong, sincere and gentle as she followed Cee, to the bedroom. "Cee, what's wrong?"

Cee maintained muteness. She opened her walk-in closet and dragged Brim out into the middle of the floor. He was duct taped and quiet as scratches and bruises decorated his face. Kay's mouth went wide. She looked at Cee in wonder, watching her kick Brim in the stomach and spit at him. Kay stood paralyzed, as Cee unbuckled his pants and yanked them down just below his buttocks, allowing his penis to flop along his thigh. Suddenly, she grabbed from under her mattress a black .357 Magnum, and placed the barrel on the head of his penis.

"Wait!" yelled Kay, shaking in fear. "Cee we can't go through this shit again. Please put that gun down."

Cee, cried hysterically while holding her aim. The more Kay talked, the harder she cried.

"And why not, Kay!" she blurted, looking deep into Kay's face.

As Kay pieced things together, her heart dropped. All she could do was place her palms over her mouth and cry.

"Cee, I..."

"Shut up, bitch! You and him have been fucking all this time! Why? Kay why? You're all I got, all I had and you knew how I felt about him." Cee's tears turned into rage. Kay looked on noticing Cee hands trembling while holding the gun.

"It wasn't even like that Cee, I..."

Before Kay could finish trying to explain, Cee fired the gun, making Brim's penis headless. She then pointed the gun at his head and fired. Kay went into extreme fright. As Cee, pointed the gun at her, Kay thought about her kids. "What about my kids!" she yelled. "Think about your kids also, Cee."

Cee's eyes were crazed, and deranged. "No, bitch, you think about 'em," she said, then fired two shots into Kay's chest, making her fly back into the wall.

The blast from the shots snapped Cee, out of her psychotic trance. She ran over to Kay's body, and couldn't believe what she has just done.

"I'm sorry. I'm sorry, Kay. Please don't die it wasn't meant for you. I just wanted you to know that I was mad," Cee, begged rocking back and forth holding Kay's bloody body.

Kay listened as she fell in and out of consciousness.

Thinking that she had killed Kay, Cee placed the gun to her own head, inhaled, and calmly fired the weapon.

When Kay fell back into consciousness, she managed to drag her bloody body across the bedroom. She grabbed the cord to the phone, yanked it from the nightstand, and dialed 911 before passing out. When she awoke, she saw the faces of her and Cee's kids crowded around her hospital bed. Their faces were deeply saddened. Behind them was a woman, around fortyish, with dark skin and jet-black hair reaching shoulder length. She excused her way to the bed and smiled.

"Hello. How are you feeling?"

"Fine," Kay struggled.

"I am Delores Winters. I work for the Corbitt & Corbitt, Life Insurance Company for Mrs. Ciara Collins. Apparently, she has you down as her next of kin. It seems as if Mrs. Collins has breached her contract. Naturally it states, that if something was to happen to her then the life insurance money would go to you upon affirmation that you will take care of her children; however, if you do decide not to take care of them, then the money would normally go in a trust fund for her kids until the age of eighteen."

Kay slowly eased her body upright and swallowed before speaking in her low, scratchy, and dehydrated voice.

"What do you mean *normally?*"

"Well, since Mrs. Collins committed suicide, she forfeited the money, and if you don't take the children, they'll go to the state. Now, I don't mean to be rude, but I have six hospital rooms to visit and yours is just the first. So, Mrs. Frazier, do you have any idea what your intentions will be?"

Kay burst into tears. She looked at Cee's Kids, thought about Cee, and signed the custody papers.

Earrrrly! She said, mocking Cee's famous Statement!

THE END!

The Davis Project, LLC
Presents

Scruplez

Written By: JOHN MOORE
Co-Author: MAYNE DAVIS

Printed in the United States
by Baker & Taylor Publisher Services